THE PILLARS OF ENOCH

TEMPLARS AND THE MELUNGEON LEGACY

DAVID S. BRODY

Eyes That See Publishing

The Pillars of Enoch:

Templars and the Melungeon Legacy

Eyes That See Publishing

Newburyport, Massachusetts

ISBN 978-0-9907413-9-8

Cover by Kimberly Scott and Renee Brody

Printed in USA

DEDICATION

To Allie, Renee, Jonathan, Ben, Matt, Sarah

Sometimes I listen to the people who say
our country's next generation of young adults
is somehow subpar.

Then I think of my amazing
daughters, nephews and niece.

ABOUT THE AUTHOR

David S. Brody is a 7-time Amazon #1 Bestselling fiction writer named Boston's Best Local Author by the *Boston Phoenix* newspaper. His children call him a "rock nerd" because of the time he spends studying ancient stone structures which he believes evidence exploration of America prior to Columbus. He serves as a Director of the New England Antiquities Research Association (NEARA) and has appeared as a guest expert on documentaries airing on History Channel, Travel Channel, PBS and Discovery Channel. A graduate of Tufts University and Georgetown Law School, he resides in Newburyport, MA with his wife, sculptor Kimberly Scott.

The Pillars of Enoch is his 15th novel.

For more information, please visit DavidBrodyBooks.com

NOTE TO READERS

1. **Though this story is fiction, the artifacts, sites and works of art pictured are real. See Author's Note at end of book for more detailed information.**
2. **This is a stand-alone story. Readers who have not read the first eleven books in the series should feel free to jump right in. The summary below provides some basic background for new readers:**

Cameron Thorne, age 47, is an attorney/historian whose passion is researching sites and artifacts which indicate the presence in America of European explorers prior to Columbus. His wife, Amanda Spencer-Gunn, recently died; she had moved to the U.S. from England and was an expert on the medieval Knights Templar. Cam and Amanda adopted Astarte, who is of Native American descent, when she was a young girl. Astarte is now eighteen and attending college in Montana. Cam resides in the Massachusetts suburbs. This story is set in a post-COVID world, where the virus has been mostly brought under control.

CHAPTER 1

Cameron Thorne stared at his laptop screen, jaw clenched. He was already in a bad mood because Astarte had just flown back to college after winter break. Not to mention the furnace in his apartment had crapped out on the coldest weekend of the year. A cold home—made colder.

Now he had received an email from a dead man. In his experience, dead men rarely wrote with good news.

He pounded at the keyboard, fingertips barely able to feel contact. *Is this really Bruce Arrujo?*

The reply came immediately. *Come on, you knew I wasn't really dead.*

That was true. Both he and Amanda had suspected Bruce had faked his death to avoid jail or a mob hit—or both. So why had the rogue attorney, who specialized in fencing stolen paintings, resurfaced now?

Hands tucked under his armpits for warmth, Cam didn't have to wait long for his answer.

I came across a painting. I don't think it's worth much, at least not as artwork. But I think it may have some historical value. I thought of you. Free for a chat?

Pacing in front of a space heater, Cam dialed the number Bruce provided. They skipped the small talk. Neither saw the need to pretend to be friends, though Bruce knew he could trust Cam—Bruce's longtime love interest, Shelby Baskin, and Cam had been close for two decades.

"I'm in North Carolina, by the way," Bruce offered. "Asheville."

"Never been. Big arts community, I heard."

"You heard right. I bought into a small gallery. Art follows money. And there's plenty of money down here."

"I'm assuming you're not using your real name. Being dead and all."

Bruce made a noise deep in this throat. "Not a single letter. And I keep a low profile. But this seems like it might be important. I'm on a burner phone, obviously. Shelby thought it was worth the risk to reach out to you."

Cam knew Shelby was still in Boston. Somehow she and Bruce made it work long distance. It probably wasn't ideal, but it was better than nothing. Sighing, Cam felt the familiar pang of Amanda's loss. It had been almost a year. He'd kill for a weekend in North Carolina with her.

Bruce continued. "So, like I said, I'm not sure what to do with this. A guy brought a painting into our gallery. Late 1700s. It's a family portrait. Probably worth a couple hundred bucks, if that." He paused. "Or maybe a couple of million."

Cam laughed to himself. *A couple of million.* That explained why Bruce had risked reaching out to him. "Why the discrepancy?"

"Because it may be a portrait of the Hanks family."

Cam froze. "As in Nancy Hanks Lincoln?" Cam was a big fan of the sixteenth president. He knew there were no surviving portraits of President Lincoln's mother, and she died before photography was invented. In fact, surprisingly little was known about her, other than that she had been born out of wedlock, was said to have a bold personality, and died when the future president was only nine.

"In the portrait, she's only about ten years old. She was living with her grandparents at the time. The names of all the kids are written across the back, so I'm pretty sure it's her."

"That would be a big find. Nobody even is sure what she looked like."

Bruce paused. "Well, that's the thing. The reason I reached out. I need your help. And I'm willing to pay for your time and expenses. Looking at this portrait, I would say Lincoln's mother was Black."

✡ ✝ ✡

After getting Cam to sign a non-disclosure agreement, Bruce agreed to email Cam a copy of the portrait. Cam made a fire in the living room fireplace and stared into it, wondering how he had ended up here, in Newburyport, in a rented apartment. It had been a spur-of-the-moment decision to rent out his Westford lakefront home. A visiting executive offered him a boatload of money—"My wife and I just got divorced, and my boys really don't want to leave their friends and come live with me this coming summer, but I thought a lake might win them over." And Cam thought it might be good to get away from so many reminders of Amanda. Plus, Newburyport had a lot going on, especially downtown. And it turned out the real estate broker for the guy wanting to rent Cam's house knew of a furnished sublet that just hit the market. It would be like an extended vacation, Cam thought. But he had imagined some heat.

Waiting for Bruce to email the portrait, he walked to the front window of the Colonial-era ship captain's mansion, Venus by his side. The grand structure had been cut into six condos, the sublet unit consisting of two bedrooms in the basement and an ornate living room with kitchen area and porch on the first floor. He gazed out over the frozen Frog Pond on Bartlett Mall. For the past few weekends, he had been on the pond with neighborhood kids playing pond hockey. But today a swirling wind and temperatures in the single numbers kept even the hardiest skaters indoors.

He yawned. He hadn't slept well last night, strange dreams keeping him on edge. A haunting song, a refrain—*I am gone but in your dreams I live*—echoing in his skull still, like an earworm on steroids. As far as he knew, he'd never heard the song before. He rubbed his eyes. Oh, well. He had regular conversations with his dead wife, Amanda, which his therapist said was normal—well, not exactly normal, but an acceptable coping mechanism. Was it really so surprising that his dreams were messed up as well?

Cam pulled up a 1963 portrait of Nancy Hanks Lincoln, painted by a Lincoln historian asked to make his best guess as to her appearance.

1963 "Portrait" of Nancy Hanks Lincoln

Cam rolled his eyes. Nancy was depicted as demure and respectable —none of the boldness for which she was known. Cam guessed her pale skin tone was inaccurate as well in light of Bruce's painting. The 1963 depiction was, he thought wryly, a true "whitewash" of history.

He wondered what the historical record said about Nancy's appearance. There wasn't much, but this description spoke loudly: "Her skin was dark; hair dark brown; face sharp and angular." Well, they got the face part right in the 1963 portrait, at least.

Cam's computer dinged. Bruce's email. Cam studied the Hanks family portrait, along with the back side which listed the names. Joseph and Ann Hanks sat in the middle, unsmiling. Four children fanned out on either side. The smallest, Nancy—their granddaughter—stood at one end, next to Lucy, her birth mother.

The "dark skin" description was accurate. Not deep brown, but definitely biracial. And it was only Nancy—the rest of the family was lighter-toned. The inference was that Nancy's father—unknown to history—was probably dark-skinned. Cam sat back. So, did it matter? Did it matter that the president who freed the slaves may himself have been part Black? Or, instead, did it matter that the president who—as many modern critics liked to point out—delayed freeing the slaves for political reasons may have been betraying his own people?

Cam knew it was dangerous to look back 150 years and try to analyze and understand things using modern values. But Lincoln was an icon, near the top of every historian's list of most influential Americans. Understanding Lincoln meant, in many ways, understanding America. And, of course, the racial divide that tore the country apart during the Civil War had still not healed. If any American family was worth putting under a microscope, Lincoln's was.

And that microscope had, surprisingly, just revealed colors that were anything but lily white.

✡ ✝ ✡

Amanda's voice popped into Cam's head as he crouched in front of the fireplace, his hands tucked into the fur around Venus' neck in an attempt to stay warm.

Go, already. Pack a bag, grab some dog food, get in the car.

"Where?" he replied aloud.

North Carolina. Go look at the painting. No sense sitting here freezing your ass off. Even I'm cold, and I don't feel bloody anything.

Cam thought about it. A fourteen-hour drive. He could do a chunk today, find a hotel, then finish the trip tomorrow. And he had nothing urgent keeping him in Newburyport. Plus, his parents had retired to Chapel Hill, so he could swing by on the way home for a visit.

Even so, he voiced his trepidation. "We agreed I'd lay low, stay out of danger. You know, try not to get myself killed."

Yes, we did. But that doesn't mean being a shut-in. You haven't been out of this condo since Astarte left three days ago. Frankly, Cameron, you're turning into a bore. And that's saying something, coming from someone who lives only in your head.

Chuckling, Cam stood. "Come on Venus. Time for a road trip."

Then he caught himself. "Amanda?"

I'm still here.

"Did you hear that song overnight? I think it was a dream, but it seemed so real."

Don't be silly, Cameron. I live in your mind. If you heard it, I heard it.

"But did you? Hear it?"

Did you?

He laughed. "I guess I should know better than to try to win an argument against a voice in my head."

Don't kid yourself. You never won an argument when I was alive, either.

Venus looked up at him and whined. Cam checked his watch—sure enough, 3:30. Somehow the dog knew the exact time. They had developed a routine over the past few weeks. Leave the condo at 3:30, walk to a coffee shop down the street, grab a hot chocolate and a dog treat, then continue down to the riverfront park where dogs were allowed to be off-leash beginning at four. No matter how cold the day, Venus raced and rolled and frolicked in the park until Cam could finally cajole her away with the dog treat.

Cam grabbed his parka, hat and gloves and allowed Venus to drag him down the street. He was happy to match her pace, jogging alongside to keep warm. They reached the coffee shop in less than five minutes.

Cam pushed through the door and froze. A thin young woman sat on a stool, her face framed by straight dark hair, strumming a guitar and singing. *I am gone but in your dreams I live; I mean no harm but answers I must give...* "No way," Cam whispered. He edged closer, watching, listening. No doubt, it was the same song he had heard in his dreams. Venus whimpered. "One second, girl."

He stood, listening, waiting for the song to end. The singer looked up and smiled shyly. "I hope you liked it," she offered.

"I did." He shifted. "Did you write it?"

"Yes. It's new."

"Really?" He looked around. "I've never seen you playing here."

"Today's my first day."

He didn't want to appear creepy, but he also wanted some answers. "That song, is it based on anything? What do they call it, a derivative?"

Her eyes narrowed. "No. Like I said, I wrote it."

Weird. "Oh. Okay. Thanks."

"I can sell you a CD if you want."

He pulled out his wallet. "No, thanks." He dropped a ten-dollar bill into her guitar case. He was trying to get the song *out* of his head. "But thanks for letting me listen."

Just over an hour later, with Venus wiped out from her romp in the park, they pulled onto Interstate 495 heading southwest, the late afternoon winter sun refracting through the swirling, wind-driven snow dust. Still shaking his head over the song, Cam cranked the heat, tossed Venus a rawhide bone to gnaw on in the back seat of his new Jeep Cherokee, and hit Astarte's number on his speed dial.

"You free to talk?"

"Sure, Dad. Classes don't even start until Monday. What's up?"

He told her about the painting and what he knew about Lincoln's mother. "So I'm driving down to see it. Figured I'd test out the new car." In addition to moving, he had traded in Amanda's Subaru. Just too many memories. "What do you think? Is it worth my time?"

"Definitely. But I have a thought. Maybe she's not Black. Maybe she's Melungeon. This is Appalachia, right?"

"Interesting idea." Cam had heard of the Melungeons, but knew little about them.

"I did a paper on them last semester. Nobody's sure where they came from. They live in Appalachia, like I said. Based on recent DNA tests, they seem to be a mixture of Portuguese, Sephardic Jews, North Africans and Native Americans, mostly Cherokee. That's apparently where the name came from, Melungeon being a take-off on the French word, *mélange*, meaning mixture."

"But you said Portuguese, Jewish, African and Cherokee. None of them speak French."

"I know. It's part of the mystery. They might have come over on Spanish or Portuguese ships in the early Colonial period. Nobody's sure. But Hanks is a common Melungeon name."

"You said African. So then Lincoln's mother could be Black, right?"

"Yes, but I wasn't being clear. What I meant was that they don't seem to be related to Black slaves, most of whom were not from Northern Africa. The Melungeons have African blood, but it probably predates them coming to America. There was a Tennessee Supreme Court case from after the Civil War that decided that the Melungeons were Portuguese, descending from the ancient Phoenicians." Cam guessed that's where the African blood would have come in—the Phoenician territory extended to North Africa.

"Phoenician, huh?" Cam bit his lip. If they were Phoenician, they could have come to America in pre-Colonial times. Cam's research indicated that ancient Phoenician traders may have come to America to trade for and mine copper—needed during the Bronze Age—around 3,000 years ago.

"Could be, Dad. Nobody's sure how long the Melungeons have been here. Based on the DNA, the court could be right: They could be ancient Phoenicians who intermarried with the natives."

They were getting ahead of themselves. There was no indication that Nancy Hanks Lincoln was of Melungeon descent. Other than the 'Hanks' name. And her skin color. And that she grew up in Appalachia. Cam blinked. "Can you send me that paper you did?" His skin tingled the way it did when he sensed he was on the verge of some important discovery.

He knew what he'd be reading tonight in his hotel room.

Astarte hung up with her dad and leaned back into Matthias' arms, the springs of her Montana State dormitory bed squeaking beneath them.

He patted her butt. "Too big a lunch, maybe?" He could say it because they both knew she was in great shape, having spent much of her winter break cross-country skiing with her dad in Newburyport.

She slapped him playfully, turning to stare into his dark eyes. "Maybe you can help me burn some calories."

He grinned. "That's quite an offer, but I've got a meeting I can't miss. Will the offer still be good in an hour?"

"I'll give you forty-five minutes. After that, I'm heading over to frat row to do shots of tequila."

The truth was, she hoped the offer would be good for, well, the rest of her life. What had begun as a freshman-orientation infatuation had grown into an 18-month mature relationship. She knew she was still young and that things might change. But he checked all the boxes for her —they had great chemistry, he was her intellectual equal, he was kind and devoted, and they shared an indigenous heritage. And, crucially, he was supportive of the whole Fortieth Princess legend, the Mandan tribe's prophecy that Astarte was destined to lead the Native Americans—and perhaps all Americans—on some kind of spiritual awakening. It was a lot to put on her, and on him as well. If she didn't end up marrying Matthias, she hoped it would be someone just like him.

They shared a languid kiss at her doorway before Matthias jogged away. Astarte began to close her door when a stocky, middle-aged woman appeared at the top of the stairs, a few doors down from her room.

Huffing, the woman pulled herself up to the fourth-floor landing and caught Astarte's eye. "It's you," she breathed, placing her hand over her chest as she dropped her wicker carrying bag. She let out a long breath and stood motionless.

"I'm sorry?" Astarte replied. The woman looked Native American. Reddish-brown skin, high cheekbones, dark hair pulled back, a wide mouth. And bags under her narrow eyes.

"Astarte. The Fortieth Princess." Not a question, a statement.

Astarte took a step forward. "Yes, that's me. How did you know?"

The woman's weary eyes shone. "Your picture, my dear." She pulled a Polaroid from the pouch of her brown and beige wool poncho. "I have been traveling for three days, by bus. From Arizona, the Hopi Reservation." She smiled, showing a mouth crowded with small white teeth.

"Whatever for?"

"To see you, of course." She took a deep breath. "We need to warn people. The Blue Star is set to return."

✡ ✟ ✡

An hour after the Hopi woman appeared at her dorm, Astarte met Matthias at the dining hall for an early dinner.

"Sorry I had to call off our rendezvous."

He smiled. "Is that because of the squeaking springs joke I made?"

"No, it's because there's a Hopi woman sleeping in my bed." Astarte explained her guest's arrival and their quick conversation. "Poor thing hasn't slept in days, afraid someone would rob her on the bus. So I left her to sleep, told her we would talk tomorrow."

"I'm sorry, a blue star?"

"No idea. Like I said, I put her to bed."

✡ ✟ ✡

Rather than angling southwest through New York City, Cam stayed north of the metropolitan area. His prior research had uncovered evidence of a Templar journey to the Catskill Mountains of New York in the late 1100s. A fellow researcher had invited him to view a recently discovered carving of a Templar cross on the banks of the Hudson River not far from where the Templars would have disembarked to explore the Catskills. This trip south was a good chance to stop and check it out. His post-dinner arrival coincided with low tide, and the bright moon illuminated their hike through the woods and then north along the west bank of the partially frozen river.

"Thanks for coming out last minute on a cold night to show me this," Cam said as they walked, his breath visible.

"Not a problem." The bearded man, in his thirties, moved effortlessly across the rocky path. A person comfortable in the woods.

Twenty minutes after parking, his guide pointed a gloved finger at a boulder a few feet from the river's edge at a point where the river made a sharp bend. "There it is. Facing the river."

Using a bright flashlight, Cam bent to view it. A clear cross pattée in the style of the Templars, with arms narrow at the center and flared at the outside. He snapped a series of pictures.

Templar Cross, Hudson River

"Look at all the lichen growing in the carved areas," Cam said. "That indicates it's an old carving."

His guide nodded. "When the tide is really low, you can see a stone pier extending out from the carving into the river. I'm guessing the carving was a mark, or signpost."

Cam peered out at the Hudson. "Here, at the bend, is a perfect spot to put a hidden pier."

A half-hour later, he was back on the highway, heading south. Outside of Allentown, Pennsylvania, still nine hours from Asheville, Cam pulled into the parking lot of a dog-friendly motel. It was only eleven o'clock, and he could have driven for another couple of hours, but he wanted to read Astarte's paper on the Melungeons. As a diabetic, he also needed to eat.

He had listened to a podcast on his phone while he drove, discussing the Melungeon people and their history. The truth was, nobody was certain where they came from or how long they had lived in Appalachia. Daniel Boone was Melungeon, as was Elvis Presley. Tom Hanks, also—in fact, he was a distant cousin of Nancy Hanks Lincoln, as was George Clooney. The actress, Ava Gardner. Cher, the singer. Cam thought about the list: Most were swarthy, and they all shared dark, thick hair.

He checked in, ordered room service, walked Venus, and threw his bag on one of the twin beds. "Try not to snore," he said to the dog as his phone rang. He checked the number. Unknown. Shrugging, he answered.

"This is Cam."

"And this is Rivka."

He dropped onto the bed. They had not spoken in over a month. Last he heard, she was on a mission in the Baltic region. "Hi. Are you okay?"

"I'm alive. That's always a good thing."

She sounded distant, detached even. "Are you hurt?"

She sighed. "Like I said, I'm alive."

Cam stared out the window, not sure how to respond. They were in a strange place, not yet lovers but seemingly on that path. She, being a Mossad agent, couldn't really share much. And that was when she didn't drop off the radar entirely.

But he sensed something was wrong. He pushed a bit. "Are you hurt?"

He heard a gulp of air, which could have been a sob. "A little. My mission is over. I have two weeks off. I thought I could come visit. I could use … a friend."

"Of course. I'm actually on my way to North Carolina. You want to meet me there?"

She let out a long sigh. "Will you buy me a drink? And make me laugh?"

She wasn't normally so ... vulnerable. A former professional beach volleyball player, she combined a hard body with a soldier's willpower and discipline. It must have been a tough mission. "Of course. In fact, the more you drink, the funnier I get."

"I don't know. I'm afraid I won't be very good company."

"That's okay. I'm here to work anyway. Plus, I'm in a bit of a funk myself since Astarte went back to school. And the guy I'm meeting—his name is Bruce—is himself a killjoy. You'll fit right in. Maybe it'll even rain."

A small laugh echoed across the miles. "Okay, Cameron. I'll text you my flight info. And thanks."

He spent the next hour reading through Astarte's research paper. Aside from being impressed by the quality of her work, he was intrigued by the mystery of the Melungeon culture. How could a people know so little about its heritage? There were legends, of course. But apparently they had been living in Appalachia for so long—alternately avoiding contact with mainstream society and trying to assimilate into it—that the truth about their past had been lost to history.

Some clues remained, however. As Astarte said, DNA testing tied them to Portugal and North Africa, with some intriguing Sephardic Jewish blood mixed in along with the Cherokee influence. Cam had done a lot of research on Christopher Columbus and his ties to the outlawed Knights Templar—Columbus married into the same prominent Templar family as had the granddaughter of Scottish explorer Prince Henry Sinclair, purported to have visited New England in 1399. It stood to reason that Columbus would have had access to maps showing the route to America. And the timing of Columbus' departure from Spain coincided exactly with the effective date of a royal decree mandating that Jews of Spain either convert or flee. As a result, a number of Jews served aboard the ships of Columbus and other explorers—many of them Portuguese—in the late 1400s and early 1500s. Some of them could have found their way ashore and inland into Appalachia, perhaps with remnants of the outlawed Templar order. After the Templar put-down in 1307, most of the knights fled either to Scotland or Portugal. Cam didn't know as much about the Portuguese refugees from the Templar put-down as he did the Scottish. He had a feeling that would need to change.

Fresh in his mind, of course, was the Templar cross he had just viewed along the banks of the Hudson River. It was just one of many artifacts evidencing a twelfth-century Templar expedition to the area. And the Catskills range was part of the northern span of the Appalachians. If the Templars had been in northern Appalachia, why not the southern section as well?

The other clue Astarte had uncovered was an intriguing connection between Melungeon religious life and Judaism. Many Melungeons wore skull caps when praying, observed the Sabbath on Saturday rather than Sunday, read almost exclusively from the Old Testament, were married under a canopy (or chuppah), prepared a matzo-like cracker for the Last Supper (the Christian equivalent of Passover), relegated women to a separate section in the rear of the sanctuary, worshipped in a prayer hall devoid of crosses and steeples and stained glass, began the count of a new day at sundown rather than sunrise, and abstained from eating pork. And those who did eat pork slaughtered the pig following the kosher practice of slitting its throat and letting the blood drain, then scrubbing the carcass with salt.

Cam sat back. A secret sect of Jews living in the heart of America's Bible Belt? No wonder they kept to themselves.

CHAPTER 2

Astarte returned to her dorm room Sunday morning, not sure what she would find. She knocked lightly. "Hello?" she said.

The door swung open. The Hopi woman, who stood only about five feet tall, beamed up at her, her hair wet.

"Good morning. Thank you, I feel much better. I hope you don't mind that I found a towel and took a shower."

"Of course not. You know, I still don't know your name." Astarte saw that the woman had made the bed.

"Soohu. It means 'star.' You see, I was destined to watch the stars and learn their meanings. It has always been so in my family." She held Astarte's eyes. "We all have paths we must follow."

"Well, are you hungry, Soohu? It would not be wise to follow our paths on empty stomachs."

"Hungry like the wolf in winter," she replied with a toothy smile.

Over brunch, Soohu spoke between bites. She had pulled a book from her poncho and handed it to Astarte. "Have you read this?"

Astarte glanced at it. *Earth Under Fire: Humanity's Survival of the Ice Age,* by Paul A. LaViolette. "No. But I have a feeling you're going to tell me I should."

Soohu nodded. "The book explains how, periodically, the core of our galaxy explodes, sending out waves of cosmic rays which heat up our atmosphere and lead to floods and fire and vast destruction." She stopped eating. "The last explosion was about 12,000 years ago, ending the Ice Age."

Astarte nodded. She knew that almost every ancient culture had a flood legend and that most scientists agreed that some cataclysmic, climate-changing event occurred around 12,000 years ago.

Continuing, Soohu said, "Our Hopi legends speak of three epochs before the present one, each ending in vast destruction. I have been taught the prophecy, as have hundreds of women in my family before me." She closed her eyes and spoke, reciting the words from memory:

There will come a time when a blue star will appear in the sky. Its light will shatter the darkness of the night. The Blue Star will bring a wind, a wind which has not been seen on Earth since the time of the mammoths and mastodons. The Blue Star, which we call Kachina, will bring a fire. This fire will be so bright and hot that it will transform the matter of the universe. The blue light of this star is a signal which shall end the fourth world. The Blue Star will cause the oceans of the world to rise and topple upon the land, flooding the world. Almost all living things will perish in this great catastrophe.

Soohu opened her eyes, which had moistened. She took Astarte's hand. "As the prophecy says, each of the previous calamities was portended by the appearance of a blue star. This star, Kachina, appears in what is normally a black void near the Milky Way. Through modern science, we now know that the Blue Star is located, in fact, at the very center of the galaxy."

Astarte sat motionless. Clearly she had underestimated her guest, based at least partly on her travel-weary appearance and seeming lack of sophistication. But beneath that wool poncho beat the heart of a woman passionate about fulfilling her role as guardian of the Hopi prophecy. "I'm not sure I understand. If this Blue Star is so deadly, how can the Hopi have any memory of it? Did people really survive?"

"Yes, some people did. We went underground. Are you familiar with the cliff dwellings of the Anasazi?" Soohu handed Astarte a Polaroid photo.

Anasazi Cliff Dwelling, Mesa Verde, Colorado

Astarte nodded. She and her parents had driven to see them while visiting the Grand Canyon a couple of summers ago. Some dwellings consisted of as many as 150 rooms, built high into the sides of cliff faces in Mesa Verde, Colorado. Other similar cliff dwellings existed nearby.

"Well," Soohu continued, "the Anasazi are the ancestors of the Hopi. As you probably know, we are all part of what is called the Pueblo Indians. Do you know why we have that name?"

"Because you live in villages. 'Pueblo' is Spanish for village."

"Correct. Historically, we have always lived in villages. Except, periodically, when—for some mysterious reason—we relocated to the cliffs." She leaned closer. "What people don't realize is that there are tunnels leading underground from these cliff dwellings. There is a vast subterranean living area in those cliffs."

"I get it. You moved to the cliffs when the Blue Star appeared."

"Yes. Or when we feared Kachina was coming. We were high enough in the hills—at over seven thousand feet in elevation—to avoid the floods, and by being underground we avoided the fire and searing heat. The Hopi legend is that we were the only people to survive the calamity. It was left to us to then repopulate the earth." She paused. "I don't want that burden to fall solely on us again."

Astarte nodded. "Which is why you're here, obviously."

Soohu held Astarte's eyes. "Like my ancestors, I have been trained to read the stars. Unlike them, I have the benefit of modern science. The second largest telescope in the country is located in Arizona. I have been lucky enough to be allowed to use it from time to time and I see alarming activity at the galactic center." She swallowed. "I believe the next explosion is imminent. I fear that the arrival of the Blue Star, the arrival of Kachina, is near. As the book title suggests, we are about to experience an explosion which truly will put the *earth under fire*."

✵ ✛ ✡

Cam had awoken before dawn, relieved that the song had not haunted his sleep, and made great time on the highway, his eyes drinking in the beauty of the majestic Blue Ridge range—tinted blue by the hydrocarbons released from the trees—as he crossed from Tennessee into North Carolina. He pulled into Asheville early in the afternoon on a warm, sunny Sunday. He wound his way from the highway past the Art Deco-style City Hall building and a grand, brick Masonic temple, two of the many historic buildings for which the city was famous.

Bruce had given him the gallery address, in the pastel-colored River Arts District south of downtown. Cam waited as a parking spot opened up, studying the bustling city and its art-loving occupants from his Cherokee. Ironically, before the Europeans arrived, this was Cherokee country. Had the Melungeons been among the earliest European settlers? Or had they come centuries earlier, fleeing Spain and Portugal in the days of the Inquisition? Or perhaps even earlier than that, as part of a group of copper traders sailing from one of the Phoenician city-states ringing the Mediterranean? Whatever the case, Melungeon DNA testing indicated that they were part Cherokee.

Cam shook his head. He would not likely find answers inside the SUV. Venus on her leash, Cam stepped out. He looked up at Bruce's gallery, the name 'Null & Boyd' etched in gold lettering above the door of the lime-green stucco façade.

Smiling at the name, he pushed through the glass door.

"Can I help you?" asked a college-aged woman in jeans and a blouse which matched the building color.

"Um, I'm looking for the owner."

She picked up some kind of house phone, asked Cam his name, then escorted him into a back room through a thick wooden door. Unsmiling, Bruce stood to greet him. "Thanks for coming."

Bruce had done a good job changing what had once been a dark, rugged appearance. Cam remembered him as fit and square-jawed with olive skin and a full head of black hair. He was still fit—a white golf shirt showed off both his tanned complexion and his biceps. But his jaw was covered by a bushy beard and he had shaved his head. Plus, he wore thick glasses. So he looked less like a Mediterranean runway model and more like, well, an art gallery owner. An unsmiling one, closed and guarded. Only Shelby, it seemed, could break through.

They had only met a few times, always with Shelby as a buffer. Too bad this weekend did not coincide with one of her periodic visits. Cam tried to break the ice. "Cute name, Null & Boyd. Which are you?"

Bruce motioned for Cam to sit in a director's chair as he retreated around his desk. "Null. I could have chosen 'Sample,' but 'Null' went better with 'Boyd,' I thought."

Cam angled his head. "I get the 'Null & Boyd' wordplay, but I'm not tracking you with 'Sample.'"

"Right. Sorry. Not everyone is paranoid like me." He tapped at his computer keyboard for a few seconds before spinning the monitor toward Cam. A headline appeared: *Hello, I'm Mr. Null. My Name Makes Me Invisible to Computers.*

Bruce explained. "It's a bit like the Y2K problem. Most computers read 'null' to mean 'blank' or 'nothing.' Same with 'sample.' But a field can't be left blank. So computers don't know what to do when someone enters 'Null.' Some crash, some loop back and ask for the name again, some just do nothing, as if waiting for more information." Bruce offered a hint of a smile. "For someone looking to go off the grid, it's the perfect name. It won't fool Homeland Security or the FBI, but most state and local governments aren't sophisticated enough in their programming to have fixed the glitch."

"In other words, you don't exist."

"Pretty much. It makes it hard to book a plane ticket sometimes, but the flip side is, like you said, I don't show up on most databases or records searches. So even if you had my picture or my fingerprints or my DNA, you wouldn't be able to get to my name. You'd just come back with null, nothing." He paused. "First name is now Lenny, by the way." He shrugged. "I was a big fan of Lenny Bruce, the comedian."

Cam was impressed. But not surprised. Bruce Arrujo had spent a lifetime operating in the gray areas of society. Often dark gray. Lenny Null was now doing the same.

"So, can I see the painting?"

"Not until tomorrow, unfortunately. By the time you told me you were coming down, the vault where I keep my stuff was closed for the weekend."

"Vault? Is this painting really that valuable?"

Bruce/Lenny shrugged. "Like I told you, either a few hundred or a few million." He paused. "And the fact you drove fourteen hours just to see it makes me think the latter is a possibility."

"Fair point. Where'd you get it, anyway?"

"Guy walked in with it after an older relative died, same way we get a lot of our stuff. Actually, I shouldn't say 'we.' I bought Boyd out last year, a few months before he died. Tough situation. He had a bad case of dementia, was always ranting and raving. Apparently, he was an impressive guy back in his day—mayor, Master of the Masonic lodge, set up a big scholarship fund. I leave his name on the door because so many people knew him around here. Plus, they're amused by the wordplay." He shifted. "I should tell you, I got an interesting call last night. From the family lawyer. Asking for the painting back. Said it was a mistake to sell it. A family heirloom. Offered me ten times what I paid for it."

"What'd you say?"

Lenny held Cam's eyes. "I've done this my whole life. I know when someone's fucking with me. That painting's not an heirloom. At least not in the traditional sense."

"So you said no?"

"And make an enemy before I needed to?" Lenny shook his head, as if answering a stupid question. "I've got enough people pissed off at me. I told him I'd have to consult with my partner. That'll give us time to figure this out, hopefully."

✠

Astarte and Soohu had been in the dining hall for three hours and had yet to get up even to clear their food trays. Soohu had gone deep into the science of a galactic explosion, explaining both its causes and its effects. Astarte only half-understood the science—best she could understand, it was comparable to giant sun flares. But she did not need to understand the science to understand its ramifications.

Astarte rubbed her face with her hands. Of all the things she thought the little Hopi woman was going to tell her, the imminence of doomsday was not high on the list. She took a deep breath. "This Blue Star, you say you can see it?"

"Yes, but only faintly. During an explosion, you can't miss it. Based on the blue glow we see during explosions in other distant galaxies, we expect it would look something like this, the blue color caused by cosmic dust." As if dealing cards from a deck, knowing she had the winning hand, she handed Astarte another picture.

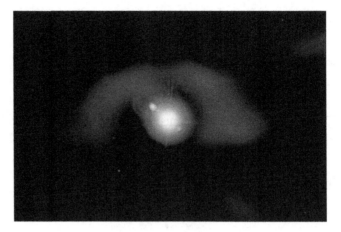

Blue Star Explosion

Astarte looked at the image. "Well, if you're only seeing a faint blue glow, you can't be certain it's really coming, right?"

Soohu nodded. "True. I understand your skepticism. And you are correct, it could be a false alarm, could be only minor activity. But the prophecy tells us exactly where to look. And the glow is in the exact spot." She pulled yet another image from her folder. "Here, let me show you."

Sagittarius and Scorpio at Galactic Core

Astarte studied the image, showing animated depictions of the Sagittarius and Scorpio constellations against the night sky, with the Milky Way behind Sagittarius' bow.

Soohu explained. "Most people associate these constellations with the Greeks and Babylonians. But they are more universal than that, going back to pre-history. Ancient cultures, many of them now lost, had knowledge of the signs of the Zodiac." She gestured toward the photo. "These are the only two constellations with arrows, or pointers. Sagittarius is pointing his arrow straight across the sky, while Scorpio's stinger is aimed directly up. See how the two lines intersect at a bright spot? That's the galactic core, which is normally dark but is depicted bright to show an explosion."

"You think they are pointing at it on purpose?" Which made no sense, really, unless some greater being—whoever created the stars—intended to send a message to earthlings.

Soohu read her thoughts. "No, I don't think the gods are speaking to us. I think the constellations were *designed* by ancient humans, much as we see shapes in the clouds today. The depictions—the archer and the scorpion in this case—were invented as a message to future generations. When you think about it, you could make almost any shape or figure given the millions of stars. The archer could just as easily have been, say, an elephant. And the scorpion a grasshopper. But the ancient peoples wanted pointers, arrows, as part of a message." She pointed at the image. "This is a cypher—a zodiacal cryptogram—devised by ancient star watchers to warn future generations of a cycle of explosions at the galactic core. They are telling us exactly where to look, where the Blue Star will form. By keeping close watch, we buy ourselves some time. Time to prepare for the coming calamity."

"How much time?"

Soohu shook her head sadly. "Not much. Understand, the center of the galaxy is twenty-six thousand light years away, so it takes twenty-six thousand years for the blue light of the explosion to reach us as it barrels across the galaxy. What we experience here on earth is the result of an explosion which occurred tens of thousands of years ago. But the fact that we can see the blue light, even faintly, indicates it is fast approaching."

"Do the cosmic rays move as fast as the light?"

"Good question. The rays take longer since they are composed of dust and other mass which will not move as fast as the light—as you know, nothing moves as fast as light. Our legends tell us the lag between when the Blue Star first appears and the cosmic storm hits may be a year or two. But other things, such as a gravity wave which could cause tsunamis and volcanic eruptions, will likely hit us sooner." She shrugged. "It is impossible to predict the exact timing. But the blue glow seems to be getting brighter every day. I fear Kachina is coming."

Astarte asked again. 'Not much' wasn't really an answer. "So, if you had to give an exact estimate, how much time do you think we have?"

She sat back and held Astarte's eyes. "Based on my calculations, we could have less than three months before the fires and floods begin."

⚙ ✝ ✡

Knowing he had the rest of the afternoon to kill, Cam trudged up a steady incline from the arts district back toward Asheville's downtown area, Venus in tow, the Masonic temple his destination. Many of the older lodge buildings embedded Masonic symbolism and secrets into their architecture and design. He was not a Freemason himself but, as a Templar historian, he was always curious to learn more about Masonic history and lore. Actually, 'curious' was probably not the right word; 'obsessed' would be more accurate. There was some ancient secret or hidden knowledge at the core of Freemasonry, something they had inherited from the Templars, which was just beyond Cam's reach. He was like a kid desperately swimming after a beach ball—every time he reached out for it, his movement seemed to propel it further away. Maybe he should just relax and let the secret float back to him.

He stopped and admired the Masonic temple. Built just over a hundred years ago, the four-story brick building featured a two-story portico—complete with four granite Ionic pillars—rising above the entrance, as if trying to evoke the feeling of an ancient Roman temple. *Roman.* The back of Cam's neck tingled. Why would Freemasons want to evoke anything Roman in their architecture? If anything, Rome—specifically, the Vatican—was the enemy of Freemasonry, the Pope having decreed that being a Mason was a grave sin, disqualifying members from receiving Communion. And there was little in Masonic ritual or symbolism which related to Rome—instead, the rituals tended to harken back to Jerusalem and ancient Egypt.

Studying the building, Cam recalled something the patriot Thomas Paine—who authored a treatise about Freemasonry—wrote: "Freemasonry is derived and is the remains of the religion of the ancient Druids; who, like the Magi of Persia and the Priests of Heliopolis in Egypt, were Priests of the Sun." Was sun worship therefore the Masonic connection to ancient Rome? Rome did not officially adopt Christianity until the fourth century; prior to that, many Romans (especially those affiliated with the military) worshiped Mithras, the sun god, and/or Sol Invictus, the 'Unconquered Sun.' Cam would need to explore this connection further—perhaps it was key to understanding the secret at the heart of Freemasonry.

But, for today, he would just admire the Roman-style building and enjoy the warm afternoon sun on his face, putting aside for now the question as to whether the two were somehow related.

✦✝✡

Matthias loped into the dining hall and joined Astarte and Soohu at around three o'clock.

"You guys must have been hungry," he said with a smile, grabbing a cold piece of bacon off Astarte's plate.

Astarte introduced them. "Soohu, would you mind repeating what you've told me? Abbreviated version, of course. I want Matthias to hear it. Plus, it would help me to get it a second time."

Forty minutes later, Matthias leaned back, balancing on the rear legs of his chair. "Wow. I'm part of the Blackfoot tribe, and we have some crazy legends. But you get the gold for this one." He eyed Soohu across the table. "Do other cultures have this legend?"

"Almost all of them, in fact. The Aborigines of Australia have a myth of people and animals moving underground to escape a global fire. The Chinese speak of a time of great destruction when the sun had the strength of ten suns. The Hindus speak of a calamity brought on by a wind-driven fire sweeping the earth, followed by the whole world covered in water. The ancient Britons speak of a small group of people surviving a time of burning and flooding by secreting themselves in an underground enclosure." She shrugged. "I could go on."

Matthias took a deep breath. "Are any of them specific as to the Blue Star prophecy?"

"Yes, the Egyptian." She pulled another photo from her pouch and placed it on the table. "One of the effects of the explosion is that cosmic dust begins to swirl around what used to be the dark center of the galaxy. At times, it appears to be more than just a blue star. You end up with something like this."

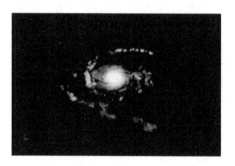

Blue Star Explosion with Cosmic Dust

Soohu continued. "Does that look familiar to either of you?"

Matthias angled his head. "It looks a little like the Eye of Horus."

Astarte pulled up an image of the Eye of Horus on her phone and nodded. "It sort of does."

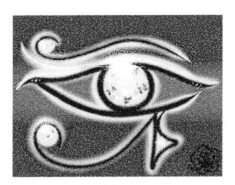

Eye of Horus Depiction

Soohu smiled, turned to Astarte, and gave her a look as if to say, *He's a keeper, this one.*

Instead, she said, "You could see how the ancient peoples would have thought so. What's interesting," Soohu continued, "is that the ancient Egyptians have a legend about a great eye in the heavens inflicting punishment on mankind, as if the eye were some kind of angry god. In fact, the name 'Horus' means, 'He who is above.' So it's entirely possible that the Egyptians looked up and saw the Eye of Horus in the stars just before, or as, the cosmic calamity hit earth. Remember, this is an area in the sky which is normally black, then all of a sudden the eye appears. Those few who survived may have attributed the destruction to an angry god, in this case, Horus."

They sat in silence for a few seconds, contemplating Soohu's words.

Astarte spoke first. "Okay, so what do we do? I think we have to assume this prophecy has some validity. And we can't just let the world, you know, come to an end."

Matthias smiled. "I'm grabbing my sleeping bag and staking a claim to one of those cliff rooms."

Astarte cuffed him playfully. "Come on, seriously."

Matthias looked at Soohu. "Have you gone to the authorities with this?"

She exhaled. "I've tried. Other than a few astronomers who've seen the same blue glow I've seen, nobody will listen." She shrugged. "I don't have a formal education, much less a degree in astronomy. And our tribe went through an ugly power struggle about ten years ago. My group, unfortunately, lost." She held up her hands. "So the Hopi tribal leaders are skeptical of anything I say."

Astarte nodded. "It sounds like that Jennifer Lawrence movie, *Don't Look Up*. A meteorite is about to hit the earth, and nobody'll believe her."

"Yeah, well, that's just a movie," Matthias said. "This sounds like it's for real."

◈ ✝ ✡

Cam had spent twenty minutes studying the Masonic temple—Venus interrupting periodically by barking at a squirrel—and was ready to call it a day when a voice behind him spoke.

"Can't go in there with a dog."

Cam turned and smiled politely at a gangly older man, hunched over his cane, wearing an Irish flat cap. "No, I suppose not."

"An insult to the dog, I say." He turned away from Cam and spat through yellow teeth, the movement causing his smudged glasses to slide down his nose. "They take in much worse."

Venus looked up at the man with wide eyes. She was normally a good judge of character. "How so?" Cam replied.

"If you had an hour, I'd fill your head with stories about these hypocrites."

"I don't have an hour, but I wouldn't mind the abridged version, if you don't mind."

Grunting, the man led Cam to a walkway running through the land-scaped front lawn of a bank across the street. He sat on a boulder, peering at the imposing brick Masonic structure which took up more than half the city block.

"They claim anyone can join. But that's rubbish. Not down here, at least. Not if you're Jewish. Or at least not in 1962."

Cam sat on an adjoining landscape boulder. "1962?" A decade before Cam was born.

"My father tried to join. I was fifteen at the time. He and a couple of his buddies. They got in. He didn't. Blackballed. For being Jewish. His buddies were Christian."

Cam knew that being blackballed was a literal thing—when voting on new members, each Mason was given two marbles, one black and one white, to drop anonymously into a box. If the candidate received even a single black marble, he was considered 'blackballed' or rejected. But what Cam didn't know was that Masonry was anti-Jewish. He supposed that, in the South, things might be different from the Northeast. And what he also didn't know was why something that happened in 1962 still mattered so much. So he merely nodded and waited for his new friend to continue.

"My dad took it hard. Started drinking. Lost his job. A year later, he stepped in front of a Greyhound bus." His rheumy dark eyes held Cam's. "My mother told people it was an accident, but I knew the truth." He lifted his chin. "Being blackballed killed him, sure as if one of those Freemasons had pushed him into that bus." He exhaled. "Fifty-nine years. And I'm still bitter."

Cam said, "I'm sorry," then they sat in silence for a few seconds. Was there more to this?

"So I decided to get back at them, to avenge his death." He lowered his voice. "I actually considered burning down their temple at one point, but they have insurance and would just rebuild. So I decided I'd hit them where it really hurts. I'd figure out the secrets they're trying to keep and then tell the world."

"And? Did you?"

The man waved Cam's comment away. "Turns out the secrets are not all that interesting. No treasure or taking over the world or anything. The world wouldn't really care."

Masonic secrets? "Well, I care. I've been trying to figure these guys out for years."

The man grinned. "Well, then it looks like you're going to need to give me that hour after all."

Lenny Null drove fast, his BMW 8 Series convertible hugging the narrow mountain road as he accelerated through a tight turn. He wasn't big on gadgets and toys, but he loved a quality automobile. And if he was going to drive a half hour every day to the gallery, he was damn sure not going to do it in a minivan. As he reflected on it, there really was nothing surprising about him driving a luxury coupe at this point in his life. What was surprising was that he was doing so in Appalachia.

Not that his life had been predictable in any way. An art thief in college, he had gone to law school and landed a job with a top Boston law firm because he figured scamming institutional clients from the inside would be safer than breaking into museums from the outside. He was correct in that assumption and would have been content to swindle his way to a small fortune had he not met Shelby Baskin. She had cursed him with the worst thing a crook could be saddled with—a conscience. She had, in short, made him want to be worthy of her. As if that could ever happen.

But he tried. He went straight, building a successful career consulting with museums and their insurance companies about security protocols. In other words, he'd case places so they could prevent people like himself from breaking in. For a fee, of course.

That had all been fine until an old job had come back to bite him. The mob had put a price on his head, so he had pulled off one last scam—a multi-million-dollar real estate play stinging a Saudi prince—before faking his own death and going underground. Resurfacing in Asheville, he changed his look, kept a low profile, and counted on the 'Null' name to keep him off the grid.

His leather gloves gripped the steering wheel. The temperature had been in the fifties in town, but as he climbed—Mount Mitchell, the highest point east of the Mississippi, visible in the distance—it had dropped fifteen degrees. He had come to appreciate the mountains of Appalachia, both for their beauty and for the isolation they provided. Throughout American history, settlers had ventured into the mountains to hide from the law or escape discrimination or simply find solitude. Of course, few of them had millions of dollars to buy dozens of acres of secluded mountain land and build a retreat like Lenny did.

It would have been nice if this were one of the weekends Shelby was visiting. She could have entertained Cam, asked him about his daughter's prophecy and told stories and showed him around town. But they limited her visits for safety reasons, and even then she would fly into Charlotte rather than Asheville and drive two hours in a Honda—registered to Null —which Lenny kept garaged near the airport. They both knew that if someone really wanted to hunt Lenny down, they probably could. But they weren't going to make it easy.

Lenny had not lied to Cam about the vault being locked for the weekend. Or at least had only half-lied. The vault wasn't a bank vault like Lenny had implied; rather, it was part of an elaborate, secure complex of underground rooms Lenny had built beneath what looked from the outside to be a modest mountain home. Partly this subterranean complex served as a deluxe safe room should someone come looking for him. But it had a second benefit as well. Lenny had spent a lifetime studying how to rob institutions like banks and museums—no way was he going to entrust those idiots with his treasures.

◈ ✚ ✡

Cam had bought a hot chocolate for himself and cup of coffee for the elderly man as the late afternoon sun began to set. The man had identified himself as 'Paris,'' which Cam assumed was his surname.

"Back then, it was hard to get information on the Masons. No internet, no TV documentaries. So I started watching the obituaries. Whenever one of these guys died, they'd put the lodge affiliation in the obituary, right? Then I'd wait for the estate sale. That's where I got a bunch of books. Mackey, Anderson, Coil, all the encyclopedias." He shrugged. "And I started reading."

"And you figured out the secret?"

"It wasn't that hard, once you take away all the pomp and circumstance and silly aprons and marching around." He studied Cam. "In fact, I bet you could figure it out. You seem like a smart guy. And if you get the same answer I got, then I'll know I'm right."

Cam smiled. "I'm only here for another day or two."

"Then I'll give you three hints, sort of like a genie. Payment for this cup of coffee." He counted them off on his fingers. "First, most of the Masonic rituals, the degrees, involve priests from the Old Testament. Some kings, yes, but mostly obscure priests. Why is that?" He paused, taking a breath. "Second, you need to look closely at the story of Josephus, the Jewish historian. He was captured during King Herod's war around 70 AD—he was a Jewish general. But somehow he was able to get himself pardoned. He even got himself adopted by the Roman emperor. There had to be something going on there, right?"

"Okay."

"Third, the whole story about Freemasonry evolving from the old stonemason guilds is bullshit." His voice rose. "It's a cover story to keep people from figuring out the truth. No way would the old English gentry join a social club with a bunch of dirty laborers. Just wouldn't happen."

Fair point. Cam nodded. "Okay, you've given me some good homework. Some good things to chew on tonight." He was supposed to meet Lenny at the gallery at eleven the next day to see the portrait. And then Rivka's flight landed at three. "Can we meet back here tomorrow at, say, nine o'clock?"

Paris smiled. "Not like I have anything else going on." He pushed himself to his feet, rubbed Venus on the head, began to walk away, and stopped. "Oh, one more thing. I saw you eyeing that Roman portico on the temple. You're right—that's a clue also."

Cam nodded. "Thanks. That's a good deal—buy three clues, get one free."

Paris shrugged. "Even genies like happy customers." He took three steps before adding, under his breath, "Just don't tell anyone. I'm supposed to be angry and bitter. Don't want anyone to think I've gone soft."

⚒ ✝ ✡

A dejected Astarte sat in the passenger seat while Matthias navigated the streets of downtown Bozeman. He had borrowed his roommate's car, and they had dropped Soohu at the bus station for her long trek back to northern Arizona. She had left Astarte with a thick binder full of documentation and images and reports, not to mention a heavy, sinking feeling in her gut. And also a boatload of questions.

Exhaling, Astarte asked the obvious one. "So what am I supposed to do?"

"Tell people. That's all you can do."

She could always rely on Matthias to be practical. But his suggestion wasn't much of a battle plan. "Warning people about a galactic explosion isn't my prophecy. I'm supposed to unite the Indians and lead us down a new spiritual path. Not into underground bunkers."

He glanced over and smiled sadly. "Can't unite us if we're all dead. So, first things first."

"That's another thing. Soohu wants me to only spread the word to Indians. She says there's not enough room underground for everyone, and we should save our own people first." She frowned. "I'm not sure I can do that."

He nodded. "I hear you."

"And who's to say it will even work, going underground?"

"Well, it worked three times before, according to Hopi legend. I'd rather take my chances underground, in the mountains, than, say, along the coast."

Astarte tried to picture how it would all work. Soohu had explained that the best locations, based on Hopi lore, were located at high altitude (to stay above floodwaters) and featured naturally occurring underground caves; in addition, since ash from all the fires would block the sun's rays and cause the earth's temperature to drop, southern locations would be more survivable than northern ones. But what about food? Oxygen? And how would the animals survive? Should they take them, two-by-two, like in Noah's Ark?

She sighed. "I glanced through that book she gave me, *Earth Under Fire*. You know what the author suggests? He says we should build a giant shield on the edge of the solar system to deflect the cosmic rays. Like that's going to happen."

"That's it, that's his advice?"

She sat back, dejected. "He also says we should pray."

✦ ✚ ✡

Cam had checked into a pet-friendly hotel in downtown Asheville after his encounter with Paris at the Masonic temple. Not wanting to leave Venus alone, he had planned to order room service. A phone call from Astarte interrupted those plans.

"How's my girl?"

"Other than the world coming to an end, I'm fine."

"Come on, it can't be that bad."

"No, seriously, the world is coming to an end. Ever hear of the Blue Star, or Kachina, prophecy?"

Twenty minutes later, he had forgotten about dinner. "Are you serious? Wow. That is heavy stuff."

"I'm not sure what to do."

He wasn't sure how seriously to take this prophecy, but Astarte clearly was concerned. "What about the NCAI folks?" he asked. The leaders of the National Congress of American Indians, based in Washington, D.C., had reached out to Astarte a year ago to tell her they were aware of her prophecy and supportive of her efforts to unite the tribes. And Cam was assuming that Indian groups would be most receptive to a message of an Indian prophecy. "I mean, why reinvent the wheel? They have a national organization already in place. They easily could arrange for you to spread the word."

"Good idea."

"In fact, why didn't the Hopi woman do that?"

"Apparently, there was a power struggle in her tribe and her side lost, so she's sort of *persona non grata*. She also said she thinks it would be more impactful coming from me, anyway. The Blue Star is still really faint, and she's worried they won't take her seriously."

"But you believed her."

"Yes."

"So why wouldn't they?"

"I don't know, Dad." He noticed an edge to her voice, probably because of the pressure she felt. And because, well, kids always tended to be short with their parents. Even kids as level-headed as Astarte.

She continued, "Maybe because I'm young and naïve and impressionable."

"I'll give you 'young,' honey," he said with a chuckle. "But I get your point. The Hopi woman probably thought it was best to pass this off to you, that you would have the best chance of being heard."

"Yeah, well, no pressure. All I have to do is convince three million Indians to pack up, head to the mountains, and begin digging caves. Shouldn't be too hard."

"Just Indians?"

"I'll tell anyone who will listen, Dad. But we're talking about a Hopi legend merging with a Mandan prophecy. I don't expect the Rotary Clubs of the world to pay much attention to me."

◈ ✛ ✡

Cam hung up with Astarte, ate dinner, and walked Venus, his thoughts on the Blue Star prophecy. In some ways, it reminded him of the Mayan calendar scare of 2012. On the one hand, it was just a legend. On the other, it had people pretty nervous. In the end, the possibility of the world becoming engulfed in fire and flood was too monumental just to ignore. He left a voicemail for a buddy from his softball team who worked at the MIT Haystack Observatory in Westford.

"Hey, it's Cam Thorne. Can you give me a call when you get a chance?" He chuckled. "Nothing important, just the end of the world."

Back in his hotel room, he opened his laptop and spent the next four hours ferreting around in the dark, dusty corners of Masonic history, illuminated only by the faint glow of the clues Paris had given him. He found online articles, purchased obscure books (fortunately, almost everything was available for download these days), and visited discussion forums populated by conspiracy theorists and nut jobs. Everyone, it seemed, had an opinion about the Freemasons.

Cam focused first on Paris' observation that most Masonic rituals involved priests (many of them relatively obscure) from the Old Testament. These priests—the descendants of Aaron, Moses' brother—were the caretakers of the Temple of Solomon (and later, when it was rebuilt,

King Herod's Temple) and in charge of rituals within it. Cam found a book which confirmed Paris' point and took it one step further:

> *Masonic rituals and legends always refer exclusively to fundamental episodes in the history of the Judaic priestly family. For example, the rituals from the first to the twelfth degree all revolve around the building of the First Temple—not from a historical perspective, as told in the Bible, but from the point of view of the priestly family.*

The author then went on to make the same point about Masonic degrees thirteen through thirty-two—the rituals all recounted stories of the Bible, told from the point of view of, and with a focus on, the priestly families.

Why would the Freemasons focus with such single-mindedness on obscure priests of the Old Testament? The answer, Cam guessed, was the same reason people obsessed over their family trees: These priests, *being their forefathers*, were important to them.

Cam sat back. Something resonated in the back of his mind. He did a quick internet search. *There.* He read that, under Masonic tradition, the son of a lodge brother automatically qualified for membership. Such a candidate was called a 'Lewis.' The name, Cam knew, was the Anglicized version of 'Levite'—the tribe of the Biblical Jewish priestly family. It wasn't even subtle, a secret hidden in plain sight. The Masons passed on the priestly title—a 'Lewis'—to their sons just as the Levites of the ancient Temple had passed on priestly honors to theirs.

Sensing that Paris was on the right track, Cam moved on to the second clue, Josephus. History remembered him as the chronicler of Jewish history, author of *Antiquities of the Jews*. But, according to Paris, there was more to his story.

Cam quickly confirmed this. Josephus was born into the Jewish priestly class in the first century, just after the death of Jesus. In the early years of the Jewish revolt against Rome, Josephus—a skilled tactician—led Jewish forces against the Roman general, Vespasian. Faced with certain defeat, he surrendered and, taking advantage of his priestly status, won Vespasian over by claiming a Jewish prophecy existed declaring that

Vespasian would soon be emperor. Flattered, Vespasian granted Josephus his freedom. Josephus then defected to the Roman side, was granted Roman citizenship, and—when the prophecy came true—was eventually adopted into Vespasian's family, where he lived a life of leisure and luxury.

But the story was more nuanced than that. Cam learned that Josephus, before leaving Jerusalem, had somehow negotiated the freedom of 240 prisoners, all friends and family of his and all members of the Jewish priestly class. Given that most Jewish prisoners were slaughtered—or at least enslaved—after the revolt, Josephus must have offered something of incredible value to Vespasian to secure the freedom of these prisoners. By most accounts, few members of the priestly class families, beyond this group of 240, survived. Cam also learned that, as part of the deal, the prisoners had to agree to leave Jerusalem and accompany Josephus to Rome, Vespasian being fearful that the Temple would be rebuilt and the Jews would rise up again (as, in fact, they did during the Bar Kokhba revolt approximately 60 years later).

Cam stood and stretched. He didn't have all the pieces to this puzzle, but it wasn't hard to fill in the gaps. Josephus had clearly paid a ransom to Vespasian to ensure the freedom of his family and friends. As priests of the Temple, they would have been in charge of the Temple treasures and entrusted with hiding them from the invading Romans. History was clear on one thing: Vespasian had used the wealth he acquired from sacking Jerusalem to fund his rise to power. Cam had little doubt where much of that wealth came from. In fact, one of the most famous tourist sites in Rome even today was the Arch of Titus, featuring a carving of Vespasian's soldiers marching through Rome carrying treasures—including the Golden Menorah—from the Temple of Jerusalem. Cam had no trouble finding an image of the carving.

Arch of Titus, Rome

Cam turned to the third clue, the legend that Freemasonry originated when the gentry and noblemen of Europe decided to join the stonemasons' guilds. It had never occurred to him before, but Paris was correct: The idea was absurd. The class-conscious nobility of Europe during the late medieval time period and centuries that followed simply did not mix with commoners. Rather, Cam's research indicated that the Masons descended from the Knights Templar, outlawed in the early 1300s— calling themselves 'masons' and adopting many of the rituals of the stonemason guilds was simply a cover, a way for surviving Templars to maintain their order in secrecy. The Freemasons did not evolve from the stonemason's guilds any more than the Templars had been formed—as some historians claimed—merely to protect pilgrims on their way to Jerusalem. Rather, the truth, as was often the case when it came to secret societies, lay hidden in the dusty corners of history.

Just the places Cam liked to ferret about.

Cam slept fitfully, his dreams disjointed and erratic.

Amanda's voice, strained. "Cameron, you need to find the treasure. Find the treasure. Find the treas—"

He jolted awake to see Venus alert, upright. He put a hand on her, settling her. Did she hear it also?

Venus, whining now, swung her head, her ears perked.

"What do you hear, girl?"

Venus continued whining, almost as if in pain, clearly distressed.

Cam heard nothing. Swinging his legs off the bed, he strode to the window, pulled the curtain aside, and peered out. Nothing. As he released the drape and turned back toward the bed, a flash of illumination backlit the curtain. Turning, he froze. Venus barked. A woman's face. *Amanda?*

And then it was gone. But he had seen it. Her face, her features, her hair. Ephemeral, and vaporous, but her. Blinking, he peered outside again. Still nothing. He rubbed his face. It was gone so quickly, he couldn't be certain. But Venus had clearly sensed something, perhaps a presence. And Amanda's voice, her message.

Find the treasure.

Taking a deep breath, Cam crossed to the bathroom and threw cold water on his face. He didn't believe in ghosts. Never had. He swallowed. But the voice. And the face. And Venus' reaction.

It didn't feel like three times a charm.

CHAPTER 3

Yawning and still unnerved after his sleep-deprived night in the hotel, Cam parked in front of the Masonic temple at 8:45 on Monday morning. Seeing the gangly Paris leaning on his cane, already waiting, did not surprise him.

"Back to our boulders?" Cam asked with a tired smile. He was glad to have something else to occupy his mind.

Paris, bundled in a parka with gloves and his Irish flat cap against the morning chill, rubbed Venus' neck and nodded. "I've been sitting on that boulder for so many years that I'm practically part of the landscaping. Even so, I carry a bird-watching book to make it look good."

"Does it help, watching from out here?"

"It does when you have binoculars and can see them enter the security code on the alarm."

Cam chuckled. "So you've been inside?"

"A few times. They have quite a library in there. Some books you just can't find at estate sales. I even put a listening device in there once—heard some good stuff for about a year, until the battery died."

"You want coffee? Maybe a muffin? I stopped at that double-decker bus a couple of blocks down Broadway."

Paris grinned. "Tourist trap. But I won't say no."

"Those were good clues," Cam said as he handed Paris a bag. "I spent the night doing research. You may be on to something."

"Well, I've spent my adult life working on it. Over fifty years." He took a sip of coffee and let out a long breath. "Do yourself a favor. If someone screws you over, just let it go. I'm an old man and all I really have left in life is my anger." He shook his head. "The bastards killed my father and now they've sucked the life out of me."

Cam redirected the conversation. "I think, based on the clues you gave, that you believe that Freemasonry descends from the priestly families of Jerusalem."

"Bingo." Paris grinned like a proud parent. "They even named their lodge buildings *temples*, just so even a *schmendrick* like me could figure it out." He brought the muffin to his mouth and took a bite, like it was an apple, as if in celebration. "Go on."

"The details are fuzzy, but it seems to me that the priestly families ransomed their way to Rome with Josephus and formed a secret society to guard their secrets and their treasures—they gave a bunch of stuff to Vespasian to buy their freedom but must have kept some wealth for themselves. I think, originally, this society took the form of Mithraism."

Cam looked up to see if he needed to explain that Mithraism was a cult popular with members of the Roman military who worshipped Sol Invictus, the 'Unconquered Sun.' Paris nodded, indicating the explanation was unnecessary. "Josephus, with his military background, would likely have belonged to the cult." Cam exhaled. "That's as far as I got."

"Well done." Paris nodded again. "I'll take it one step further. If you look at Mithraic ritual in Rome, you see a lot of similarities to Masonry—sun worship, secrecy, a system of degrees, male only, an initiation ceremony almost identical to Freemasonry, June 24 being an important date."

It was Cam's turn to nod. "I'm with you."

"The priestly families weren't allowed to practice Judaism, so they needed some kind of structure or organization, a way to remember and honor their family history. So they created rituals and ceremonies that got passed down over the generations. If you follow the history of these families, you can see them moving westward across Europe. I can give you all my research on this, but just as one example, they played a key part in the Carolingian dynasty—you know, King Charlemagne—in France in the eighth and ninth centuries. In fact, these priestly families became part of almost every royal family in Europe."

Cam knew where this was going. "But they never forgot their roots. They were the priestly families of Jerusalem."

Paris showed his yellowed teeth. "You get it, you see it." He sipped his coffee. "Like you said, they never forgot who they were. And when they finally gained enough power, a thousand years later, around the year 1100, they made their move. Time to take back Jerusalem. Time to rebuild the Temple and take their rightful place as its caretakers and guardians."

Cam nodded. It made sense. "When you say take back Jerusalem and rebuild the Temple, you're talking about the Crusades." Recapturing Jerusalem, in fact, was the main goal of the Crusades.

"Yes. And going hand-in-hand with that was the creation of the Templar Order. An army loyal to the priestly families. An army that would help them take back their birthright." He turned to face Cam. "If you really think about it, the whole idea of the Crusades made no sense. The holy sites in Israel had no strategic value. And European monarchs practically went bankrupt. Not to mention the loss of life—as many as two million European soldiers died. And for what? For the most part, the Muslims welcomed Christian pilgrims already. So why bother?" He sat back. "There had to be some secret motivation."

Cam played devil's advocate. "They wanted to save their souls?"

"By fomenting war and mayhem and rape? Come on." He shifted. "Look, maybe the Church had a religious motivation. But for the royal families, something else was going on."

Cam nodded. "Okay, I'm with you. Continue."

Paris spread his arms. "That's pretty much the whole story. The Crusades failed. The Templars were outlawed and became the Freemasons. Mission unaccomplished."

"So why are the Freemasons still around?"

"Inertia, best I can tell. Most of the members have no idea about any of this. Hell, a couple of yahoos blackballed my father because he was *Jewish*, for God's sake. I mean, they use the Hebrew calendar—the Masonic year is 5781, just like the Jewish year. But it never occurs to them to ask why. I'm guessing they only tell you the truth when you reach the thirty-third degree."

"So this big secret is pretty anticlimactic."

"I told you it would be. Nobody cares. So many generations have passed that all these families and their bloodlines have been watered down. And nobody's seriously talking about rebuilding the Temple again in Jerusalem." He shrugged. "Basically, the secret at the center of Freemasonry is a giant nothing." He shook his head. "The joke's on me. My great revenge. I could scream it from the rooftops and people would just yawn."

Cam stared across at the Masonic temple. Something didn't add up. "I'm not so sure you're right about that. There has to be some reason beyond inertia that Masonry has continued on for the past, what, seven hundred years."

"Well, if there is, I haven't figured it out."

Cam continued to stare, the germ of an idea beginning to take root. He allowed himself a small smile. It was a longshot. And he had a lot of work to do before he'd even give voice to it. But if it grew into something, it definitely would be a game changer.

He stood and shook Paris' hand. "You've given me a lot to think about." He handed the elderly man his card. "Don't be so sure you haven't stumbled onto something truly monumental."

Paris shook his head. "That's it? You're not going to even give me a hint?" He chuckled. "Recall, I gave you three."

Cam smiled. "Fair enough. Think about this. The priestly families were in charge of the Temple treasures—not just the tithes, but, like you said, the religious artifacts like the Golden Menorah and the Ark of the Covenant and the Table of Shewbread and the Rod of Aaron and the Ten Commandments. Vespasian wouldn't have cared about them, except maybe for their value in gold. Well, they've all been lost to history. None of them has been seen since the Romans destroyed the Temple. They had to have gone *somewhere*."

"You don't think?" His eyes had widened, especially at the mention of the Ark of the Covenant. "Wait a second. I told you I bugged the place. One time, I heard them talking. It was the Master of the lodge, talking to the incoming Master. He said that once a year, on the September equinox, it was his job, and I'm quoting, 'to open the pillar and check on the treasure.' He said nobody else could be there, it had to be him alone, and only once a year."

Cam nodded. "Sounds like the head priest inspecting the Temple treasures in the Holy of Holies. Once a year, on Yom Kippur, in the fall."

Paris licked his lips. "I made the connection in my mind to the high priest and the Holy of Holies. But I figured it was just one of their Masonic keepsakes. But you think it might be something else, like a real treasure?"

Cam turned his palms to the sky. "I *think*, but I don't know. Give me a couple of days, then give me a call."

◈ ✛ ✡

Paris decided to walk a few blocks toward his apartment to get a little exercise before hailing a taxi. It was a pleasant January day and he was feeling rejuvenated, his encounter with Cameron Thorne giving him a spark of energy he hadn't felt in years. The man was clearly an accomplished historian—Paris had found the book Thorne had written about exploration of America before Columbus on the internet. And Thorne thought Paris was on the right track. Maybe the last fifty years hadn't been a waste after all.

Actually, that was not true. He had never married, never had children, never accomplished anything of any note. He worked as a part-time accountant, helping other CPAs during tax season. During the rest of the year, he did some bookkeeping. Once in a while, his rabbi asked him to do a *mitzvah*, a 'favor for his people,' which usually involved forensic accounting—a fancy way of saying he spied on clients who for some reason had been identified as a threat to Jews and/or Israel. He earned enough so that he could afford his apartment near the synagogue a mile north of the Masonic temple. And his lifestyle gave him enough free time to study the Freemasons and their rituals. But it was a skeleton of an existence. Other than his single passion and the occasional *mitzvah,* he merely endured.

He passed under the highway, turned down a side street, and stopped to rest, leaning against a telephone pole. People—healthy people, that is—took for granted simple things like walking along the sidewalk. Since his broken hip, even the most mundane tasks had been, well, a task.

Something Thorne had said kept echoing around in his head. He mentioned the various treasures the priestly families were in charge of, including the Table of Shewbread. The table, overlaid with gold, sat in the Tabernacle—on it were placed various gold utensils and serving implements, along with the holy bread used as an offering to God. Paris, in his decades of studying and spying on the Masons of Asheville, had on a handful of occasions heard senior members of the lodge speak reverently of a sacred 'table' of some sort kept hidden in the Asheville temple. Was it possible that this 'table' was the sacred Table of Shewbread? He pursed his lips. Like Thorne said, it had been lost to history. It had to be somewhere...

The screech of tires jolted him out of his musings. Turning, Paris saw a thick young man in a baseball cap lunge at him from the rear of a black SUV. *What the?* Paris lifted his cane in defense, but the man easily knocked it away, grabbed him by the coat collar, and flung him into the back seat. The vehicle roared off before Paris could right himself.

"Who are you?" Paris stammered, fighting to lift himself into a sitting position. "What do you want?" He tried the rear door. Locked.

The reply came from the front seat. An obese, middle-aged woman with pale skin, bright red lipstick and narrow slits for eyes studied him in a mirror attached to the passenger-side visor. "Mr. Paris. My apologies for the rough treatment. We are not thugs. We will treat you humanely. Assuming you cooperate, that is."

He swallowed, his heart racing. "Cooperate? I'm just a bookkeeper, a nobody. What could you possibly want from me?"

"We want you to tell us everything you shared with Cameron Thorne, and he with you."

"And then you'll let me go?"

Her red lips formed into a smile above the folds of her chin. "Let you go?" She nodded to the man seated next to him, who suddenly jabbed Paris in the upper arm with a needle. "No, Mr. Paris. I said we would treat you humanely if you cooperate. But I said nothing of letting you go."

✦ ✝ ✡

Sitting in his SUV in front of the Masonic temple, Cam did a quick Google search on his phone. He had a few minutes to kill before meeting with Lenny at the art gallery, and his conversation with Paris had sent his mind racing. Again, it was good to have something to take his thoughts off his ghost sighting.

What was it, exactly, that Josephus could have offered Vespasian for his freedom?

According to contemporary accounts, the Temple treasures were immense. Based on accounts in the Bible, King Solomon received 25 tons of gold for each of the 39 years of his reign. When added to riches amassed from taxation and trade, his personal fortune would have surpassed $2 trillion in today's money, making him one of the richest people in world history. (By comparison, Solomon's relative wealth was ten times that of Jeff Bezos, the richest person alive today, whose net worth reached $200 billion in 2020.)

The Jewish king spent much of that fortune furnishing and decorating the Temple. But the real wealth of the Temple would have been found in the Tabernacle. In the outer sanctum of the Tabernacle, the Israelites placed the Golden Menorah, the golden Table of Shewbread, a golden incense altar, and elaborate golden candelabras, all as described in the Old Testament. In the inner sanctum, called the Holy of Holies, rested the Ark of the Covenant with the Ten Commandments inside, along with Aaron's Rod, a pot of manna, and another mysterious inscribed tablet.

These treasures were viewed only once a year, on Yom Kippur, by the high priest.

All of these treasures, along with the tithes regularly collected from the Israelites (which Cam knew were called 'levies,' from the Levites who collected them), would have been in the control of the priestly families, available to ransom their freedom. Cam shook his head. How could Vespasian have said no?

The question, of course, was how tough a deal did the emperor-to-be negotiate? On the one hand, he held the priestly families prisoner. On the other, they had hidden the treasures before the Romans breached the city walls. It would have been a high-stakes barter, one in which the priestly families would surely have paid dearly for their freedom. But one thing seemed obvious: Vespasian would have put little value in the religious artifacts kept in the inner sanctum. He would have valued the tithes and the gold furnishings of the outer sanctum, of course—the carving on the Arch of Titus, which Cam had viewed last night while doing his research, showed that the Golden Menorah and Table of Shewbread were included in the treasures taken by Vespasian. But that didn't mean they had been melted down. Perhaps, in fact, these sacred items were reacquired by the priestly families while in Rome. And what of the Ark of the Covenant, the Ten Commandments, Aaron's Rod? Had all these treasures been lost to history?

Cam doubted it. The priestly families took their job more seriously than that.

He checked his watch. "Enough of that, Venus. We have another meeting to get to. We can look for Aaron's Rod later." He rubbed her neck. "But, no, we're not going to play fetch with it."

Ten minutes later, he strolled into Lenny's gallery. Lenny, of course, didn't bother with any pleasantries. "There it is," he said, pointing to a horizontal painting propped against a wall. "Like I said. Either worth a fortune or pretty much nothing at all."

It struck Cam that he really hadn't needed to drive all the way to North Carolina to view it. He knew practically nothing about art. And the question at hand—was Lincoln's mother portrayed as a Black woman—

could be answered just as easily with a high-resolution email image. But there was something about being able to touch history, to smell it, even.

He moved closer, reached out—

"Don't touch it, please. Not without gloves."

"Oh. Okay."

Cam spent the next ten minutes examining the portrait, using a magnifying glass, focusing on Nancy Hanks Lincoln. No doubt that the artist had given her skin a significantly darker tone than her mother, her mother's siblings, and her mother's parents. Beyond that, Cam had nothing of substance to contribute. He shrugged. "Maybe it was summer and she tanned easily."

"Date on back of portrait is March."

Cam flipped it over and examined the date along with the list of family names, all scrawled out in pencil in a neat but faded cursive. "I assume these names are historically accurate?"

Lenny nodded.

"All right, we have a historical mystery on our hands. So what's the next step?"

Lenny smiled wryly. "*You* are the next step. I called you, the *historian*."

"Fair point." Cam chewed his lip. "There's a third possibility, something not really Black or White. It's possible that Nancy was Melungeon."

Lenny nodded. "I've heard of them. Lots of them live in the mountains around here. Where did they come from?"

"That's the thing. Nobody knows for sure."

⬥ ✚ ✡

Even as his heart raced in fear, Paris felt the warm glow of whatever they had injected him with enveloping his body. The sun shone through a window onto his face, and the movement of the SUV made him recall days as a child, driving home from synagogue with his parents, trying to stay awake in the back seat…

"Can you hear me, Mr. Paris?"

He opened his eyes, not sure if he was really awake or just dreaming. They were no longer in the vehicle, but the room was dark other than the light shining on the fat woman's face.

He nodded.

"Good. My name is Dr. Little. I'm a hypnotherapist. I've given you a drug to calm you and make this easier on you."

He nodded again. She seemed nice. He smelled a floral perfume on her—mean people didn't wear perfume. But had she said she was going to kill him? No, that must have been part of his dream...

"First, I'd like you to imagine you are a bird, soaring over the trees. A gentle wind caresses your face, the sun keeping you warm. You are free, content. You are a young bird, and mom and dad birds are with you, protecting you. Your stomach is full—you have just had your favorite meal, with a cookie for dessert." She paused. "Can you feel it, little bird?"

He nodded, at peace, the air like a cushion beneath him.

"Good. Now, I need you to stand, to flap your wings, to raise yourself higher in the sky."

He stood, flapping, feeling his body soar.

"Excellent. That's high enough. Now, your mother is asking you a question. She wants to know about your new friend, Cameron Thorne. What did you and he talk about? And you know how moms are—she wants to hear every detail." She lowered her voice. "Especially anything about a *treasure*."

✦ ✝ ✡

Cam killed most of the two-hour drive to the international airport in Charlotte to pick up Rivka listening to a podcast discussing the Temple of Jerusalem treasures. Parts of it were too detailed for his purposes, going into the specific design features of the various artifacts as specified in the Old Testament. One thing, however, did catch his ear: Apparently, in addition to the Ten Commandments, God imparted to man a second stone tablet, called the Tables of Testimony, upon which he disclosed the secrets of number, measure and weight. These secret formulas were known as the Cosmic Equations. Cam shook his head. This was the mystery tablet. In all his years of researching the Templars, he had never heard of the Tables of Testimony. It was as if they had not only been lost to history, but forgotten as well. But if there was some set of Cosmic Equations, and the Templars had somehow discovered them, it would go a long way toward explaining the Order's mysterious and sudden ascent to power and wealth in medieval Europe.

The podcast continued, highlighting how zealously the priestly families guarded their role as caretakers of the Temple and priests of the flock —even after three thousand years, these families were afforded preferential treatment over other Jewish families. Cam remembered going to synagogue with his grandparents and watching as men with the last names derived from 'Cohen' and 'Levine' (which Cam knew were the names of the priestly families) were called to read the Torah first, before other congregants. In some ways it was like the caste system in India. And, of course, the custom mirrored the Masonic use of the name 'Lewis' as designation for those born into the Order.

Just before the podcast ended, his friend from Haystack Observatory called. "End of the world, huh?"

"Even so," Cam replied, "it took you half a day to call back."

His friend laughed. "I know you're a drama queen."

Cam explained the Hopi prophecy and the Blue Star. "Make any sense to you?"

"Sure, it's possible. We see explosions in other galaxies all the time. And the cosmic dust could turn the light blue."

"But would it, you know, cause fire and floods and the end of the world?"

"Depends on the size of the explosion. But, theoretically, yes." He paused. "In fact, I was just reading some new data that came in from Greenland. Scientists have been drilling down and taking core samples from the ice. Each layer of ice tells a story about what life was like when that layer of snow fell," he explained. "Things like dust, ash and pollen get captured and frozen in place for thousands of years, providing evidence of events like volcanic eruptions. What's relevant to your question is that they found high levels of cosmic dust—marked by iridium, which is rare on earth but common in outer space—in an ice core dating to the end of the last Ice Age. That would be consistent with what you are saying, some kind of galactic impact event causing the Ice Age to end."

"So this prophecy is more than just possible."

"Well, maybe. But we're a long way from *likely* still."

Cam exhaled. "Supposedly, this blue glow is at the very center of the galaxy. Can you take a look for me?"

"Can you afford a case of Misguided Angel IPA?"

Cam laughed. The softball team had visited a brewery in New Hampshire a few months back to celebrate a winning season. "Deal. But just in case this prophecy is true, you better drink it fast."

Cam chewed his lip as he hung up. What was one supposed to do to prepare for doomsday? Live it up? Perhaps greet a beautiful woman at the airport and take a chance on her?

He was now twenty miles away. He glanced at Venus. "Well, girl, what do you think? Are you excited to see Rivka?"

Venus angled her head, her eyes wide as if wondering the same of him. "I'm not sure, actually," he replied to the unasked question.

With a long sigh, he rubbed his hands dry on his blue jeans. He and Rivka had spent lots of time together, but it had always been professional. She had been assigned to recruit him as a Mossad asset while he was researching Roman artifacts in America; from there, things devolved into murder and mayhem and betrayal and treachery. They had grown closer within the heat of this crucible, though Cam had resisted allowing things to ignite because he had not fully finished mourning Amanda. Now, four months later, he felt ready to begin to date again. But what were he and Rivka supposed to do—what were they even supposed to talk about—now that the rollercoaster ride was over? Hell, he didn't have a clue as to what her hobbies were or whether she was close to her parents or even if she had been married before. He could live with the possibility that they might end up not liking each other. But what if they just found each other uninteresting?

Amanda's voice popped into his head. *You know, you sound like a teenage girl.*

He smiled. "Is that really you? Or is it your ghost?"

Is there a difference?

"Well, I know this voice is just in my head. Last night, I saw your face. And I think I heard your voice out loud, while I was sleeping. And Venus sensed your presence."

I suppose if you're going to act like a teenage girl, you might as well stay up and tell ghost stories.

"Seriously. Was that really you last night?"

You know how this works, Cameron. I'm in your head, not mine. I don't exist anywhere else. There might be another me floating around out there—literally. But, if so, she's as mysterious to me as she is to you.

"Okay." Cam chewed his lip. "And I guess I really do sound like a teenage girl. But in my defense, I really do hardly know her."

I might remind you that you and I had a similar start to our relationship. On the run together, full of adrenaline and danger, not knowing boo about each other.

"But I was younger then, still had all my hair. I knew you'd find me irresistible."

Please. But I was attracted to your decency, your passion to do the right thing, your strength of character. Those things haven't changed about you. Dollars to donuts that's what Rivka's attracted to as well. Who cares if she doesn't know what you like in your coffee. She's looking at the big picture stuff. And I'm guessing you are as well.

He nodded. Nothing like getting solid dating advice from your dead wife.

With a deep breath, he took the airport exit.

Oh, Cameron. One more thing.

"What?"

Big picture stuff is crucial, like I said. But some flowers might not be a bad idea also.

Alone in her dorm room, her eyes on the orange sun setting above the Rockies, Astarte let out a long breath and ended her phone call. "Well, that sure changes my life," she said aloud.

She had just spoken with one of the board members of the National Congress of American Indians in Washington, D.C. She had called to tell them about the Hopi prophecy, to ask if they had any suggestions about the best way to spread the word. Two hours later they had called back and dropped a bombshell: They wanted her to go on a nationwide speaking tour, which they would fund. "Many of the tribes have already heard about you, about the Fortieth Princess prophecy. And now we have the Hopi Blue Star prophecy. You should know, the Hopi delegate objected, saying he didn't even know this Soohu woman, that she was apparently part of a splinter group that broke away from the tribe ten years ago. But the delegate acknowledged that the Kachina prophecy is real, so the majority decided we needed to take action. This is a good chance for you to get out there, Astarte. If it turns out you're right, it'll just enhance your reputation. And if you're wrong, well, that's fine too because it means we've somehow avoided the doomsday scenario. Win-win."

Astarte disagreed that it was a 'win-win' situation. If it turned out she was wrong, she'd look like a fool. So she would need to be careful about how she presented the evidence, couching it as a possibility rather than an inevitability. The situation, in fact, was more of a 'lose-lose'—either catastrophe struck, or she had wasted months preaching about and preparing for a giant nothing.

She rubbed her face. The whole thing, in fact, was a minefield. But after a lifetime of hearing about her prophecy, of wondering what it really meant and how she could possibly fulfill it, here she was. For better or worse—about to live it.

⬩✠✡

As luck would have it, Rivka's flight was delayed. Waiting in his SUV, Cam decided to kill the time researching the Tables of Testimony tablet he had just learned about from the podcast. The tablet was, apparently, kept with the other sacred objects within the Ark of the Covenant—the Ten Commandments, the Rod of Aaron and a pot of manna. So why did nobody talk about the tablet. And where did it go?

As Cam dug deeper, he was surprised to learn that, in ancient times, the Tables of Testimony were both well-known and well-documented. In Mesopotamian mythology, they were called the Tables of Destiny. The ancient Greeks referred to the tablet as the Emerald Tablet. The Egyptians knew of it as well, crediting its teachings with the technology needed to build the Pyramids. In Freemasonic teachings, the tablet was secreted in robust pillars called the Pillars of Enoch (or, alternatively, carved directly onto the pillars), thereby allowing the tablet to survive the Great Flood. This pillar theme was carried forward to medieval times in both Tarot practice (where the high priestess card featured pillars) and mystical Cabalism (which featured pillars on the tree of life). Egyptian, Hindu and Islamic traditions contained similar legends. In all cases, the sacred tablet/pillars were said to contain the Cosmic Equations, disclosing the secrets of number, measure and weight. And in all cases, the pillars were built to save the Cosmic Equations from catastrophic flood and/or fire.

Cam sat back. For something which was featured so prominently in ancient times, the Tables of Testimony sure had faded into obscurity in modern times. Cam had extensively studied the Templars and Masons, but had only seen passing mentions of the Pillars of Enoch. Somehow these pillars had saved the accumulated knowledge of the ancient world from being lost during the Flood. Something similar would come in handy if the Blue Star prophecy proved to be real.

He checked the time. Thoughts about ancient knowledge and the end of the world would have to wait. Rivka's flight had landed.

Ten minutes later, feeling a bit cliché holding a bouquet of airport-bought flowers, Cam waved to Rivka from the sidewalk as she strolled out of the airport terminal. It was not hard to spot her—she moved with the grace of a professional athlete and had the legs of a runway model. Plus, she had added a swath of royal blue color to one side of her thick, dark hair. More than a few heads turned.

"Those for me?" she said with just a hint of an accent.

He handed her the bouquet, the gesture substituting for a hug or a kiss. "Venus thought you might like them." He smiled. "I'm glad I didn't get colors that would clash with blue."

She crouched, allowing Venus to nuzzle her. "Venus is a sweetheart." She stood, eyed him, and surprised him by leaning in quickly to kiss him on the lips. "But I didn't fly all this way just for flowers. Of any color."

Okay, then. Cam recalled the scene in *Annie Hall* where Woody Allen asked if he could kiss Diane Keaton early on their date so they wouldn't have to stress over it all evening. Maybe that's what Rivka had in mind.

He grabbed her suitcase, and she took his arm. "So," she said, "what's the plan?"

"Asheville's got some great breweries. I thought maybe a burger and some craft beers and some live music?"

"Sounds great. I haven't had a drink in weeks."

He knew that she was not supposed to drink while on assignment. "Tough mission?"

She swallowed. "It's always tough when families are involved. These people we target are horrible, awful people. They do unspeakable things. And they truly do deserve to die. But they have children, wives, mothers." She shuddered. "To a five-year-old, Dad is just, well, Dad."

At some point, he'd need to deal with the question of whether he could be with a woman who actually killed people as part of her job. He thought he was okay with it—soldiers did so regularly, and the Mossad presumably only targeted those engaged in acts of war against Israel. So it seemed like her actions were justifiable. But what about those gray areas, when the Mossad targeted people who may not be quite so awful? Would Rivka even agree to go along with that? From what he knew of her, she wasn't afraid of standing up to her boss in order to do the right thing...

She interrupted his musings. "No, I wouldn't."

"Wouldn't what?"

"You were wondering if I'd kill someone who wasn't truly evil."

"How did you know that?"

She leaned against him. "You're not the only one who can read people, Cameron Thorne."

He stopped and looked at her. "No, seriously. How'd you know?"

"Your arm muscle tensed, as if you were thinking about violence. And you turned away from me, breaking our intimacy for a second. I put two and two together."

"Wow. I'm impressed."

"That, and last time I saw you I put a mind-reading chip in your frontal lobe."

He chuckled. "I can see I better be on my toes."

She breathed in the bouquet. "True that. I expect nothing less than your 'A' game."

◈ ✚ ✡

Naked, Rivka laid a bath towel on the tile floor, stretched her body to its full length, and—feet wedged against the bathroom door—methodically executed fifty military-style pushups. From her overnight bag, she then removed a chin-up bar, draped it over the door, and performed thirty chin-ups, her head lightly grazing the ceiling as she did so. Lastly, she laid on her back and did 200 crunches. Her breathing slightly elevated, she studied herself in the mirror. Not the hard body she had as a pro volleyball player, but not bad.

Languorously, she allowed the hot water to wash over her. She had been traveling for almost 24 hours, from Estonia to a long layover in Frankfurt—where she had added the blue stripe to her hair—and on to Charlotte. At some point, she'd need some sleep. But her body was trained to deal with jet lag. And if she slept now, at seven in the evening, she'd never get her body clock set to American time.

Not that she wanted to waste the evening on sleep. She hadn't been on a date in, well, she didn't know how long. She and Cam had gone out to dinner back in September but—though things turned a bit flirtatious—that had been more of a business meeting, debriefing each other after a wild adventure involving ancient Roman artifacts. The flowers, and her spontaneous kiss in response, indicated they both wondered if tonight would lead to romance.

Learning the answer to that mystery required, at a minimum, that she stay awake.

Twenty minutes later, she threw on a pair of jeans and simple white blouse. She brushed out her still-damp hair and spritzed herself with some perfume. She didn't bother with makeup, though she did drop some Visine in her eyes to wipe away some of the jet lag. Standing in the mirror, she shrugged. Tall, olive-skinned, shapely, fit. There was a lot to like, even without the mascara and eyeliner. Her sense—and her hope—was that Cam would agree.

She strolled out of the bedroom area to find Cam on the couch in the outer room. She appreciated that he had arranged for a suite, allowing each of them some personal space (and also a pull-out couch) as they danced around the infancy of a romance.

"That was quick," he said, standing.

"I'm working on no sleep. If we don't go soon, I might not make it at all."

Walking in the cool January air, her arm linked around his, they reached the brewery in ten minutes.

"Can we get a table away from the band?" she asked. "I like music. But I also want to be able to talk."

"Of course. But after an hour of listening to me babble, you might reconsider."

"I've heard you babble before. I don't hate it."

He chuckled. "Good. Babbling is one of my most endearing qualities."

"If it gets too bad, I could drag you onto the dance floor."

"I do some of my best babbling while dancing."

Laughing lightly, she leaned into him. She liked that he didn't take himself too seriously. Being a Mossad agent—being around death and mayhem so often—had changed her, had caused her to realize how unimportant the superficial things were. Cam, unlike many men, seemed to be more interested in the steak than the sizzle.

They sat and ordered beers and potato skins. "So, why the blue?" he asked.

"To match our flag," she replied with a smile.

"I like it. It tells the world that you play by your own rules."

"Truthfully, I needed something frivolous after the mission. Something goofy and lighthearted. I thought about a tattoo, but what if I didn't like it? At least the hair will grow out in a couple of months."

As he sipped his beer, she touched his other hand. "Last time we were at a restaurant, I was telling you that I knew where the Golden Menorah was." Her boss, not wanting the artifact to destabilize the Middle East, had chosen to throw it overboard in the Atlantic, not knowing she had attached a tracking device to it. "But we've been together, like, four hours and you haven't asked about it. Aren't you curious?"

He leaned closer. "Of course I am. But I figured you'd tell me when you're ready. I know it's complicated."

It was. "Thanks for understanding." Her allegiance was to her country. But both she and Cam felt strongly that the Menorah deserved a better fate than to languish at the bottom of the ocean. "It hasn't moved. Still in the same place."

Cam chuckled. "I half-expected to see it on the six-o'clock news, dragged up in a fishing boat's net."

She sipped her beer, savored it. "Maybe that'd be best. I hate that it's down there."

"Funny you bring it up. I met with a guy this morning who went deep down the rabbit hole on the origin of the Freemasons."

"I'm guessing you were only too happy to join him down there."

He smiled. "True. Anyway, he thinks that Freemasonry—that is, what today we call Freemasonry—was founded by the priestly families after King Herod's War as a secret society to guard their secrets and their treasures and try to stay in power." He paused. "So I started thinking about that, about what their treasures might be."

"The Golden Menorah," she interjected.

"And not just that. All the Temple treasures that have been lost. The Ark of the Covenant. The Ten Commandments. Aaron's Rod. A pot of manna. Something called the Tables of Testimony, carved onto a stone tablet. They all disappeared after the Temple was destroyed, never to be seen again. Well, they have to be somewhere."

"And your friend thinks the Freemasons have them?" She smiled. "Well, we know they don't have the Golden Menorah. But the rest of them?"

"Actually, he didn't take it that far. He figured out the stuff about the priestly family being at the roots of Freemasonry. He was focused on who they were, not the Treasures necessarily. Not to get too deep into it, but essentially most Masonic rituals are stories of the Old Testament told from the point of view of the priests. And some of these priests are pretty obscure. Who would care about these guys other than their own family?"

"It's like those family histories that people publish. Nobody reads them other than a few of their relatives."

"Well, in this case, you've got, like, six million Masons acting out rituals featuring these ancient priests. Trust me, they have no idea why they're doing it, other than that's the way it's always been done. The only way it makes any sense is if this guy Paris is right, if it really is just a fancy way to record and remember and even glorify the family history." He spoke theatrically. "Look, here's Great-grandpa Zabud, advising King Solomon. See how important he is?" Cam shook his head. "The reality is that Zabud was a nobody, a minor priest only named once in passing in the Old Testament. But for some reason he plays a big role in a bunch of Masonic degrees. It'd be like telling the story of the United States by focusing on minor Congressmen."

"Which would make sense if they happen to be your ancestors." She paused. "And if they also happen to be the caretakers of some ancient treasure."

He lifted his glass and nodded. "Exactly."

Rivka was interested in Cam's research, both personally and professionally. But the Americans had an expression she liked, about how all work and no play made Jack a dull boy. She stood. "Let's dance."

"Okay."

She was glad she had chosen flats, given that Cam was probably an inch shorter than her. He was a surprisingly adept dancer, leading her in a series of simple swing moves. Actually, it wasn't so surprising. He seemed like the type of person who was competent at almost everything.

And he knew enough to keep his eyes on her, despite a group of bois-
terous young women dancing near them.

The music flowed through her, washing away the trauma of her recent
mission. She leaned into Cam and closed her eyes. No dull boy this one.

✦ ✝ ✡

Three beers and a shot of tequila later, Cam and Rivka—her arm again in
his—weaved their way back to the hotel. Neither was fit to drive, but
they both had their wits about them.

"That was fun," she said. "I haven't gone dancing in ages."

"Me either. There was a time when all our friends were getting
married and it seemed like we were always on the dance floor."

"Was Amanda a good dancer?"

He liked that she didn't shy away from touchy subjects. "She was a
gymnast, and dancing of course is a big part of the floor routine."

They reached the hotel lobby. "You want a nightcap?" he asked.

"I think I had my nightcap three drinks ago."

In the elevator, Cam leaned in and kissed her lightly. Nothing too
rambunctious—he still wasn't sure if he was ready for this. It felt strange
to be tasting and smelling and sharing personal space with someone who
wasn't Amanda. But Amanda wasn't Amanda anymore, either. He half-
expected Amanda to chime in, the voice in his head, and tell him to go
for it. Instead, he pulled back and said, simply, "I agree. That was fun."

Venus greeted them at the door. "I need to walk her. Back in fifteen."

She yawned. "Want me to come?"

"That's okay. You must be exhausted."

He returned just before midnight to find her sprawled on one side of
the king-size bed, dressed in shorts and a t-shirt, snoring lightly. Venus
looked at him as if to ask where she should sleep. "Good question, girl.
But I'm not even sure where *I* should sleep."

In the end, he decided to follow Rivka's lead. He threw on shorts and
a t-shirt of his own, washed up, settled Venus at the foot of his bed,
turned off the light, and eased himself down onto the other side of the

bed. Quietly, he leaned over and kissed Rivka on the cheek. "Sweet dreams."

✡ ✝ ✡

His own "sweet dreams" words echoing in his head, Cam fell asleep. At some point, he awoke to find Rivka's hand resting on his arm. Later he dreamt, a vivid dream of a sultry woman gently opening his mouth to hers, her lips and tongue probing his, her hands touching, caressing, stroking. Unlike last night's dream, this one did not feature Amanda. And the woman didn't disappear in a flash. Trancelike, Cam's body moved with hers, slowly, languidly, as if sensing that too much rigor would break the blissful reverie. It went on for what seemed like hours, until, with a start, he realized he might not be dreaming. He pushed the thought away, descending back into the warmth…

He awoke suddenly to daylight pouring through the hotel room window. Blinking, he checked his watch. Past eight. A note rested on Rivka's pillow.

I'm out walking Venus. Be back soon with breakfast.

When he came out of the bathroom, Rivka was in the living area unpacking muffins and breakfast sandwiches. He hugged her from behind and kissed her hair. "Good morning."

She turned to face him. "You know the one thing a lady can't resist is a gentleman."

"So you had the same wild dream I did?"

"Wilder."

He gestured toward the food with his chin. "Middle of the night sex *and* a breakfast run. Wow."

"Wait until you see what I do on birthdays."

"Really?" He grinned, raising an eyebrow. "Chocolate chip pancakes?"

She licked her finger. "With whipped cream."

Cam had decided to suggest they return to bed once they finished eating—planning to joke that this time he'd like to remember all the lurid details. But a knock on the door brushed aside thoughts of amorous activity.

"Cameron Thorne?"

Shit. "Who is it?"

"This is the Asheville police. Open the door."

Standing, he turned to Rivka. "You paid for the breakfast, right?"

Smiling, she cuffed him on the shoulder as he walked around the table. He opened the door. "I'm Cameron. What's this all about?"

"A man is dead." The officer held up Cam's business card. "We found this in his pocket."

CHAPTER 4

Seated in a small conference room at the Asheville police station on the edge of downtown, Cam told a female detective what he knew about Nathan Paris.

"I met the guy outside the Masonic temple. We both study Masonic history. Studied, I guess." He swallowed, saddened by the loss of his new friend. Paris had obsessed for decades over the Masons and now, with Cam, he had finally found someone with whom to share his research. Finding a fellow researcher may not have given Paris a full life, but it had been a bright spot in what seemed like an otherwise dreary existence. "I gave him my card so he could update me on his research. That's it."

"When was the last time you saw him?"

"Yesterday morning, at a park next to the lodge."

"He didn't get into your vehicle?"

"No."

"Witnesses say they saw him get into a black SUV a couple of blocks from the lodge. Next time anyone saw him, he was stepping in front of a bus."

"Ugh." Cam took a deep breath. "I drive a black SUV. But it wasn't me."

They went back and forth a few times, until Cam finally convinced them to call Lenny Null to check his alibi.

"You can go," she said, returning to the room ten minutes later. "But we'd like you to stay in Asheville."

"I was planning to drive back to Massachusetts later this week."

"I'm going to have to ask that you change those plans, Mr. Thorne."

◈ ✝ ✡

Humming, Rivka tidied up the hotel room as she waited for Cam to return from the police station. She was certain he had nothing to do with the man's death. But she would include it in her report nonetheless.

Cam was, now, her lover. But he was also an asset. Her boss, Menachem, had made it clear that she could sleep with, even fall in love with, whomever she wanted. "But your primary allegiance must, at all times, be to the Mossad. More so than to your lover, more so even than to yourself."

And, as it turned out, Menachem had an assignment for her. "Relax, enjoy yourself," he said, with the French-like Israeli accent that many older Israelis employed. "But keep your eyes and ears open. Something is going on. I can feel it." He had tapped the side of his nose. "I can *smell* it."

Seated next to each other on the flight out of Estonia, Menachem had given her more details, explaining how Jews in America were at a crossroads politically. She was always surprised to look down at him, to see the top of his shaved head; in her mind, he towered over his operatives, though in reality his hard body stood only five foot six inches. "You know that it is essential that Israel maintain the support of America. The best way to ensure that is for American Jews to support candidates who are friendly to Israel. Recently, it has been the Republicans who have been the most pro-Israel—many Fundamentalist Christians believe the Second Coming can only happen when Israel is controlled by the Jews, so they see a strong Israel as crucial to their very salvation. Plus, many Democrats have focused on human rights and the plight of the Palestinians." His dark eyes held hers, reading her, making sure she was following. Apparently satisfied, he continued. "The result is that American Jews—who have traditionally supported the Democrats—have increasingly switched allegiances to the Republicans."

"Okay, I'm with you," she had replied.

"The problem for Israel is that the election pendulum has now swung away from the Republicans. If it swings further, we could find ourselves with an American government which is less than friendly. We went through that once with Barack Obama. We prefer not to have it happen again."

"I get it. But we need to be careful not to appear like we are interfering."

"Yes. It is a dance, in a way. We want the Republicans. But the Jews of America are predominantly Democratic. If we make our intentions known, we risk alienating our own people." He had offered a rare smile. "So we need to be subtle. Sneaky even. That's where our agency comes in."

"But what does this all have to do with Cameron Thorne?"

Menachem had blinked. "I'm not certain. Perhaps nothing. That's what I want you to find out. Thorne's research seems frequently to intersect with areas of Israeli concern. My instincts tell me it may be happening again." He had given her a hard stare. Everything about him, in fact, was hard—his body, his features, his attitude, even the jagged scar running up the side of his face. "I'm not asking you to spy on him. But I am asking you to keep me apprised of what he is doing."

It had been a fair ask. And she had, from the beginning, made it clear to Cameron that her loyalty was to her country.

So why did she feel a pang of guilt at what she knew she must do?

♦ ✚ ✡

Cam stepped out of the police station into what had turned into a warm, sunny day. Rather than going straight back to the hotel, he walked the half mile up past the Masonic temple and under the highway to where Paris had been hit by the bus.

The police had shown him a photo of the scene. Cam crossed the street, stood on the corner where Paris had—apparently trance-like—stepped from the sidewalk into the path of a fifteen-ton mass of hurtling steel. He looked around. It looked like any street corner in urban America—graffiti scrawled on a bus shelter, an empty bottle of Mountain Dew wedged into the grates of a storm drain, sand and rock salt piled against the curb, blotches of motor oil staining the pavement. He shrugged. Nothing which would even begin to explain his new friend's odd behavior.

His cell phone rang as he turned to walk back to his hotel. Astarte. "Hey, how long you going to be in Asheville? Looks like I'm coming to North Carolina this weekend."

"Longer than I planned." He explained the death of Nathan Paris.

"You do know that people around you have a funny way of ending up dead?"

"I noticed."

"Seriously, why do they suspect you? How did he die?"

"He stepped in front of a bus. Weird coincidence, same way his father died. But people said he was, like, in a trance when it happened. Like he'd been drugged. I guess they think he was in my car and I gave him something."

"Did they do lab work?"

"Hasn't come back yet. Which is why they want me to stick around. But if you're going to be here, I'm fine with it. Where and when you coming? And why?"

"Saturday. They gave me a list of five or six reservations to choose from. I knew you were down there, so I chose the Eastern Cherokee Reservation. It's less than an hour from Asheville."

He stopped at a crosswalk. "I'm assuming the Blue Star prophecy?"

"Yup. Nothing attracts a crowd like a doomsday prophecy."

He could tell she was trying to put a brave face on this, but also that she was distressed. "I know the Hopi woman seemed convincing, but the earth has survived a whole lot of doomsday predictions."

"My head hears you. But my intuition can't seem to let this go."

"And even she says she might be wrong. It might be a false alarm. I reached out to a buddy of mine who's an astronomer, asked him to look into this."

"Thanks." She exhaled. "The thing I'm struggling with is that I'm in a unique position to do something. Even if there's only a one percent chance the prophecy is true, don't I have to do everything I can to warn people?"

"I hear you. The stakes, obviously, are high. So I think you're doing the right thing. Spread the word. But tell people it's just a possibility. No reason to get everyone panicking."

"That's what Matthias said also."

"Smart boy." He tried to lighten the mood. "So, for your lecture, can you get me a comp ticket?"

"Do you promise not to heckle?"

He grinned. "For sure. And it'll be great to see you." He exhaled. "You should know, I'm here with Rivka."

A pause. "I suppose you'll want a comp ticket for her also?"

"Right."

Another pause. "I guess I'm okay with that."

"You sure?"

"It's been, what, nine months? And I like her well enough. But don't expect me to give her a Mother's Day card or anything."

"Of course not. And thanks."

"Hey, Dad."

"What?"

"This Paris guy died just after meeting with you, and the cops think it's suspicious. Maybe you should be careful?"

"I'm always careful. It's the people around me who take crazy chances."

"Yeah, right. Bye Dad, love you."

As he hung up, his phone dinged again. His softball buddy.

"So I took a look at this blue glow at the center of the universe."

"And?"

"And it looks like a blue glow."

Cam switched the phone to his other ear as he walked. "I knew I was right to bring this to a scientist."

"Seriously, something is going on out there. There is, or was, some kind of explosion. A few guys have been chatting about it already in a discussion room I belong to. The question is, how large was it? I'm guessing it's just a run-of-the-mill cosmic event. No big deal."

"But you're just guessing."

"Right. And some of the chatter is that it could be pretty significant. I'll keep an eye on it, see if it grows."

"So there's a chance this prophecy could be right?"

"In a word, yes. There are such things as galactic explosions large enough to cause a cataclysm here on earth. I'm not saying this is one of them. But it is possible."

"But wouldn't we have more warning? Wouldn't the blue light fill the sky before it hit us? It's just a glow now."

"Technically, you are correct. But, if this is a big explosion, by then it would be too late. The best way to explain it is that, once the first light reaches us—and it apparently already has—other stuff is right on its tail. Nothing moves as fast as the speed of light, but lots of things come close. Some stuff would hit months later, some years later, some decades later. One danger is that an electromagnetic pulse, followed a few days later by a massive gravity wave, could hit within the first few months. That gravity wave is like, well, the first wave of attack. Theoretically, it could already be on the way. It all depends on how big the explosion was."

"Gravity wave? That doesn't sound good."

"You've heard of lunar high tide? Well, multiply that by a thousand. We're talking tidal waves and tsunamis. Probably enhanced volcanic activity also."

It took Cam a moment to reply. "Wow. That's sobering."

"If it was a big explosion, yes. And, Cam?"

"Yeah?"

"Speaking of sobering, any chance I could get that beer soon? You know, just in case?"

Cam suddenly had a lot on his mind—and not just the small matter that the earth might become engulfed in flood and fire. A new love interest. A new friend, now dead. A new Amanda ghost in his hotel room to go with the old one inside his head. A new theory about the secret at the center of Freemasonry. Not to mention the painting he was here to examine. And now Astarte flying in. He let out a long breath as he walked. It was a lot. Probably too much to all be a random coincidence.

Not five minutes after admitting to herself that she felt guilty about 'handling' Cameron like an asset, Rivka's cell phone rang. *Menachem.* As if he could sense her ambivalence. With a sigh, she sat on the hotel suite couch and answered.

"Yes, boss."

"Why is it that trouble follows Thorne like toilet paper on a shoe?"

"How so?"

"One of our assets in North Carolina is dead." The Mossad had informants and enablers—Jews loyal to Israel—in practically every city in America. "You're in Asheville, right?"

"Yes." She swallowed. "Was it an old guy?"

"It was. My sources tell me Thorne is a suspect."

"He didn't do it."

Menachem exhaled. "Of course he didn't. He had no reason to. But someone did it, and *they* must have had a reason."

"What kind of stuff did he help us with?"

"Apparently, he worked part time during tax season for a big accounting firm. There's a defense subcontractor in the area that we suspect is selling specs of our missile defense system to Iran. Our guy was following the money, looking for the paper trail."

"And you think that's what killed him?"

"Maybe. But that was over a year ago, so maybe not. I need you to poke around. Somebody wanted him dead. And Thorne spending time with him is too much of a coincidence to ignore."

Lenny Null paced around the back room of his gallery, letting his mind wander. There was a possible play here, no doubt. He just needed to figure out the best way to navigate his way through it.

It wasn't like he *needed* another score. Not in the financial sense, at least. But he definitely *craved* one. He was addicted, unable to resist the allure of the perfect scam, the flawless swindle. As a kid, his favorite movie was *The Sting*—he had watched it at least twenty times. And when he wasn't watching it, he was playing Monopoly with his friends. It hadn't taken Lenny long to figure out how to load a dice and hide a few five-hundred-dollar Monopoly bills in his shoe to ensure victory over his middle-school friends. As an adult, he still played Monopoly, except now for real money. Again, he didn't need the cash—his previous scam had set him up for life. In fact, he usually gave most of his earnings to charity. But accumulating wealth was the way Americans kept score— winners walked away with the cash. And Lenny had become addicted to winning. A shrink would no doubt tell him his obsession with money stemmed from growing up as the poor kid in a rich town. Whatever.

Not that he shared this side of his life with Shelby. She probably sensed when he was working on something, but years ago they had reached a silent understanding regarding Lenny's business dealings: As long as he wasn't scamming the innocent or vulnerable, she'd look the other way. Which was the one benefit of them living a thousand miles apart.

The innocent and the vulnerable. That was the other thing about a perfect sting—ideally, there should be no victim, nobody to complain or seek revenge. Lenny had made his first fortune buying real estate at fore- closure auctions, manipulating the bid process in unseen ways. If he purchased a house at a foreclosure auction for fifty cents on the dollar because, say, everyone believed the siding contained asbestos, and it turned out it in fact did not, who was actually victimized? The fore- closing bank, perhaps. But banks were not people. Hell, most *bankers* he knew were not people.

All of which was why he was pleased—and not at all surprised— when Thorne texted him a few minutes ago that he would be sticking around a few more days because his daughter Astarte would be speaking at the Eastern Cherokee Reservation this weekend about a Native American doomsday prophecy.

Lenny would not miss it.

◆ ✝ ✡

Cam strode down the hotel hallway, not at all sure what he would find when he pushed open the door to his room. He didn't know Rivka that well, but one of the few things he did know about her was that she was unpredictable.

Yet the last thing he expected to find was her staring at a computer screen with a picture of Nathan Paris on it.

"Wait," he said. "How could you know that's the guy who got killed?" He knew the police hadn't released any information yet. "The Mossad didn't have anything to do with his death, did they?"

She shook her head, a mane of blue fluttering as if in the wind. "No. But Menachem wondered the same thing about you. Nice that you guys are so *simpatico*."

He moved closer. "Then I don't get it."

"Apparently, he was one of our informants. Menachem wants me to find out what happened."

"Paris, a spy?" Cam shook his head. "I suppose he had a perfect cover. He basically just sat at home, other than when he was stalking the Freemasons."

She looked up at him and smiled. "The good news is that this means I'll need to stay in town for a while."

He put his hand on her arm. Should he have kissed her when he walked in? "That is good news."

Cam checked his watch. "I was supposed to drive out and talk to a local historian. A guy who knows a lot about the Melungeons. I can go alone if you have work to do."

"You think the Melungeons might have something to do with Paris' death?"

"I'm not sure. But my gut tells me this is all related."

"Well, that settles it, then." She grinned. "Much as I hate the idea of spending more time with you, duty calls. You're stuck with me for at least another day."

"If you make it four days, you'll see Astarte." He explained the Hopi prophecy. "I have a buddy who's an astronomer. He says the galactic explosion is actually possible."

She shrugged one shoulder. "Doomsday prophecies are like a national pastime in Israel. Every religious group, every sect, thinks they've deciphered some hidden code in the Bible. You could go crazy trying to keep up."

"Well, at some point one of them is going to come true. Just the law of probabilities."

"That sure is comforting, Cameron."

"Sorry." He smiled. "Like you said, you could go crazy worrying about stuff like this. But in my experience, it's usually the stuff you *don't* see coming that gets you. COVID-19. September 11th. Pearl Harbor. AIDS. Obsessing over all the things that *might* happen can be paralyzing."

She stood. "Agreed. Let's go learn about the Melungeons."

Fifteen minutes later, they exited the hotel, Rivka holding Venus' leash. A female guitarist busked next door in front of a café where diners lunched at umbrella-covered tables. Cam froze as the song hit him. *I am gone but in your dreams I live; I mean no harm but answers I must give...*

"What is it?" Rivka asked.

He swallowed, his body tensing. "That song. It's been, like, haunting me."

"What do you mean?"

"I first heard it in my sleep a few nights ago. Then at a coffee shop in Newburyport. Now here."

"So? Maybe it's a popular song."

"That's the thing. It's not. The singer in the coffee shop said she just wrote it."

Cam studied the busker as she sang. Heavy-set, close-cropped hair, easy smile, college-aged. As she finished the song, Cam strode over and dropped a twenty-dollar bill into her guitar case. "I liked that song. Where's it from?"

"Thanks. I just wrote it."

He eyed her "Really? Wow. It's catchy."

Her blue eyes held his. "Thanks." Non-committal.

"I was wondering, how do you write a song? Does it just pop into your head."

She strummed her guitar, transitioning into her next number. "This one did, yeah. While I was sleeping. It was weird."

Cam blinked. "Yeah. Tell me about it."

His mind still on the song, he led Rivka to his Cherokee parked around the corner.

"You seem preoccupied," she offered.

"Sorry." They weren't at the stage yet where Cam wanted to discuss his mental health. He smiled. "I'm fine."

She let it go. "So tell me where we're going?"

He had given her a quick overview of what he knew about the Melungeons. "I can't think of another group of people who know so little about themselves. From what I read, I think it's because they were trying so hard to blend in. Almost all of them were fleeing persecution, so nobody wanted to do anything that would make them be singled out. So they didn't really socialize in groups. It was mostly families marrying back and forth into each other." He read from his phone, a passage from a Melungeon historian:

The Melungeons, pushed off their lands, denied their rights, often murdered, always mistreated, became an embittered and nearly defeated people. Over the ensuing decades—in a vain effort to fit in with their Anglo neighbors, they lost their heritage, their culture, their names, and their original religion.

She nodded. "When you get that isolated, it's hard to keep your culture and history."

"Right. Appalachia is one of the poorest areas in America," Cam explained. "More than half the adults don't have a high school diploma.

Many are illiterate, which obviously doesn't help with keeping track of their history."

"Neither does their poverty. There's an old saying, 'Hunger steals the memory.'" She smiled sadly. "When people go to bed hungry, it's hard to focus on bedtime stories."

He navigated the SUV north out of the downtown area. "Having said that, there's a professor at the college here, UNC Asheville, who's an expert on Melungeon history."

Five minutes later, they parked and found their way to the academic quad, a large grass-covered area framed by flat-topped, yellow-brick buildings that looked like they had been built in the 1960s. "There," Cam pointed, "that's the history building."

A tall, blond woman in her late thirties, dressed stylishly in a herring-bone blazer and matching skirt, stood as they knocked on her open door. "Professor Campbell-Klein?" Cam asked.

"Yes, come in."

They made introductions and small talk, then Cam asked, "So, how does one become an expert on the Melungeons?"

The professor smiled. "In my case, entirely by accident." She explained that she had been raised Presbyterian outside of Knoxville, Tennessee, about a hundred miles west of here. She then fell in love with a Jewish man. "He asked me to convert, so I started doing research on Judaism—not just the religion, but its customs. I was amazed to find out that my paternal grandparents practiced many of the so-called Jewish customs. As an example, my grandmother used to light candles for Friday night dinner—she said it was a way to celebrate the end of the week. My grandfather was a jeweler, a classic Jewish profession. And all the people in my family tree have Old Testament names. Then, when I went to the old graveyards, I found flat burial stones with Stars of David on them."

Rivka smiled. "Hard to explain that one away."

"Right. So, being a historian, of course I dug deeper. And the deeper I dug, the more I came to realize that the WASPy girl who looked back at me every morning in the mirror was, in fact, the granddaughter of crypto-Jews. Outwardly Christian, but secretly practicing Judaism." She shook her head. "It turns out our family name—Campbell—was really Campanal, a Sephardic Jewish name. My family came from Portugal, not Scotland."

"Your husband must have been pleased," Cam said.

The professor rolled her eyes. "Not nearly as pleased as his mother." She shrugged. "Long story short, I'm Melungeon. My family's been here for centuries. Most of that time they lived in the mountains, like other Melungeons, just trying to blend in." She smiled sadly. "Hoping the KKK didn't figure out who they really were."

"But they left the mountains for the city," Cam said.

"Yes. After World War II, I guess they finally thought it was safe. And it's hard to be a jeweler out in the woods someplace. So they moved into Knoxville." She held Cam's eyes. "Which is why I can't be as much help to you as you probably hope. I'm an academic. I study the Melungeons. But I've never actually *lived* like one. I think that if you really want to understand them, you need to go into the mountains. That's what I did. Let me tell you, it was a culture shock. I felt like Dorothy, not in Kansas anymore."

✧ ✝ ✡

Astarte sat across from Matthias at the dining hall table, trying to keep her voice modulated. "I'm sorry, I don't agree."

They were having, she realized, their first fight.

He tore into a bagel, shaking his head. "What do you think would happen? They would take the caves for themselves, just like they took our land. And leave us all out in the open to die."

"You don't know that."

"Come on, Astarte. Maybe not all of them, but there are, like, tens of thousands of Survivalists out there. And most of them are heavily armed. Once they hear about this prophecy, they're going to pack up and head straight for our cave dwellings."

"Can you blame them?"

He leaned closer. "No. Of course not. But that's exactly the point. They'll do what they can to survive." He lowered his voice. "Just like we should do. This is an *Indian* prophecy and *Indian* caves. We need to save ourselves first."

It wasn't that simple. At least not for her. What was she supposed to do, just leave her father out there to die?

Matthias, being one-hundred percent Blackfoot, simply couldn't relate to what she was going through. Sniffling, she stood. "I need to get to class."

He nodded. "Okay. I'll walk you."

"That's all right." She touched his hand. "I wouldn't mind some time alone to think."

✦ ✝ ✡

Professor Campbell-Klein gave Cam the name and address of a Melungeon family she thought might be receptive to a visit. But she could not give him a phone number—they didn't have a phone.

"Go in slow and easy," she had warned. "And best be out of there before dark. They're not always happy to have visitors."

Using a hand-drawn map the professor gave them, they wound their way west into the mountains, the SUV barely able to fit on the narrow, pitted dirt roads. As Cam drove, doubling back and climbing, Rivka tapped at her phone, which surprisingly still had service.

"Aren't you getting carsick?"

She laughed. "No. Even as a kid, I loved rollercoasters."

"What are you looking at?"

"When I did a search for 'Melungeon,' one of the first things that came up was a short story about the boogeyman. The professor's comment about getting out before dark got me curious. So I'm reading the story. Listen to this." She read aloud:

I first heard the word 'Melungeon' at my father's knee as a child in the mountains of Eastern Tennessee, and the name had such a ponderous and inhuman sound as to associate them in my mind with the giants and ogres of the wondrous tales I listened to in the winter evenings before the crackling logs in the wide-mouth fireplace. And when I chanced to waken in the night and the fire had died down on the hearth, and the wind swept with a demoniac shriek and terrifying roar around and through the house, rattling the windows and the loose clapboards on the roof, I shrank under the bedclothes trembling with a fear that was almost an expectation that one of these huge creatures would come down the chimney with a rush, seize me with his dragon-like arms, and carry me off to his cave in the mountains, there to devour me piecemeal.

Cam smiled. "I don't have to outrun the boogeyman. I just have to outrun you." It was a favorite joke he often shared with Amanda. Somehow it seemed okay to bring Rivka in on it.

"Good luck with that."

He was almost back to one-hundred percent physically after the car accident which killed Amanda, and he jogged regularly, but even at his best he doubted he could keep up with Rivka for more than a couple of hundred yards.

Swinging left, he reached a fork and chose the right side, heading higher. The professor had told them to crest the ridge and then come down a few hundred yards on the back side. A minute or two later, he frowned. "Does this look familiar to you?" They had reached an elevation where a thin layer of snow covered the wooded areas on either side of the road, making the landscape blend together.

She blinked. "Not sure. I was looking at my phone."

He continued on, reaching another fork. Or perhaps the same one. Again, he chose the ascending route. And, again, things began to look familiar again. "Wait, this isn't right."

"No," she said tersely. "No, it's not. Cameron, look."

Two gangly men had emerged from the brush, camouflaged, brandishing hunting rifles. One fired a shot over the top of the SUV. Cringing, Cam hit the brakes.

In the time it took the SUV to finish its skid, Rivka had drawn a handgun, shoved back her seat, and dropped to a defensive position behind her door. "Get down," she hissed.

"I think that was just a warning shot. Easy," Cam said.

"Where I come from, there are no warning shots." She lowered her window and peered out, ready to return fire. "I think there's only two of them. I'm going to engage them. Once I do, drive like hell."

"Wait, Rivka, seriously. The guy shot over the truck. I'm guessing this loop we're on is meant to catch trespassers like us." The lower fork, which at first blush looked to be descending, was probably the route which led upward. This one just circled around, giving the locals time to watch and observe. "Catch, not kill."

Weighing his words, she let out a long breath. "Okay, this is your gig." Her eyes remained focused on the men with the rifles. "But I'm not putting up with any bullshit."

"Fine. I have no interest in being a character from the *Deliverance* movie."

Cam placed his hands on the steering wheel where the men could see them. The older man approached Cam's window while the younger man, who could have been his son, held his rifle steady. Both were dark-skinned, the older man leathery. Cam rolled down the window. "No need for the guns. We're just looking for the Levi Goings family."

The man leered at Rivka for a few seconds and then grunted. Cam could only imagine what he thought about the blue hair. "They kin of mine." Cam noticed the man had six fingers on his right hand, which Cam had read was common among the Melungeons. "Nobody said nothing about no visitors."

It took Cam a second to process the heavily accented words. "Professor Campbell-Klein, from the university, sent us." Cam held up the hand-drawn map. "Maybe I took a wrong turn."

"I expect you did."

"Well, um, could you point us in the right direction?"

The man chewed on a piece of grass. "I suppose it depends."

"On what?"

His eyes narrowed. "On what business you have."

Cam did his best to make his body language open and unthreatening. "I'm doing some research on the Melungeon people. Like I said, the professor thought Mr. Goings would be willing to meet with me."

The man tossed the piece of grass aside. "Leave your vehicle here."

The younger man patted-down Cam to make sure he had no weapon.

As he approached Rivka, dressed in jeans and a belted, beige leather jacket, she lifted her chin and placed her hands on her hips. "Don't even think it."

Kicking the dirt, he looked to his father for guidance.

The older man sighed. "Leave her be. But show me what you got inside that bag of yours."

She unzipped her leather purse, displaying a cellphone, chewing gum, ChapStick, tissues and a travel hair dryer, along with her wallet. Her gun, Cam knew, was tucked in a holster under her arm.

Walking single file, the older man leading and guns still out, they pushed their way through dense woods on a slush-covered trail, angling their way down the backside of the ridge. A frozen pond appeared before them in a clearing; a log cabin sat on the opposite shore, smoke wafting from a stone chimney at one end. Beyond the cabin, the slope fell away to an undisturbed valley below.

"I don't like this," Rivka breathed. "Nobody knows we're here. And here is the middle of nowhere."

"That's the point. People come here to be alone," Cam replied. "Been that way for centuries. I think our escorts are just being careful."

"And I think you're too trusting." She lowered her voice to a whisper. "I could take them out. Just give the word."

Cam was tempted. But both their captors were armed, and he wasn't certain Rivka could back up her boast. At least not without risk. And who knew how many more men were in the woods watching? "Not yet. Give it a few more minutes."

They walked straight toward the pond, as if to cross it. Cam spoke. "That ice can't be safe." Certain areas, in fact, remained unfrozen.

"Nope," the lead man replied, continuing to trudge toward its shore.

As they got closer, Cam could see that the pond was actually a pooled area of a decent-sized river. The river itself was definitely not frozen. And he didn't see any boats to help them cross.

"Hope you don't mind getting your boots wet," their guide said simply as they reached the shoreline.

Picking his way carefully, the older man stepped from hidden stone to hidden stone, each concealed an inch or two below the waterline, angling away from shore and then back and then out again like a lightning bolt.

"Ingenious," Cam said. If you didn't know where the stones were, no way could you get across unless you were willing to swim. These people took their isolation seriously.

"This would be the best time," Rivka whispered. "Easy to push them into water."

Cam considered it. Their rifles would still work, but they'd probably be flailing around so much it won't matter. Especially once they saw Rivka was armed. But his gut told him no. He shook his head. "I think we're good."

The simple rectangular cabin was small but appeared well-kept. A set of solar panels covered the southern slope of the roof, the modern technology starkly contrasting with the rudimentary architecture and materials of the structure. Good for them, Cam thought. Many homes in Appalachia did not have electricity.

As they approached, a girl scurried into the doorway, sweeping, apparently tidying up for their approaching guests. A man chopping wood spotted them, nodded to their guide, set down his ax, and trudged toward them. Levi Goings, Cam guessed.

With a grunt, their escorts turned and re-crossed the pond. Levi—a bearded, short-legged man with a barrel chest—squinted at his visitors. Thick dark hair to match his beard, olive skin, sharp features. "You the reason for the gunshot I heard?"

Cam smiled. "Yup."

"Not much Southern hospitality in these parts." He shook his head. "We can't afford it." He hitched up his pants. "The professor send you?"

Cam nodded. After introducing Rivka and himself, he reached into his jacket pocket and withdrew a package wrapped in red tissue paper. "She wanted me to give you this."

Goings squeezed the gift and smiled, surprising Cam with straight white teeth—Cam knew dental care was hard to come by in Appalachia. "Pistachio nuts, I reckon. My favorite." He winked. "Don't tell the kids, or I'm afeared I'll have to share them." His accent was not as thick as the men in the woods, though Cam still had to concentrate to get every word. Levi turned toward the cabin and yelled, "Esther, we got company."

A lanky, thirty-something woman, her hair tucked under a black bonnet, appeared at the door. She held a baby while two young boys hung on her skirt and the older girl, still holding the broom, hid shyly in the shadows. All three children stared at Rivka's mane of blue hair. After contorting her frame into a gangly curtsy, Esther looked up, her gray eyes striking against almond-colored skin. "Welcome. We'd be right pleased if you came in."

As Esther set a pitcher of apple juice and a plate of biscuits on the kitchen table, Cam noticed that the sleeves of her black blouse and the bottom of her gray skirt were tattered. He hoped their visit would not be a hardship. He suddenly felt guilty for not bringing anything beside the pistachios.

Grinning, and requesting a kiss on his cheek in return, Levi gave each of the three older children a handful of pre-shelled nuts and told them to run off to play. Popping the nuts into their mouths as they ran, they scurried into the living area, the only other room on the cabin's main floor. A wooden ladder in the corner of the kitchen led to a loft, where Cam guessed the family slept.

The four adults sat on what looked to be handmade wooden chairs, Esther still holding the baby. She said, "I'm sorry we cain't offer you nothing fancier."

Rivka leaned forward and covered Esther's hand with hers. "Of course not. You had no idea we were even coming."

Levi shifted in his chair. "What is it we can do for y'all?"

Cam nodded. "I'm researching the Melungeon people."

"A shame you didn't arrive last week. Esther's mother just passed on a few days back. She was the historian of our family."

"I'm sorry to hear that," Rivka said. "May her memory be a blessing."

"Thank you."

Cam asked a number of questions, mostly related to Goings family history. It turned out Esther's mother was also Levi's second cousin, consistent with what Cam had read about Melungeon families' insular nature. "I read that most people from Appalachia descend from Scottish settlers," Cam said.

Levi made a face. "I suppose that could be for some folks, but I ain't never heard no talk of the Goings being Scottish. I always learned we was Portuguese."

Not wishing to overstay their welcome, and remembering both their rude welcome in the woods and the professor's admonition to leave before dark, Cam stood after an hour. "I'm sure you folks have things you need to do. Thanks so much for your hospitality."

Levi offered to walk them back to the road, but Cam declined. "Just guide us back across the pond, if you would."

On the far side, Levi offered Cam his hand. "I don't reckon you learned much from us. Truth be told, we don't really know much about ourselves. Most folks think we've just always been here, in these woods. Never occurred to us we might have come from somewheres else."

"Actually, I learned a lot," Cam said. He smiled. "Not the least of which is that you were wrong about there being no Southern hospitality in these parts. You and Esther are gracious hosts."

Rivka took Cam's arm as they crossed the meadow on the far side of the pond, following the footprints they had left in the snow.

"Definitely Jewish," Rivka proclaimed.

"Wait, what? Why do you say that?"

"You're not as observant as you think you are, Mr. Thorne. I'll tell you, but it's going to cost."

"Cost what?"

"A nice dinner. I'm in the mood for sushi. And, fair warning: I eat sushi like Levi's kids wolf down pistachio nuts."

"I'll call the credit card company and increase my limit. But only if your intel is good."

"Okay, first clue. The girl, when she was sweeping, was pushing the dirt into the house, not out."

"So?"

"It's a Jewish tradition never to sweep the dirt toward the mezuzah because it's disrespectful to God. My *Bubbee* taught me when I was little."

"But I didn't even see a mezuzah on the doorframe."

"True. But the tradition, apparently, lives on. Otherwise, why sweep *into* the house?"

They reached the edge of the clearing and began to ascend through the woods. Cam grabbed a thick branch to use as a hiking stick. "Fair point. What else?"

"Did you notice the rips on Esther's clothes? A Jewish name, by the way."

"I did. But, I mean, these people are pretty poor."

She shook her head. "Poor, perhaps. But everything in the house was tidy and well-kept. Her clothes weren't ripped, they were *rended*."

Cam nodded. "Right. The Jewish tradition of ripping clothes during a period of mourning. Esther's mother just died."

"Which leads me to another clue. They had a small mirror near the front door. It was covered by a cloth. Another Jewish mourning tradition."

Shaking his head, Cam exhaled. "I missed that also."

"And I'm guessing you also missed when Levi mumbled a quick blessing after finishing his biscuit."

"I heard him say something."

"It was just a quick thanks. But Christians say grace before eating. Only Jews do so after."

Cam remembered that from family dinners with his grandparents. He smiled. They were halfway up the hillside. "I guess I owe you some sushi."

Suddenly, Rivka froze, stopping Cam with a grab of his arm.

"What?" Cam asked.

"Movement, up ahead."

"Maybe our friends with the rifles?"

"I saw blue jeans. Those guys were in camo."

It was beginning to darken in the late afternoon. "I suppose not hard to find us. Just wait for us to come back on the same trail we went in on."

Rivka pulled out her phone and held it in front of her face.

Cam gave her a funny look. "How is that helping?"

"I'm using the camera function to look behind me. More movement. We're being followed."

"How many?"

"At least four—two ahead and two behind."

Cam exhaled. Presumably all four carried hunting rifles. Versus Rivka's handgun and the hiking stick Cam was carrying. "I don't imagine that phone of yours has any service."

"Negative. Not that there's really anyone to call."

"So what's the play? Head back? Get off the trail?" Cam wasn't willing to risk the chance that these guys meant them no harm. He had seen the way the younger escort had leered at Rivka.

"It's going to be impossible to lose them in the snow because of our tracks. Unless…" She approached a thick tree. "Here, give me a boost."

He helped her up to the lowest branch." She smiled. "I just have to out-climb you."

"Very funny."

She hoisted herself higher. About thirty feet up, she called down in a low voice. "I can see the road from here. The SUV is still there, at least."

He shivered against a growing wind. "See anything else?"

"Two men waiting by the road, two following from behind, like we thought. All armed. Definitely seem to be waiting for us. Give me a second."

"Should I come up?"

"No. I have a better idea." She scurried down. From her purse, she removed the hair dryer.

Cam gave her a funny look. Then it hit him. *The Mossad.* And of course she wasn't the type to carry a personal groomer.

The hair dryer quickly morphed into a parabolic listening device. Earbuds in, Rivka aimed the mechanism back along the trail. Shaking her head, she handed the device to Cam. "I can hear them, but it's like a foreign language. You try."

He listened for a minute. "Okay. They're not sure what to do. They can see the trail ahead of us and know we haven't passed that spot yet. They're wondering if we went off trail and got lost." He held her eyes.

"It's safe to say they mean us harm." Cam left out the details of what they hoped to do with Rivka and her blue hair back at their barn.

She nodded. "At some point, they'll come looking for us, wondering why we seem to have stopped."

"Agreed."

"And they think they have us outnumbered."

"They do."

"Let's even things up." She removed her jacket and slipped her sweater over her head. Standing only in her bra, she smiled. "Don't get any ideas." She then put her jacket back on. "Do the same," she instructed.

On one knee, she stuffed her sweater and Cam's shirt with snow and old leaves, propping them both up against the trunk of the tree she had climbed. From fallen branches, she crafted human legs. Lastly, she took Cam's baseball cap and her scarf and fashioned heads for the dummies with snow. She stepped back. "How do they look?"

"Should fool someone from a distance, at least. But why would we be just sitting there?"

"How's your voice?"

"What do you mean?"

"Can you give me a loud howl, like you broke your leg?"

He smiled. "Sure." For five seconds he hollered and cursed and agonized, bellowing in the direction of the men on their trail.

"Good. Now come on."

Leading them off the path, Rivka doubled-back, the plan being to circle behind the men as they pushed forward to investigate Cam's histrionics.

"Get down," she ordered. They stayed still as the men passed. "Okay," she said. "The dummies won't fool them for long. Come on."

Staying low, realizing the men had likely spent most of their lives in these woods, they followed in the fading light. The men stopped twenty yards from the dummies, taking cover behind trees on either side of the trail. Cam watched as they silently motioned to each other, much as Cam imagined they would while hunting a deer or bear. As one man inched closer, Rivka made her move.

Gliding between the trees like a woodland fairy, she closed on the rifle-wielding adversary. From behind, she delivered a sharp chop to the side of his neck with her left hand while simultaneously relieving him of his rifle with her right. Covering his mouth as he collapsed, she whispered something into his ear. Cam guessed they were not words of comfort. She motioned Cam forward, handed him the rifle, and crossed the path to pursue the man's partner.

Cam sat on the man's back and stuffed leaves into his mouth. "You move and I put a bullet into the back of your head. Understood?"

The man grunted. He looked to be about eighteen, perhaps buddies with the younger escort from earlier today. Probably hoping to spend some time in the woods with Rivka. Well, careful what you wish for.

Reaching behind him, Cam caught the young man's boot and pulled out a shoelace. Pulling his arms behind his back, Cam hogtied him, yanking the lace a notch or two tighter than was necessary.

Meanwhile, Rivka had closed to within a few feet of the other man. She had placed the dummies on the far side of the tree trunk, so he still hadn't ascertained that they were not real. As he crept to within ten feet of the tree, she lowered herself and lunged, kicking his feet out from under him and dropping a knee into the small of his back. Even from fifty feet, Cam could hear the spasm of air escaping his lungs. Holding her handgun to his ear, she reached over and took his rifle. Still kneeling, she aimed the rifle at the tree trunk and fired, the gunshot echoing through the woods.

She turned and glanced at Cam. "That should bring the other two." She wiped her mouth with the back of her hand. "I just hope they hurry. I can't stop thinking about that sushi."

Cam shook his head. Who knows where this relationship would go? But one thing was clear: If he ever was going to break up with her, he'd best not be an asshole about it.

☆ ✚ ✡

Astarte had spent the afternoon deep in thought, barely aware of going to class and then wandering over to the library. It wasn't so much that she and Matthias had fought—that was part of every relationship. It was that they had *disagreed*. Normally they viewed the world through the same lens. But this time, incredibly, he thought it was okay for her to warn Indians of the pending cataclysm but to leave the rest of the country blissfully unaware.

She had been told her whole life that she was destined to lead her people on some kind of spiritual revolution. Was it really supposed to be based on selfishness and mean-spiritedness? The world didn't need Astarte to teach that lesson.

She took a deep breath. The truth was, this disagreement with Matthias masked a much larger problem. It didn't matter who her audience was, Indian or Caucasian. There was no guarantee anyone would listen. The world was awash in conspiracy theories—everyone with an internet connection seemed to have one. Her dad had once commented that the 'conspiracy revolution' was a product of what he called the *participation-trophy generation,* where all the kids on the soccer team were praised for their excellent play, patted on the head, and handed a shiny trophy. "Well," Cam had said, "the truth is that some of the kids didn't even really try. But little Johnny thinks that's okay. Then, when Johnny grows up, he comes up with his own half-baked conspiracy theory and expects to be patted on the head and told how smart he is. Well, the reality is, Johnny is a freaking idiot and his theory is garbage."

How would Astarte's message break through all the white noise, all the end-of-world predictions? Not to mention the Fundamentalist Christian belief in the pending arrival of the Antichrist. Sure, she had the Indian Congress behind her. And that would help her messaging get through to the tribes. But would the rest of the country listen?

In the end, maybe her fight with Matthias didn't matter. She could scream and holler all she wanted about Doomsday, show her charts and images and reports. But if nobody listened, there'd be plenty of room for anyone who wanted to take refuge in the cliff dwellings. Plenty of vacancy at the Cliffside Inn.

Cam drove the SUV out of the mountains, still shaking his head at what he had just witnessed.

After taking out the first two hillbillies, Rivka had made equally short work of their two buddies, aided by the fact that the hair dryer/listening device also functioned as a night-vision monocular. Leave it to the Mossad. No doubt the thing probably actually worked as a hair dryer as well.

Rivka hadn't needed Cam's help, other than deciding what to do with the miscreants. In the end, they had taken their weapons and their boots, kept their hands tied, and left them to trudge home through the woods in the dark. They might suffer frostbite, but that should be the worst of it. Might even teach them a lesson, though Cam doubted it.

"I may need a glass of wine to go with that sushi," Rivka announced.

"Deal." He checked the dashboard clock. "It's just after six. Half-hour drive and quick showers, then seated by eight." He continued. "Hey, something Levi said about being Portuguese. The professor said the same thing. So does the DNA testing. And I read that in Europe the term 'Portuguese' became synonymous with 'Jew' because so many Jews fled from Portugal to other countries during the Inquisition."

She turned toward him. "That's an important point. So when they say they're 'Portuguese,' what they might be saying is that they're 'Jewish.'"

"Right. And it makes sense. If you're being persecuted for being a Jew, and someone refers to you as 'Portuguese,' you might just shrug and accept it, figuring it's safer that way."

"Well, one thing is certain. Levi and Esther look a lot more Portuguese—whatever that means—than they do Scottish."

"So if the Melungeons really do descend from Jews fleeing Portugal, I guess the question is, why? Why leave Europe? Why come to America? And, then, why settle in Appalachia?"

She smiled. "I know one place to find answers."

He pointed his thumb toward the rear window. "I'm not going back into those hills."

"I don't mean there." She pointed out the front window, toward the east. "I mean Portugal."

CHAPTER 5

The wake-up call came at four. His mouth like cotton, Cam rubbed his face and gulped from a water bottle on the side table. At least no ghosts had disturbed his sleep.

Disentangling herself from him, Rivka leapt from bed. "Sorry, I need to pee."

Blinking, he turned on a lamp. After dinner and drinks and a blissful hour in the Jacuzzi in their suite, they had only slept for three hours. It felt like three minutes. Probably not enough time even for a ghost to swoop down.

"Do I have time for a run?" Rivka called from the bathroom.

"We need to be on the road by five." While driving back to town last night, Rivka had found reasonably priced tickets on an early-afternoon flight to Lisbon out of Charlotte which would get them back to North Carolina in time for Astarte's Saturday arrival. Cam had never been to Portugal, but the country—especially the city of Tomar—played a crucial role in Templar history. Even if they were unable to unravel the Melungeon mystery, the trip, albeit a whirlwind, should be worth the effort. And also worth potentially incurring the wrath of the local police, who had requested he not leave town. So he had cajoled his cousin Brandon to drive to Newburyport, retrieve Cam's passport, find a late-night FedEx drop-off, and ship it down to a law firm in Charlotte where one of Cam's old classmates was a partner.

"There a girl involved?" Brandon had asked.

"In fact, there is. Rivka."

"That crazy Mossad agent?"

"Not crazy. Just ... different."

"Dude, she almost killed you."

"But that was before she knew me."

"That is different, you're right. Most people want to kill you *after* they know you."

In the end, it cost Cam another case of Misguided Angel IPA. He should have invested in the brewery.

Rivka peeked her head out. "Five is fine. Three miles and a quick shower, then throw my stuff in my bag. Plenty of time."

He smiled. He liked her spontaneity, her energy, the fact that she was low maintenance. "I'll walk Venus and get the valet to bring the SUV," he replied—he had parked in the hotel garage in case the mountain boys came looking for revenge. He had also called his parents last night and convinced them to meet him at the Charlotte airport and take Venus for a couple of days. The chance to have breakfast with his new love interest no doubt played a part in their decision.

By five, they had checked out and were on the highway. Ten minutes into the drive, Cam turned off the heat fan. "Do you hear something? Singing?" *I am gone but in your dreams I live; I mean no harm but answers I must give...*

Rivka angled her head. "No. But I don't have great hearing. I suffered a bit of hearing loss in the army."

"It's gone now, but I'm sure I heard it. A song." *The same damned song.*

"Is your radio on?"

He glanced down. "No."

This song thing was getting weird. Two different singers, plus in his dreams, and now in his car. Either he was going crazy, or someone was fucking with him, or ... what? Was there a third choice? Was this some kind of message from an alternative reality?

Shaking the thought away, he drove east, toward the rising winter sun, its rays bathing Rivka in an amber glow as she read from her phone. He thought about how easy spending time with her the past couple of days had been. From his years of practicing law, he had noticed a pattern in real estate transactions: At some point in every deal, there was going to be some fireworks. With hundreds of thousands of dollars at stake, inevitably the buyer and/or seller would push for concessions or advantages. If the deal survived the game of brinkmanship, it was usually smooth sailing to the closing. He and Rivka had had their fireworks early on. Now, it seemed, the seas were calm. Would they—to stretch the analogy—eventually make it to some kind of closing? The truth was, it was way too early to even ask the question. For now, he would just enjoy the wind at his back and sun on his face.

Just after seven they arrived at a Cracker Barrel a few miles from the airport in Charlotte. Rivka had spent most of the drive arranging a rental car and hotel in Portugal and researching possible sites to visit. Only when they pulled into the parking lot did she focus on breakfast. "So, what do I need to know about your parents?"

"Both retired. Accountant and elementary school teacher."

"Good for your mom. Teachers are the best."

He smiled. "Everyone makes that mistake. It was my dad who was the teacher."

"Are you close?"

He shrugged. "Not as close as we used to be, since they moved down here. But, yes."

They got out of the Cherokee. "We should get our story straight," she said. "I'm guessing it's best not to tell them I work for the Mossad. So how about we just say I play volleyball still."

"Okay, but you're still Israeli. Mom's always hoped I'd come home with a nice Jewish girl." Cam's mom was raised Jewish, his dad Catholic.

"Can't say I've ever been called *nice* before." She took his arm. "Not sure how I feel about it."

Two hours later, under a bright morning sun, they returned to the

SUV, Cam having walked Venus, said his goodbyes, and transitioned the dog to his parents' car. Pick up the passport, then on to the airport.

"Been a long time since I met the parents," Rivka said.

Cam gave a final wave across the parking lot and elbowed her playfully. "Well, they didn't hate you." He smiled. "Other than your hair. Mom especially liked how you figured out the tip in your head."

"Right. Being an accountant. And I suppose your dad liked it when I raised my hand before speaking."

Something about Rivka's passport allowed them to zip through the security checkpoint. In the terminal, Rivka bought a couple of large water bottles. They found seats in the crowded terminal. "Alcohol and flying lead to dehydration." She leaned in. "So does sex. So drink up."

He smiled and touched his bottle to hers. "Cheers."

"So," she said, "I've made a list of the top tourist sites. But I'm guessing you have specific spots in mind. And we only have two days."

"Right. Here's the thing. Most people think the Templars were founded by French noblemen around 1118. But there's evidence the order was actually established a decade earlier than that, in Portugal. As the theory goes, the Cistercians—who were the sister order to the Templars —installed one of their own as King of Portugal and made it a Templar nation. They wanted to be on the other side of Europe from Rome, away from the eyes and ears of the Vatican. At that time, Portugal was pretty much a backwater and considered unimportant. But later, of course, it became a jumping-off spot for exploration of America."

"And you think our Melungeons were part of that."

"I think so. When the Templars were put down in 1307, the Portuguese king delayed implementing the Papal decree. My guess is that a number of Knights took that opportunity to leave Europe and find a safe haven. That would have been the first wave. In fact, many historians believe that the Templar treasure left with them. There are stories of a group of Templars sailing with the treasure from La Rochelle, on the west coast of France, perhaps to America. Later, around 1317, the Portuguese king allowed the Templar order to reconstitute itself as the Knights of Christ. They even used the Templar cross. Basically, it was nothing but a name change. But, by then, the first wave had already settled in America."

"But where does the Jewish blood come from? The Templars were Christian."

"Some of the Templars were probably from families who had converted, so they would have had Jewish DNA. But I think most of the Jewish influence came from a second wave. Not only was Portugal a safe haven for outlawed Templars, it was also a safe haven for the Jews of Europe. The Inquisition hadn't started yet, but lots of countries had turned against the Jews. It's well documented that many Jews held senior positions in the Portuguese government. What I think might have happened—and this is where Nathan Paris' research comes in—is that these Jews were the descendants of the priestly families who fled to Rome after King Herod's war. And Paris thought these families secretly controlled the Templars. So when the Inquisition hit Portugal and Spain in the late 1400s, there was a second wave of refugees fleeing Portugal. A Jewish one."

"And they knew where to go. Follow the first wave."

"Right. The Portuguese in the 1400s were the leading maritime power. A lot of that had to do with the Templars. They knew how to cross the Atlantic."

She nodded. "It all holds together. And it would explain the Jewish DNA and all the Jewish customs of the Melungeons. Not to mention that they call themselves 'Portuguese.'"

"And it also explains the darker skin. These Jewish families originally came from the Middle East."

She stared out the terminal window, putting the pieces together. "So, if your theory is correct, and the priestly families had the Temple treasures, does that mean the treasures are now in America?"

He smiled. "I think we're getting ahead of ourselves. So far, this is all just a theory. An informed one, but still a theory. In Portugal, hopefully we'll find evidence."

Dr. Gertrude Little shifted her girth, fighting to get comfortable in the airport terminal seat. A standard twenty-incher. Not as bad as the planes themselves, with their sadistic seventeen-inch widths. But half of America was overweight—why not design furniture to match the people?

Not that squeezing her hindquarters into this seat was the biggest problem of her day. The whole morning, in fact, had been a major pain in her ass. Waking well before dawn. Tracking Cameron Thorne halfway across the state. Scrambling to purchase a plane ticket—money completely pissed away—so she could follow Thorne past the security checkpoint. And then wandering the terminal, searching for him. Not to mention the gum-chomping coed talking loudly on her phone, making it hard for Gertrude to eavesdrop on Thorne and his new girlfriend. She shook her head. It was almost enough to make an honest dame out of her. Almost.

Taking a final sip from her almost-full Mountain Dew, Gertrude casually knocked her elbow against the bottle, splashing the yellow liquid onto the coed's overnight bag. "Oh, so sorry," Gertrude exclaimed, offering a thin tissue.

The coed's eyes widened. "Damn," she exclaimed, loud enough for people to turn to see what caused the commotion. "I'll call you back."

As the coed rushed to the bathroom to clean her bag, Gertrude refocused on Thorne's conversation. She was glad she had decided to do the eavesdropping herself. Her two sons were good boys, and they worked hard, but they had their father's intelligence—a couple of fries short of a Happy Meal.

There. The Israeli woman, the new girlfriend, had asked the key question: Were the Temple treasures in America? If so, Thorne would be just the man to lead Gertrude to them. And she was glad the Israeli woman was still in the picture. Gertrude's son had been one of the men on the dive team recovering the old Roman shipwreck in Newburyport last summer. Rumors had swirled that a golden candelabra—quite possibly the famous Golden Menorah of Old Testament fame—had been found in the wreck. But the candelabra had disappeared, with Thorne and the Israeli woman at the center of things. Gertrude wasn't picky—she didn't care which of the Temple treasures she discovered. Paris, in fact, had been excited about the possibility of the Asheville Masonic temple housing the sacred Table of Shewbread and had said Thorne even thought it was possible that the Ark of the Covenant was hidden in the area. With both Thorne and the Israeli woman in her crosshairs, she figured she had doubled her chances of success.

Not that she was going to follow them to Portugal. She hoisted herself out of the chair. She had plenty of things to do in Asheville to keep herself and her two boys busy.

◈ ✝ ✡

Rivka shifted in her airplane seat, her legs jammed beneath the seat in front of her. Being close to six-feet tall had been an advantage in her life —on the volleyball court, in the military, as a Mossad agent, working as a model in Tel Aviv while in college. But it was no fun when crammed into coach on a transatlantic flight.

Cam snored lightly next to her, his head against the bulkhead. She watched him, wondering when was the last time she had cared enough to observe as someone slept. Somehow, even asleep, he looked both strong and kind—or perhaps she was seeing what she wanted to see? She had been in relationships before, with both men and women. And she had engaged in sexual liaisons before as part of her job as a spy, again with both men and women. But this was the first time those worlds could potentially intersect. It might get dirty, ugly, messy. But it also might be worth it.

Using her phone, she typed a quick email to Menachem, updating him. "You said to keep an eye on Thorne. He's flying to Portugal. I am next to him, doing my patriotic duty."

The reply came immediately. "That is fine. Enjoy. I just hope you are not expecting reimbursement for airfare."

She retorted, glad that she could joke with her boss. It hadn't always been such a warm relationship. But she had earned his trust. And his respect. "Who said anything about reimbursement? I used the agency credit card."

She knew she should try to get some sleep herself. They would land at 8:30 in the morning in Lisbon, with a full day ahead of them. Leaning her head on Cam's shoulder, she sighed and took his hand in hers. She had told Menachem she was just doing her patriotic duty. But she knew it was becoming more complicated than that.

✡ ✝ ✡

Lenny Null stepped from the front door of his gallery into the bright afternoon light. He carried a painting wrapped in packing paper—at 24 by 18 inches, the frame tucked neatly under his right arm. In his left, hidden in his overcoat pocket, he gripped a Glock 43. He didn't plan on having to use it. But, of course, that was the point of the weapon—it was like insurance, not needed until it was needed.

He had put off the lawyer and the family for three days, making excuses. An hour ago the phone had rung, the lawyer using his tough guy voice. "Time's up. My clients are coming for the painting. I suggest you don't disappoint them." The two ruffians huddled in a doorway across the street confirmed that time, indeed, was up. They were no longer asking nicely for him to return the Nancy Hanks Lincoln portrait. Which only reaffirmed its value.

Waiting until he made sure they spotted him, Lenny froze, feigning fear, and turned to his right. Painting still under his arm, he began to jog along the sidewalk. He reached the end of the row of pastel gallery buildings and continued to the end of the block, where he cut to his right into a dirt parking lot next to a coffee shop. Glancing back, he saw that two men had become four. Four versus one, unfair odds. They should have brought six.

Lenny had always been a natural athlete, but for this pursuit he adopted a clumsy, shuffling gait, befitting a middle-aged art gallery owner. Panting, he followed a path leading through a cluster of trees and a hundred feet later broke into a clearing alongside a middle school track. A trash barrel sat next to the track. Hidden momentarily by the trees, Lenny dropped the painting into the barrel and quickly covered it with a pizza box. Spinning, he continued running, still on the outside of the track, making sure to stay out of sight of the middle school.

The first two pursuers caught him ten seconds later, one man kicking out his feet and sending Lenny sprawling in the frozen dirt. The other sat on his back. Lenny turned his body so they wouldn't feel the hard stub of his Glock.

"What do you want," he gasped.

"The painting." The man shoved his face into the ground. "We saw you with it. Where'd it go?"

"I don't know what you're talking about."

"Really?" The man spun him onto his back and slapped him with an open hand across the face, his ring bloodying Lenny's lip. "That spur your memory at all?" He raised his hand a second time, this time making a fist.

"Honest," Lenny murmured. "I don't have any painting."

This time the man hit him with a quick right to the jaw, causing Lenny to see stars. He followed with a palm to the nose, shattering it. "Last chance." The ruffian took out a pair of brass knuckles. "The next one will hurt."

The two other pursuers arrived, no doubt anxious for action. Blinking, Lenny figured he had played the patsy long enough. "Okay, stop." He held his hands in front of his face as blood spurted from his nose. "The garbage can back there. The painting's in there."

It only took them a few seconds to locate the painting and rip off the paper. The ruffian removed his knee from Lenny's chest but did not help him up. Without a word, the four men jogged off, painting in hand.

Holding his nose, Lenny stood. He patted his Glock, glad things hadn't gotten so rough that he needed to use it. He spat blood from his mouth and smiled. The family may, in fact, have needed six men rather than four to steal the actual painting. But Lenny was only too happy to let them run off with a fake.

⬥✝✡

Matthias surprised Astarte by waiting outside the door of her afternoon Psychology class. Stomping his feet to stay warm, he handed her a single flower. Eyes wide and serious, he said, "The ultimate test of a relationship is to disagree but to hold hands." With his free, gloved hand, he took hers.

He was so earnest that Astarte almost laughed aloud. But, thankfully, she bit her lip and matched his solemnity. "Thanks," she said, leaning into him. "I know we're not going to agree on everything." She smiled. "I just have to accept the fact that sometimes you're not going to see the light."

He grinned, anxiety draining from his face. Apparently, he was even more upset about this little spat than she had been. It made her feel bad that she had left it to him to make the grand gesture. "I wish I had a little gift for you."

"That's okay. I know you've got a lot on your mind, saving the world and all. But maybe you could kiss me?"

She did, lingering.

"Can I at least buy you a hot chocolate?" she asked.

"With marshmallows?"

They began to walk, their feet crunching against frozen snow. Montana had seemed like a fun idea when she made her decision back in April of her senior year in high school; in January, not so much. "Hey," he said. "I've been doing some research. I found two things that are pretty interesting. First of all, I asked my great aunt—she's the one you met, Flowing River, the tribal elder—what she knew about the Hopi and their legends. The first thing she said was that the Hopi are the oldest of all the American tribes."

"So that's consistent with what Soohu said, about them surviving all the cataclysms."

"Right." He pushed open the student center door. They grabbed hot chocolates and found a table in front of a plate-glass window over-looking a frozen pond.

Matthias continued. "The other thing is that we have a guy in our tribe named Dusty Crawford. He has the oldest DNA found in America. It goes back seventeen thousand years."

"I read about that. Another nail in the Clovis First coffin." The Clovis First theory, still stubbornly supported by some in the archeological community despite growing evidence to the contrary, posited that the earliest Indians—makers of the so-called 'Clovis point' tools—arrived via the Bering land bridge approximately 13,000 years ago. It was the type of institutional arrogance which drove her father batty.

"Anyway," Matthias went on, "the DNA originates in Arizona."

"But the Blackfeet are in Montana."

"And we used to be further north than that. So, the question is, what were Dusty Crawford's ancestors doing in Arizona?"

Astarte smiled and nodded. "Surviving a cataclysm, of course," she said. "His ancestors were Hopi. They lived through the Blue Star explosion." She leaned forward. "That's good stuff, Matthias. Thanks."

"Your dad would probably call this corroborating evidence. You know, if you're on the right track, all the small pieces of evidence you come across should fit into your case theory." He shrugged. "If they don't fit, you probably have the wrong theory."

She leaned back and sighed. "This is one time I wished we actually were wrong. It's not exactly great news that our doomsday prophecy looks like it's going to come true."

CHAPTER 6

The pilot's voice woke Cam from what had been a sound sleep. "Welcome to Lisbon. The current time is eight o'clock and the current temperature is fourteen degrees, or fifty-seven Fahrenheit. The forecast today is sunny with temperatures warming a few degrees. We will be landing in twenty minutes. *Bem-vindos a Portugal.*"

He stretched, gulped some water, and smiled at Rivka. "Did you sleep?"

"A bit. Not as much as you."

"You weren't being guarded by a trained operative."

"Neither were you. I spent most of the flight playing strip poker in the back with a bunch of rugby players."

He pretended to scan the back of the plane. "I don't see any empty seats."

"I sat on laps."

"Did you win, at least?"

She waited for a count before holding up a pair of plaid men's boxers. "I did. Not that I have any use for them."

Laughing, he shook his head. He knew better than to ask where the underpants came from. Somehow Rivka, rather than sleeping, had come up with her little practical joke. Which meant that, somewhere on the plane, someone was missing their boxers.

She handed him an apple, a roll, and a box of orange juice. "You slept through breakfast."

"Thanks. You washed your hands after touching the boxers, right?"

A half hour later, they had cleared customs; two hours after that, Cam exited the highway eighty miles northeast of Lisbon and parked their rental car near the summit of a steep hill in the medieval city of Tomar.

Cam gave a quick history lesson as they ascended the slope, Rivka's arm in his. The arm-in-arm thing was new to Cam, but it was beginning to grow on him. "The city was built by the Templars in the twelfth century as the headquarters for the Order. At the top of this hill sits a massive fortress, with a church inside. When the Templars were outlawed, everything was handed over to the Knights of Christ."

"But nothing really changed. They were just the Templars with a new name."

"Right. Using this as their base, and with the Templar fleet and navigational skills, the Portuguese became the world's leading maritime power in the 1400s."

Massive stone walls of the castle rose up in front of them as they rounded a corner. Cam continued. "Templar historians generally fall into two camps on the question of where the Templar treasure might be hidden. Some say Rosslyn Chapel in Scotland. Some say here. Supposedly, there are underground tunnels leading from the castle all over the town. Workmen stumble upon them even today."

"And you think this treasure may have come from the priestly families of Jerusalem."

"That's what Paris thinks. Or thought. And he may be right. Another possibility is that the treasure had been hidden in Jerusalem and recovered by the Templars in the early 1100s when they excavated beneath the ruins of the Temple—that is, in fact, how they got their name. This is just an educated guess, but there's probably some truth in both stories. The priestly families would have taken stuff that was important to them—the actual furnishings and religious objects from the Temple, like the Golden

Menorah and Ark of the Covenant, for example. But other stuff, they would have left. Stuff that wouldn't have been so important to them, like the head of John the Baptist and the marriage contract between Jesus and Mary Magdalene and maybe other documents revealing the true teachings of the early Church or details of Jesus' life. Maybe even some gold, if they couldn't carry it all. Later, when the stuff related to Christianity was recovered by the Templars, it was really important to the Church." He shrugged. "But the Jews wouldn't have cared about it, so they would have just left it."

She nodded. "I get it. Some of the treasure was taken by the priestly families to Rome and remained in their custody for the next thousand or so years, and some of it was hidden in Jerusalem under the Temple. But in both cases, the Templars ended up with it." She looked around. "And brought it here, maybe."

"*Here* makes sense. Rosslyn Chapel wasn't built until the late 1400s. This castle was built three hundred years earlier." He stopped and glanced up at the immense stone structure as he snapped a picture. "Not to mention this place is practically impenetrable. What better place to hide a treasure."

Templar Fortress, Tomar, Portugal

Following a cobblestone walkway, the scents of oranges and lemons in the air, they passed through an ornate gate and circled around the citadel. They climbed a set of stone stairs and stepped inside an ornate round church. At the center of the church stood an eight-sided, gold-plated rotunda called the *Charola*. Built in the twelfth century, the *Charola* featured eight arches supported by eight pillars. "This Charola was built first," Cam explained as he snapped a picture. "Everything else —the church, the citadel, the walls—was built around it."

Charola, Templar Fortress, Tomar, Portugal

"Some people think this was the template for the Newport Tower," Cam said, referring to the Romanesque-style Rhode Island stone tower which a growing number of historians believed was built by the members of the outlawed Templar order a century before Columbus. "Both have eight rounded arches supported by eight pillars, the number eight being sacred to the Templars. And both are two stories. So I get why people make the comparison. But I don't see it—this is ornate and finely crafted, while the Tower is more rough and utilitarian."

"Maybe you're being too literal." She read from her phone. "Plus, it says here that all the decorations—the paintings and sculptures and gold leaf—were added during renovations in 1499. Originally it was much more basic. The exact quote is, 'devoid of all ornament.'"

Cam nodded. "Point taken. Maybe it was a template." He smiled. "A Templar temple template."

After exploring for another hour, they returned to their car and wound their way back down the hill, crossing the river into the downtown area. Cam parked in front of another Templar church, this the Church of Santa Maria de Olival, also built in the twelfth century. "This is called the mother of all Templar churches," Cam said.

At the center of the altar stood a statue of what most people believed to be the Virgin Mary, holding a child. But Cam chuckled as he moved closer. "Look at her. Auburn hair, wearing green and red. It's Mary Magdalene, not the Virgin Mary."

Altar Statue, Church of Santa Maria de Olival, Tomar, Portugal

Rivka gave him a funny look. "You can tell just by her clothes?"

"In fact, yes. The Church was obsessed with making sure the Virgin Mary not be depicted in red, because red was the color of passion. So it decreed that all depictions of her must be in white and blue, the colors of innocence, with her hair covered. Mary Magdalene, on the other hand, is usually depicted wearing green, the color of fertility, along with the red of passion. And her hair is usually down and lush."

"So if this is Mary Magdalene, who's the baby?"

"Exactly, who's the baby? It must be someone important, otherwise she wouldn't be standing on the altar with it."

"Jesus' baby?"

He nodded. "Welcome to the secret world of the Templars. The baby was a girl. Her name was *Sarah Tamar*, the word 'Sarah' meaning 'princess' in Hebrew. So, Princess Tamar."

"Wait. Is that where the 'Tomar' name comes from?"

He smiled. "Bingo. Like I said, welcome to the secret world of the Templars. They were the army of the Church, but they had a whole different belief set. Basically, they believed that Jesus and Mary Magdalen were married and had kids, and that the Church covered it all up."

"Let me guess. The Church didn't want Jesus to have a spouse, a partner. That would mean women had power and value."

Cam nodded. "That's pretty much it."

"Not that I spend a lot of time thinking about this, but the whole idea of Jesus being a rabbi and being single makes absolutely no sense. Rabbis are *required* to marry and have kids. Especially so back then."

"Yet somehow people believe the fiction that Mary Magdalene was just some sinner, some harlot, not Jesus' wife. Even though the gospels talk about him kissing her on the mouth and her washing his feet. Not to mention her being allowed to prepare his body for burial."

She leaned over and kissed him, lingering for an extra second.

"What was that for?" he replied with a smile.

"Just taking my inspiration from the Bible." She pulled at her blouse. "And my red shirt."

They both stared at the statue, Cam's heart thumping in his chest like a teenager. There was something intimate about the kiss, even more so than their lovemaking. The sex on the first night had been ephemeral, driven largely by their loneliness. The second night had been about passion, two fit adults—fueled by adrenaline from their altercation in the woods—exploring each other's bodies. But this kiss, this gesture, seemed grounded in affection more than loneliness or passion. It was one thing to be *desired*. But was he ready to be *liked*?

Taking a deep breath, he tried to keep things light. "When you wash my feet, don't forget to dry between the toes."

She slapped at him playfully but left her arm intertwined with his.

"So," he continued, returning to safer ground, "back to the Templars. Something had to give. The Templars and the Church were on a collision course with each other, the Church preaching one doctrine and the Templars believing another."

"So that's why they were outlawed."

"I make the comparison to the Mafia. Outlawed, yes. Gone, no. They just went underground or reconstituted themselves, like they did here in Portugal. Eventually they reorganized as the Freemasons."

He guided her toward the exit. "Which brings us to our next destination. Back toward Lisbon, to a city called Sintra."

◈ ✚ ✡

After lunch on the road, Cam pulled into the parking lot of a sprawling estate built over an ancient, sacred spring. Purchased and painstakingly renovated in the early 1900s by a wealthy Freemason, the complex known as Quinta da Regaleira had been in Templar/Masonic hands since at least the fourteenth century.

"This," Cam said as he stepped from the car, "should be amazing. It's a UNESCO World Heritage Site." He snapped a picture of the Gothic palace, complete with spires and turrets. And—as in Tomar—the structure featured an octagonal tower, this one on the upper left of the palace.

Quinta da Regaleira, Sintra, Portugal

Cam had explained to Rivka that the entire estate was built as a shrine to Freemasonry and the Templars. "It's like the Vatican, but everything—all the symbolism and decoration—is Masonic and Templar instead of Catholic."

She rolled her eyes. "Every time you mention the Freemasons I can't help but think about those old *Flintstones* cartoons, with Fred and Barney in the Loyal Order of Water Buffaloes."

Cam smiled. "You had those in Israel?"

"Yes, on videotape, in the kibbutz."

"The leader of the club was called the Grand Poobah. In my old law firm, that's what we called the managing partner. Not to his face, of course."

They began to walk toward the main entrance. "Did you ever think of joining?" she asked, her arm—again—linked in his.

"I've considered it. They do a lot of good work, and it seems to be a good group of guys. But I think it's hard on the one hand to tell your daughter she can be anything she wants in life, and then on the other to join a group that won't take her."

"Good point." She leaned against him. "I like that you're an advocate for women's equality."

He smiled. "How could I not be, after you saved my ass yesterday?"

He purchased tickets and consulted a site map which came with them. "From what I've read, the main palace itself is pretty amazing. But it's mostly modern stuff." He pointed to a path winding its way up through a treed park featuring ornate grottoes, wells, benches, fountains and ponds. "Up near the top is what we came to see."

Walking quickly as he consulted the map, they passed a white chapel decorated with Templar crosses. "We'll check this out on the way back down," Cam said.

Near the top of the hillside slope, Cam stopped in front of a rock formation which looked like an ancient cave. "Believe it or not," he said, "this is manmade. It's not a real cave, just a wall of stone." He turned sideways and slid between two boulders. Reaching in, he pushed against a seven-foot tall stone slab. Creaking, the hinged slab swung open.

"Imagine being a kid and having the run of this place," Rivka remarked.

"I have a feeling we haven't seen the half of it yet."

Pushing through the stone door, Cam froze in the sunlight. Rivka gasped. Before them, falling away at their feet, dropped a massive, moss-covered stone well circumscribed by an arched spiral staircase. Cam stared. The well resembled an inverted tower—the Newport Tower, in fact. He peered over the side. "It must go down eighty feet."

Initiation Well, Quinta da Regaleira, Sintra, Portugal

She took his arm. "Come on. What are we waiting for?"

They descended, Cam explaining the symbolism. "It's an initiation well. Freemasons use these for their initiation ceremonies. I'm guessing the Templars did also. Notice how dry it is. Obviously, this was not meant as a working well."

"Right. I've read about this kind of thing. The initiate goes into the womb, into Mother Earth, to be reborn."

He peered down. "Look, at the bottom. You can see a Templar cross on the floor."

"And this architecture is Romanesque. The other buildings on the estate are more modern."

Cam again thought of the Newport Tower—it, too, was built in the Romanesque style. "There's actually a second well, more rustic than this. From what I read, according to the local building records, they're both ancient."

About halfway down, Rivka stopped and pointed into the shadows. "Look, a tunnel."

Cam nodded. "Apparently, there's a bunch of them. A whole underground network."

"You couldn't ask for a better place to hold secret meetings and ceremonies."

"Or to hide treasure."

At the bottom of the well, they examined the Templar cross inlaid into the floor. Rivka pointed. "Another tunnel. This one's lit."

He gestured toward the shadows. A rope was strung across a narrow passageway. "Or we could try that one."

"The road less traveled. I like it."

They were deep underground. But, Cam figured, the tunnel had to lead somewhere. In the U.S., an underground tunnel which was in any way dangerous would have been completely blocked off. Were the Portuguese equally cautious, or would they believe a simple rope sufficed?

Rivka didn't wait for him to wrestle with the decision. And he didn't wait to follow her. Squeezing through, they wandered, using their phones for illumination.

"Any idea where we are?" Cam asked after about fifteen minutes. If anything, it felt like they had moved deeper. Which was probably not the greatest idea.

She shook her head. "I'm all turned around."

"I think that's the point," he replied. "It's a maze. There are probably secret markings on the walls for the initiates to follow to lead you out."

"Maybe you should have joined the Water Buffaloes lodge," she said with a smile.

He stopped and sipped some water. "What's that expression about when you find yourself in a hole, it's usually a good idea to stop digging? Maybe we should stop descending."

"Or maybe that's what they want us to think."

"Fair point."

On they trudged, the lawyer in Cam refusing to believe a popular tourist attraction like this would expose guests to the danger of being lost underground. But, well, here they were. And, after all, it had been their decision to duck under the safety rope.

Turning a corner, he froze. "What's that noise?"

She shrugged. "Remember, my hearing's not great."

"I think I hear falling water. Come on."

A couple of minutes later, the sound of falling water getting louder, Rivka stopped. "Turn off your light. I think I see a glow up there."

"You're right."

Fifty feet ahead, following the glow, they rounded a bend and emerged into daylight behind the thin curtain of a gently falling waterfall.

"Now what?" she asked, shielding her eyes and staring at a blue-green pond blocking their exit. "Try to find our way back the way we came and climb out the well?"

"I suppose we could swim for it."

"These Freemasons don't believe in booby-traps, do they? You know, like alligators?"

"Not that I know of." He smiled. "But I don't have to outswim the alligators, I only have to outswim you."

"Which would be hard with my hands around your throat."

He looked at the tranquil pond, not much larger than a hockey rink. "I wonder," he said, crouching. "Remember the pond at Levi's house, with the hidden stepping stones?" Using his hand, he swept at the water, making a wave. As the wave crested, the shadow of a stepping stone appeared beneath the wave's trough.

Grinning, he stood. "After you, Madame."

"Great," she said, stepping out. "But you do know the alligators could still get us."

Cam and Rivka spent the next two hours exploring the Quinta da
Regaleira grounds and palace. The most important find was an image on
the altar of the White Chapel, which itself was full of Templar iconogra-
phy. Rivka had been the first to notice.

"You said that the Virgin Mary is never depicted in red, right?"

"Right. If she is, it's probably Mary Magdalene."

She had pointed at artwork entitled *The Coronation of Mary.* "Well,
how do you explain that?"

Coronation of Mary, White Chapel, Quinta da Regaleira,
Sintra, Portugal

Cam had laughed aloud. Jesus was crowning Mary, and the Mary in
question was dressed in red and was the same age as Jesus. "That's
exactly what you'd expect in a Templar chapel. Like I said, the Templars
venerated Mary Magdalene, believing her to be the bride and partner of
Jesus. His crowning her would make it official."

By the time they were finished touring the estate, Cam had no doubt
that the entire complex was a shrine to Freemasonry and Templarism.
But he had known that going in. The real revelation—beyond the

homage paid to Mary Magdalene—was the underground wells and tunnels.

"Between the Tomar fortress and these tunnels, we have two ideal hiding spots for the Templar treasures," he said as they walked back to the car.

"But we don't really have anything connecting the Templars directly to the Melungeons."

He nodded. That was, after all, their primary goal.

She continued. "There's nothing about the Melungeons worshiping Mary Magdalene, is there?"

"Not that I know of. But that would be a good find." He exhaled. "The problem is, there's been so little written about the Melungeons. And they themselves don't even know their history."

As they got into the car, Rivka said, "Hold on. I have an idea. What are the states that comprise Appalachia?"

"If you're asking about Melungeons, I'd say the biggest ones are Tennessee, Kentucky, West Virginia and North Carolina."

She pulled out her phone and spent the next fifteen minutes pecking away at it as Cam navigated his way toward their hotel in Lisbon.

With a smile and a sigh, she lifted her chin. "Okay, I think I found something. I found a list of common Melungeon surnames. Some of them, like Reeves, were common to many cultures so I didn't use them. But some, like Goings, are rarer. Those are the ones I focused on. Then I did a search of obituaries looking for women named Mary Magdalene who also had Melungeon last names. Goings, Chavis, Bolin, some others."

"And?"

"Jackpot. Dozens of Mary Magdalenes, most of them living in Appalachia."

Cam nodded. He felt that familiar tingle run down his neck, his body signaling that he was on the right track. "Good work. Really good. Especially because it's not that common a name."

"I know in my family, names are really important, passed down generation after generation. Nobody even remembers where most of them come from, but we just keep on using them."

"Same thing happening with Mary Magdalene."

"Right," she said. "At some point, she was important to these families."

"Just like she's important to the Templars."

They found the boutique hotel which Rivka had booked, checked in, and unpacked. Cam resisted a pre-dinner nap, knowing it would mess up his internal clock. Instead, while Rivka showered, he threw on his sweats and took the elevator to the fitness center, where he climbed onto an elliptical trainer. While he exercised, he let his mind run, connecting dots, finding patterns. He knew this was his real strength as a researcher —others were more dogged, or had more knowledge of the Templars. But he had a rare ability to take data, distill it down, and make sense of it. In short, to turn data into information, and then information into knowledge.

All of which meant he was uniquely qualified to unravel this Melungeon mystery and figure out if the Temple treasure somehow tied into it. But being uniquely qualified to do something didn't mean it got done. He wiped his face with a towel. The truth was that many unsolved historical mysteries remained just that.

⚒ ✝ ✡

Rivka's arm linked around Cameron's, they stepped out of their hotel in the historic section of Lisbon into the warm evening air. She couldn't help but skip as she walked—it was so pleasant, and rare, to be in a cosmopolitan city with free time on her hands and good company on her arm.

The entire neighborhood rested on the slope of the hill atop which sat the prominent Sao Jorge Castle. Most of the red-tile-roofed buildings dated to the late 18th century, built after a massive earthquake in 1755 which destroyed eighty percent of the city. As they explored, music wafted out of the dozens of restaurants they had passed in only three blocks.

"You hungry?" Cam asked.

"Always," she said with a smile.

They ducked into a bistro and ordered a bottle of wine. Cam suggested clams with bacon as an appetizer, then caught himself. "I'm sorry, I don't even know if you keep kosher." He shook his head. "That would be like the worst choice ever."

"It's fine. At our home in the kibbutz we kept kosher, but not outside the house." She smiled. "It used to drive my grandfather crazy. 'What is this?' he would say in his thick accent. 'You want that your plates and bowls will go to heaven but you don't?'"

Laughing, he took her hand. "I'm glad we did this, glad we went on this little adventure."

"In my family, we call that a *Gladventure*." She sipped from her glass, enjoying the peachy chardonnay.

"You have a word for it?"

"My dad was a real wordsmith. He loved puns and language and linguistics. When my sister and I were little—she was two years older than me—he used to take us out on what he called *Dadventures*. Just him, not my mom. I guess they thought it was important he have some time alone with us. Over the years, we added new categories. If it was something crazy, like one time we did a scavenger hunt all around Tel Aviv, it was a *Madventure*. When he took us to the Holocaust Museum— that was a *Sadventure*. After my sister graduated from elementary school and he took us camping, that was a *Gradventure*. And then—"

He held up his hand, laughing. "I get it."

"Sorry." She sighed. "It's your fault I'm babbling. You and the wine. You're easy to talk to."

"What happened to your sister? You referred to her in the past tense."

Rivka took another sip of wine. "Killed by a bomb in the market. She was just fourteen."

"I'm sorry. That must have been tough."

"It still is. I was a shy girl, but she always let me tag along. She was really my only friend. After she was gone, I really became a loner. I think that's why I'm a little socially awkward." She smiled. "In case you hadn't noticed."

"Not awkward, just different. You say what's on your mind. Most people don't. It's refreshing, actually."

"It's also rude. I'm working on it." She shifted. "I've come to realize that I always mean what I say. But sometimes what I say is mean."

He grinned, then turned serious and leaned forward. "Is the bomb the reason you joined the Mossad?"

"Maybe subconsciously." She shrugged. "But mostly it was because the volleyball thing was getting old and I needed a real job. I had enjoyed being in the army, so it seemed like it might be a good fit."

"And?"

"Well, I wouldn't be here otherwise. And I just told you I think of this as a *Gladventure*."

The waiter arrived, saving her from tormenting Cameron with more word plays. He held her eyes. "You up for another bottle of wine?"

"Sure." She settled back in her chair, a warm feeling of contentment washing over her.

Suddenly, Cam's eyes narrowed, his visage hardening. A chair scratched against the floor and she looked up to see a thin man with a scar running down his cheek lowering himself into the seat. *Shit*. Menachem.

"Hello, Rivka, Mr. Thorne. I'm sorry to interrupt your dinner. But we have a problem." He set his jaw, the vein in his neck pulsing with determination. "We think the Ark of the Covenant is in play."

"In play?" Cam replied.

"Yes. We realize that people are searching for it constantly, and have been for centuries. But we also realize how monumental a find it would be. We can't take the chances of it falling into the wrong hands."

Rivka exhaled. "What he means is, we can't let the Arabs get it. They'd parade it all over the Middle East, use it as evidence that God has abandoned the Jews. You'd end up with millions of frenzied Muslims storming Jerusalem."

Menachem nodded. "I'm afraid she is correct."

"Well, what makes you think the Muslims are the ones who will find it?"

Menachem shrugged. "We don't. But we do believe they will be the ones to *buy* it, once it is found. In a bidding war, unfortunately, Israel would not stand a chance against the oil dollars."

Cam shifted. "I'm sorry, but what does this have to do with me?"

"Believe it or not, we think there is a possibility it is hidden in Appalachia."

"In Appalachia?" Cam replied as Rivka bit back a retort. She didn't believe for a second that this was a new development. Menachem had been keeping her in the dark, lying to her about why he wanted her in North Carolina.

Menachem nodded. "As I said, when it comes to the Ark, we need to take any possibility seriously." He stood. "I'm sorry to cut this short. But finish your glass of wine. Then you're going to need to be on the next plane back to America."

Rivka let out a long breath and looked at Cam. As angry as she was about being played, she couldn't tell Cam. But she could convey to him her dismay. "This, I'm afraid, is what we would have called a *Badventure*."

◈ ✚ ✡

Menachem at least had the decency not to walk with Cam and Rivka back to their hotel. But he was waiting in the lobby for them when they arrived.

"Sorry," she said sheepishly. "This is a favorite hotel for the Mossad." She shot Menachem a dirty look. "Even so, I thought we'd have some privacy."

"Please pack," Menachem said simply.

Cam had been chewing on this for the past fifteen minutes. "Look, I'm pretty open-minded. But I doubt the Ark of the Covenant is in Appalachia." He would have used even stronger language, but a part of him had begun to entertain the possibility that he should listen to Amanda's ghost—apparently speaking to him through the mysterious song—pushing him to find answers. And that those answers might take the form of an ancient treasure. "Yes," he continued, "the Templars may have ended up there. And they may even have brought some of their treasures, which could have come from the Temple of Solomon. But you don't just keep something like the Ark a secret for six hundred years. What, is it in someone's barn?"

Menachem shrugged. "Frankly, I agree with you. But I also have my orders. Someone thinks this is worth chasing. Maybe the Ark was hidden somewhere and lost to time."

"Well, then, it's probably going to stay lost. Appalachia is a big place."

"Or," Rivka offered, "maybe there really is a family keeping it in their barn. Keeping it secret." She shifted. "Take Levi and Esther, for example. Their family is very insular, intermarrying every generation. And they're isolated. Not to mention paranoid. Come to think of it, the name 'Levi' could be a clue. Cam, you mentioned the priestly families being custodians of the Temple treasures. Maybe Levi and Esther are part of the priestly families?"

Cam smiled. "So all we need to do is show up with a big bag of pistachio nuts and make a trade?" He turned serious. "Look, I guess it's possible. But it seems like a stretch to me."

Menachem held up his hand. "Stretch or not, we have to pursue the possibility. Like I said, time to pack."

"Fine," Cam replied. He didn't take orders from Menachem, but the reality was that if he wanted to travel with Rivka, he was stuck with her boss as well. Yet perhaps the boss could be reasoned with. "I don't think we should return to America just yet," Cam offered. "If you think the Ark is connected to the Portuguese and the Melungeons, we need to do more research on this side of the Atlantic. Otherwise we're just stumbling in the dark."

The Mossad agent's eyes narrowed. "What do you have in mind?"

"If anyone knew where the Ark was hidden, it was the Templars. It seems to me that we should look in the same places they looked."

✡ ✠ ✡

Rivka cornered Menachem in the hotel lobby. She kept her voice low, but there was no mistaking her tone. "You've been lying to me about why I'm in North Carolina. It was the Ark all along."

"Not lying. Just only telling you what you need to know."

"Well, now I need to know about the Ark of the Covenant."

"Not the Ark. The Tables of Testimony. That is our target. The Ark is just a fancy package, giftwrapping and ribbons. We care about what was inside."

"Cam mentioned the Tables of Testimony to me. But I thought you were hot for the Ark."

"The Tables of Testimony is the bigger prize, they tell me. Many people think the Tables of Testimony and the Ten Commandments are the same thing, both being carved on stone tablets. But if you read the language of the Old Testament closely, you see that's not right." He glanced down at his phone and read aloud.

Come up to me into the mount, and be there, and I will give thee tables of stone, and a law, and commandments.

"That was from the Book of Exodus. God gives Moses three things." Menachem counted on his fingers. "Tables of stone. A law. Commandments. They're not the same thing."

"Okay, I'm with you."

"And another thing. When it comes to the Tables of Testimony, it's clear that God physically wrote them out. God says, 'I will write upon these tables the words.' You've probably heard this phrase—he wrote them with his finger, the 'Finger of God.' But when discussing the Ten Commandments, he commands Moses to do the physical writing. 'Write thou these words,' whereupon Moses 'wrote ... the words of the covenant, the Ten Commandments." He looked up. "Like I said, there's a clear distinction. Moses wrote one, God the other."

She waited as Menachem let out a long breath. "It took me a while to understand the importance of this artifact," he said. "In fact, I referred to the Tables of Testimony being brought to America as like the misfit toys in *Rudolph the Red-Nosed Reindeer*."

"Really?" she laughed, surprised that her crusty Jewish boss would be familiar with the soppy Christmas special.

"Can you blame me? Nobody's even heard of the damn thing. It's like nobody wanted it. Even the name is silly—it's not a table and there is no testimony."

"You do know that the misfit toys are the heroic characters in the *Rudolph* story, right?"

"So I heard." He handed her a thin folder. "Read this. Then I need it back."

She plopped onto a sofa. There wasn't much, just that there was some kind of Cosmic Equations carved onto a stone tablet and that the government believed these equations could be crucial to Israel's national interest. She sighed. *Why* could they be crucial? *What* did the equations reveal? Of course they weren't going to give her any details. But they had apparently given enough to convince Menachem. Now it was her job to find the tablet and recover it. Somehow without letting her new lover know what she was doing.

She tossed the folder back to Menachem. "Just once, I'd like to know my mission before I start it."

Catching the folder, he held her eyes, his jaw tight. "Make no mistake, Rivka. Your mission is always the same. Serve Israel. It is only the details that change."

✧ ✝ ✡

Within an hour of Menachem interrupting their dinner, Cam and Rivka were in a private car on the way to the Lisbon airport. An hour later, seated side-by-side in an otherwise empty corporate jet, they taxied down the runway, courtesy of a wealthy Jewish industrialist willing to do the Mossad an occasional favor.

Cam squeezed Rivka's hand. "I could get used to this. You made it sound like being an agent was such a hardship."

"Um, did you notice we never got our dinner?" She leaned in. "Not to mention, I think I had a chance to get lucky tonight."

"I'm sure I could scare up some nuts," he said. Then, after a pause, "And a blanket."

As if listening, the pilot's voice rang out. "Flight time to Addis Ababa is about seven hours. We lose three hours. So we should land at around sunrise. Menachem says I need to get you to America by tomorrow night, so you'll only have a few hours on the ground to do what you need to do." He paused. "And we also lose seven years. It is the year 2014 in Ethiopia."

Cam looked at Rivka. "What?"

"Yes. They count from when they think Jesus was actually born. We actually know a lot about Ethiopia because a lot of Jews from there settled in Israel back around 1990."

"Right. The secret airlifts."

"Operation Solomon. We rescued over fourteen thousand people in two days. One of the flights had over a thousand passengers, which is a world record for number of people on a single plane." She smiled. "My dad was part of that mission."

Cam thought about how satisfying it must have been to rescue so many people from near-certain slaughter. Then he shifted back to the task at hand. "On the one hand, it's strange to think of African Jews, living there for centuries pretty much on their own. But if you think about it more, it explains how the Ark of the Covenant would have ended up down there."

She angled her head. "I'm not tracking you."

The plane rose and banked, the expanse of the darkened Mediterranean beneath them. "Sorry. You know the story of King Solomon and Queen of Sheba. She was an African queen who Solomon fell in love with and impregnated. This would have been around 950 BC. Twenty years later, the son from that liaison—named Menelik—returned to Jerusalem to meet his father. As the legend goes, either Solomon gave him the Ark as his birthright, or Menelik stole it. And it's been in Ethiopia ever since."

"That's quite a story."

He shrugged. "But that's probably all it is, a story. The Ark was mentioned in the Bible many times after Solomon. So, unless there were two of them, the original was not brought to Ethiopia by Menelik."

"So why are we on this plane?"

"Because the *Templars* believed that the story—or a variation of the story—was true. They were convinced the Ark really was in Ethiopia."

"You say *was*…"

"Right. Think about it. The Italians took Ethiopia in World War II. Don't you think Mussolini would have loved to have the Ark? If nothing else, to give to Hitler, who was obsessed with finding it. If the Ark ever was in Ethiopia, I'm betting it was long gone by the time World War II rolled around." He paused. "And if I'm wrong, if by chance it was still there after World War II, someone definitely would have grabbed it by now. Just recently, in the fall of 2020, there was an attack at the church in Axum, in northern Ethiopia, where some people say the Ark is supposedly kept. Militiamen were trying to get the Ark while priests and local villagers defended the church."

"I've seen some of those Ethiopian militia groups. Hard to believe priests and villagers could have held them off."

"That's exactly my point. The whole thing sounds … off. The Ark is, arguably, the greatest treasure in Western civilization. And it's being guarded by priests and villagers? And nobody has grabbed it yet?" His voice rose. "I mean, a da Vinci painting sold for 450 million dollars a few years ago. Wouldn't the Ark of the Covenant be worth at least ten times that?"

Rivka nodded in agreement. "So, again, then why are we flying all night to Ethiopia?"

"Because it's one thing to read from a book or the internet. But sometimes you just need to see for yourself."

"Okay. But *see* what?"

He shifted in his seat, turning to face her. "Here's what I think happened. The Ark really was in Ethiopia. But not with Menelik—that story makes no sense based on the dates. And how do we explain the Jews being in Ethiopia, the ones Israel airlifted out? It seems to me, the Ark would have been with the Jews, right?"

"Okay. Makes sense. Missing Jews. Missing Ark. The two are probably related."

"And we're pretty sure they didn't bring the Ark back on the plane during the airlift, right?"

She smiled. "My dad would have mentioned that."

"Okay, here's a theory I read that makes sense to me. We know the

Templars were looking for treasure under the Temple of Solomon. This would have been in the 1120s. They found something, I think—I've always thought it was some kind of ancient knowledge. Otherwise, they wouldn't have risen to power so quickly. But, by all accounts, they never found the Ark. Flash forward about forty years, to 1165. An Ethiopian prince named Lalibela shows up in Jerusalem. He was fleeing from his brother, Harbay, the king, who was trying to kill him. He tells his story to the Templars, begging for help. Of course, he mentions that the Ark of the Covenant is in his homeland. I think the Templars decided to take a little trip down to Ethiopia. They put Lalibela back on the throne—I'm guessing, in exchange for the Ark. This is now the 1180s. Nobody can say for sure if they found the Ark or not while there, but we do know they built lots of underground churches and chapels, all connected by tunnels, in northern Ethiopia."

"Let me guess: You have a theory for why?"

He stroked his chin like a professor and smiled. "In fact, I do. I think they built the underground churches to house the Ark. I think the Templars were biding their time. They didn't want to take the Ark back to Europe and have to hand it over to the Church. Then, later, the Ethiopians pushed back about it being taken away at all. There are some interesting sources documenting how an Ethiopian king sent a delegation to the Pope, beseeching him to leave the Ark in Ethiopia. This is 1306, right before the Templars were outlawed."

"Interesting. So now you're saying it stayed in Ethiopia after all."

"But not forever. You've heard of Henry the Navigator?"

"Yes. Early 1400s, the Portuguese Age of Discovery. They were the leading seafaring power, and Henry their foremost navigator." She smiled. "You do realize this is a roundabout way of finally getting to your point?"

"Sorry." He shook his head. "Must be the wine on an empty stomach. And also the fact that I'm piecing this all together myself in my head as I talk."

"That's okay. We have all night." She smiled. "Though I do want to get under that blanket at some point."

He met her smile. They were alone on the plane, so why not? Shifting, he hurried through his final point. "When I was in college, I did a term paper on Prince Henry. He had a strange obsession with Ethiopia, which has always stayed with me." He pulled up a direct quote on his phone. "A professor from the University of London, who was an expert on Henry, wrote, 'It is known that Prince Henry was obsessed with the notion of making direct contact with Ethiopia.' It seemed to me that the obvious reason for this was that Henry, as Grand Master of the Knights of Christ, was trying to find the Ark of the Covenant. I mean, why else the obsession? Henry was a navigator, a sailor. And as Grand Master, he got to call the shots. Why Ethiopia? Lalibela, where the Templars built the churches and tunnels, is hundreds of miles inland, remote, nowhere near any important trade routes or areas of strategic value."

"Lalibela, as in the prince who showed up in Jerusalem in the 1160s?"

"Yup. He built a new capital city in the northern mountains and named it after himself."

"So did Henry ever make it there?"

"Not that we know of. But, like the ancient Phoenicians, the Portuguese penalty for disclosing information about exploratory voyages was death."

"You think he did. And took the Ark."

"Maybe him, or maybe it happened a century later. In the early 1500s, the Muslims invaded Ethiopia. The king asked the Portuguese to send troops to help, which they did. If Henry didn't take the Ark, then my guess is the Portuguese took it later as payment for saving the king's ass. Oh, not surprisingly, the Portuguese troops were led by a member of the Knights of Christ."

"Bottom line is you think the Ark ended up in Portugal. Either early 1400s or early 1500s."

"Look, it has to be somewhere. Portugal makes the most sense. Especially if you agree it was in Ethiopia at some point, which most historians do."

"And from there?"

"Hidden in Tomar, maybe Sintra. Then, who knows?"

"Could it have been taken across the Atlantic?"

He shrugged. "Sure, for the same reason the Templars took other treasures to America. Just look at Oak Island up in Nova Scotia. The Church had turned on the Templars once. The Templars had to figure it could happen again." He held her eyes. "What better place to hide your treasures than on an unexplored continent across an ocean?"

CHAPTER 7

Cam was getting tired of waking up on planes. Rivka, on the other hand, seemed as chipper as ever as they touched down in Addis Ababa with the rising sun at their tail. Standing in the aisle, she did a series of calisthenics before gulping some orange juice. "There. Ready for the day."

"Do they teach you that in spy school?"

"Teach me what?"

"How to be, like, unaffected by air travel." But at least, again, no ghost. Maybe they didn't like airplanes.

She bit her lower lip. "No. But when I wake up, no matter where I am, I think of my sister. Life is a gift—why not enjoy it?"

He nodded and smiled. "All right, then." Dropping to the floor, he pounded out fifty pushups. He stood, breathing hard, and shook his head. "Doesn't work for me. I still want a hot shower."

She tossed him a hand towel and rolled her eyes. "Momma's boy."

The pilot had arranged for customs officials to board the plane, and within an hour they were back in the air, headed north to Lalibela, in the mountains 300 miles north of the capital. Cam peered out the window. They were far from the coast, the land isolated, barren and inhospitable —not the kind of place the Templars usually took any interest in.

Using connections in the Mossad, Rivka had arranged for a local guide to meet them at the airport. He did so in a sky blue Soviet Lada sedan. Cam leaned closer. "How nice, he picked a color to match your hair." Though austere, the car easily covered the twenty-minute drive to the site of the rock-hewn churches.

Like the Sintra and Tomar sites, the churches were a UNESCO World Heritage Site. Cam made clear to their guide what they wanted to see. "This is a fascinating area, and I hope to come back someday to do it justice. But, for today, we must focus exclusively on the twelfth-century churches." He danced along the edge of the truth. "I am a Templar historian, and these churches are instrumental to my research."

Smiling, the driver nodded. "I understand, sir. They are treasures."

"Or, at least, they may lead to one," Rivka whispered in response.

As they drove, Rivka pulled out her phone. "Want to hear a description of what we are going to see?"

"Sure."

She read aloud:

Towering edifices, the churches remain places of living worship eight hundred years after they were built. It is important to stress, however, that they were not built at all in the conventional sense, but instead were excavated and hewn directly out of the solid red volcanic tuff of which they stand. In consequence, they seem superhuman—not only in scale but also in workmanship and in conception. Close examination is required before the full extent of the achievement that they represent can be appreciated. That is because, like medieval mysteries, considerable efforts have been made to cloak their real natures: Some lie almost completely concealed within deep trenches, while others hide in the open mouths of huge quarried caves. Connecting them all is a complex and bewildering labyrinth of tunnels and narrow passageways with offset crypts, grottoes and galleries—a cool, lichen-enshrouded subterranean world, shaded and damp, silent but for the faint echoes of distant footfalls as priests and deacons go about their timeless business.

They entered a village, hundreds of simple but neat huts and shacks densely packed along a hillside. Near the crest of the hill, the driver stopped at a clearing. A number of white-robed men milled about, some of them seemingly in prayer. "This way," he said simply, leading them toward the clearing in the warm, thin mountain air. Suddenly, he stopped and pointed ahead. "The Church of Saint George," he announced proudly.

The passage Rivka had read was not exaggerating. The stone edifice literally sat in a pit, only the cross-like design of its roof visible as they approached. And not just any cross—the Templar cross.

Church of Saint George, Lalibela, Ethiopia

Cam peered over the side. "Unbelievable," he said simply. The cross-shaped church was forty feet in height—or was it depth? Either way, it was a truly remarkable achievement, and much larger than he expected. Lying on the edge of the pit, his eyes at roof level, he took another picture.

Church of Saint George, Lalibela, Ethiopia

"So," Rivka asked as he dusted himself off, "how do we get down there?"

The guide smiled. "Follow me." He led them around the pit to a narrow, concealed, man-made ramp. The ramp spiraled downwards; halfway down, the ramp passed underground, converting itself to a tunnel and further concealing its presence.

They entered, the church a good twenty degrees cooler than the outside air. A priest stood in front of a curtain, praying. "What's behind that?" Cam asked the guide.

"He will let you look if you offer a contribution," the guide replied.

Cam did so, and the priest stepped aside to reveal a replica of the Ark of the Covenant. "All the churches have these," the guide said, as if driving home the point that they were on the right path.

Reentering the tunnel, they continued underground, passing from church to church, winding their way beneath the ancient complex.

"Remind you of anything?" Cam asked as they squeezed through a narrow opening in the stone.

"Sintra," she replied simply.

He didn't need to ask the obvious question whether one site was designed after the other.

They viewed eleven churches, clustered in three different locations, all connected by the elaborate web of underground tunnels. Three hours later, they returned to the Church of Saint George.

Cam again stood on the edge of the forty-foot pit, again looking down at the cross-shaped edifice. He gestured around them. "It's all so ... *elaborate*." He shook his head. "This is why I wanted to come, to get a true sense of it. Can you imagine how hard it was to carve a church out of stone? Much less eleven of them? And all the connecting tunnels? Why would the Templars bother? Then, later, come back to save the king a second time in the 1500s? I mean, there's no military value to this place. And no real religious significance either. The only plausible reason for them to be here, to invest so much time and energy, is the Ark of the Covenant." He shook his head again. "Nothing else makes sense."

✦ ✛ ✡

The Lada bounced along, returning Cam and Rivka to the airport. Cam would have loved to continue exploring Lalibela, but the pilot had made it clear that their time was limited.

"Something you told me got me thinking," Rivka said. "You said that DNA testing revealed that the Melungeons were a mixture of Portuguese, Sephardic Jews, Cherokee Indians and North Africans. I get the first three. But the North African thing never made sense to me. Until today."

"You think Ethiopian?"

"It makes sense. We know how devoted the Levite families were to the Temple and its treasures. Presumably, the priestly families in Ethiopia who were guardians of the Ark were equally zealous. So perhaps, under duress, they agreed to allow the Templars or Knights of Christ to take the Ark to Portugal. But I'm guessing, as part of the deal, that they'd insist on coming with it."

Cam nodded. "Okay. And then, if the Ark continued on to America, the Ethiopians would have continued on with it." He smiled. "With their DNA."

"There's just one problem," she said. "You don't think the Ark made it to America."

"I don't, you're right. I admit it's possible, but to me the most likely scenario is that the Templars hid it someplace in Portugal. Maybe Tomar or Sintra."

"The problem with that theory is, why hasn't anyone found it? I'm sure people—Church officials, for example—have searched Tomar and Sintra. The fact that it hasn't been found tells me it's not in Europe. You mentioned Hitler before and how obsessed he was with finding the Ark. He had a whole team of SS operatives combing through Europe looking for it."

They stopped in front of the terminal, a yellow, two-story building with a five-story control tower behind it. "Okay," Cam said after tipping their guide. "You've convinced me." He smiled as they walked toward the terminal. "The Ark of the Covenant is hidden someplace in Appalachia. I'll take you for another sushi dinner if you find it."

"That would have to be a whole ocean of sushi."

A screech of tires froze Cam. As he turned in the direction of the noise, he saw that Rivka had the opposite reaction—instantly, she dove behind a brick stanchion and drew her handgun.

"Get down," she yelled, taking aim at three uniformed men carrying assault rifles as they leapt from a military jeep.

But before Cam could move, a rifle appeared inches from his face. A pair of strong arms locked around his bicep. He felt his body sag. There was something about looking into the black hole of a gun barrel that short-circuited both halves of the 'fight or flight' instinct.

A tall man with a jet-black face and yellowed eyes climbed from the jeep. He held his hand up to Rivka. "There will be no need for that," he said in a deep voice.

Rivka weighed her options and, apparently, found them wanting. She lowered her gun. "What do you want?" she asked.

"A word with Mr. Thorne."

Cam found his voice. "Go ahead."

"Not here. Come with me."

Rivka tensed. "You're not taking him anywhere." Something about her blue hair made her seem more formidable. Confident, perhaps.

Two soldiers trained their assault rifles on her. The leader replied, "And you are not in a position to do anything about it."

She slowly re-raised her weapon, her eyes hard and her jaw set. Had Cam not been so frightened, he would have laughed at the sight of a blue-haired woman holding her own in a standoff with a jeep full of armed soldiers.

"You can shoot me right here, in cold blood," she said. "It will be great for your tourist business. But you're not taking him anywhere."

The leader glared at her. Finally, with a snort, he motioned for his henchmen to stand down. "Very well." He pulled Cam by the arm out of earshot. Leaning closer, and showing his teeth in what barely passed as a smile, he said, "She is very devoted to you. You are a lucky man."

"What do you want?" He felt anything but lucky.

"A simple warning." Cam could smell the strange combination of milk and cigarettes—of youthful innocence and the harsh ugliness of life —on his breath. "Approximately two-thirds of our economy is reliant on tourism generated by the Lalibela churches. People, literally, are at risk of starvation. We know of your reputation as a Templar scholar—your opinions do not always reflect the mainstream beliefs."

"Are you trying to censure me?"

His eyes were hard, but Cam sensed the sincerity in his cause. "That depends entirely on what you might say about our churches."

"You have nothing to worry about." Cam was glad he didn't have to try to lie. "I happen to agree that it was, indeed, the Templars who built them. And I'd imagine the whole Templar story is good for business."

The man nodded. "Excellent." He stepped back. "In that case, have a good flight. Please accept my apologies."

Cam began to walk away, then stopped. "I'm curious. How do you know I'm not lying to you? How do you know I won't write something totally different when I get home?"

He pointed his chin toward Rivka. "Because of her. A good woman would not be willing to risk death for a dishonorable man."

✡ ✝ ✡

Cam let out a long sigh of relief as the wheels of the jet lifted off the tarmac. "I think I need a drink."

Rivka reached across to a small refrigerator built into the bulkhead adjacent to her seat. "You won't have to twist my arm."

She poured a couple of glasses of white wine.

"Cheers," he said, clinking her glass. "Thanks for saving my ass." He smiled wryly. "Again."

"Speaking of saving your ass, is it okay to drink when you have diabetes?"

"As long as I don't overdo it. In fact, recent studies actually recommend a glass of wine with meals."

She chuckled. "It's like that futuristic Woody Allen movie where they figure out steak and hot fudge are really health foods."

"Right. *Sleeper*." He smiled. "I always think of him when I'm on a plane. He had one of the all-time great lines. He said he always brings a bomb with him when he flies, because what are the odds of there being two bombs on the same plane?"

With a wide smile, she sipped her wine. "Good one. I suppose that logic applies to us as well. What are the odds of the same researchers finding both the Golden Menorah *and* the Ark of the Covenant?"

"Well, we didn't *find* the Menorah. We just happen to know where the people who did find it tried to hide it. And we haven't exactly found the Ark." He smiled. "Other than that, you're right—same thing."

She cuffed him on the arm. "Jerk."

He finished his wine and reclined his seat. "I've totally lost track of time. My body doesn't know whether to sleep or climb a mountain. And the adrenaline from having those rifles pointed at me doesn't help."

"Welcome to my world. You learn to fight through it."

Nine hours later, they landed in the Azores to refuel. Cam did some quick calculations: Three o'clock Ethiopia departure; fifteen hour flight time to North Carolina; eight hours lost to time change; an hour for refueling. "We should be landing around eleven o'clock Friday night in North Carolina."

"No doubt Menachem will expect us to get right to work."

Cam fluffed a pillow and closed his eyes. "Yeah, well, luckily only one of us actually works for the bastard."

CHAPTER 8

Cam's sleep was tortured, the lyrics of that same haunting song drifting in and out of his head as he himself drifted between consciousness and sleep. At one point he awoke and, listening intently, swore he could hear the hint of it echoing around the room like barely perceptible wafts of smoke.

I am gone but in your dreams I live; I mean no harm but answers I must give...

For the umpteenth time, he asked himself if the lyrics were some kind of message from Amanda, imploring him to find answers. Or, as her ghost had said to him, to find the treasure...

He thought about waking Rivka to ask if she heard it also, but chose instead to let her sleep. It was bad enough that one of them was being haunted.

At five, unable to sleep, he got up, threw on his sweats and running shoes, and left the hotel for a long run in the pre-dawn glow. Forty-five minutes later, the song no less an earworm despite the outside stimuli, he returned and jumped in the shower. He didn't generally believe in the paranormal, but he also knew there was much about the human psyche which remained a mystery. No one doubted that animals possessed memories and other knowledge passed down to them genetically from their ancestors, and humans were animals themselves, so who knew what was possible? Amanda wasn't his ancestor, technically, but still…

He turned off the water and grabbed a towel. Opening the shower curtain, he froze. As if in response to his unspoken question, words had formed in the fog on the bathroom mirror. *I am gone but in your dreams I live.*

He blinked, his body shuddering. This was getting weird. Too weird.

✠ ✠ ✡

Footsteps in the next room woke Rivka from a sound sleep. Light, furtive. Not Cam's. Blinking, it took her a second or two to place herself. Late night arrival, same hotel, different suite. She reached over for Cameron. Nothing. *Right.* He had awakened her and told her he was going to get them some breakfast. And something about a note on the bathroom mirror, which had made no sense to her…

Ears straining, she pulled her handgun—a BUL Cherokee—from beneath the mattress. Compact and concealable, the weapon packed a punch and also offered a good grip in rainy conditions. She flicked the safety off and swung her feet off the bed.

"Come on, Cherokee," she said to herself. She was suddenly struck by the irony of the 'Cherokee' name—why had an Israeli gun manufacturer named a model after an American Indian tribe, and what were the odds that she would find herself using it in the heart of Cherokee territory? But she pushed the thought aside and focused on the sounds from the living area of their hotel suite.

Slowly, her back against the wall, she crept forward in the faint glow of pre-dawn light. She pictured the space—a small kitchenette and the bathroom separating the bedroom from the living area. Venus was still with Cameron's parents, and it was too early for housekeeping. She was glad she hadn't needed to fire the weapon at the Lalibela airport. Hopefully, this morning would bring a similar outcome. But whomever was out there had frozen, perhaps sensing her approach.

The microwave. There was just enough light filtering in through the bedroom window for the microwave door to show a reflection. Moving her head back and forth, Rivka was able to survey most of the living area by peering at the appliance door. *There.* A movement. A man, burly, crouched, near a closet in the corner, its door open.

This was where her training kicked in. Her gun was a last choice, not a first. But 'last' did not mean waiting so long that you ended up dead.

She tried to piece things together; understanding who the intruder was would help anticipate his movements. She guessed he had entered when Cameron left, perhaps assuming the room would now be empty—a fair assumption given that her name was not listed on the reservation and that she had not been with Cam last night when he checked back in because she had needed to use the restroom. So a hotel worker? Or someone with intel from one hoping to rob the place? But she was just guessing.

She had an idea. Grabbing her night-vision monocular from her purse, she retreated back to the bedroom and closed the curtain. The suite fell into darkness. One hand holding the monocular and the other her gun, she moved forward in the green light of night-vision technology.

Suddenly, a thump-thump of footsteps sounded and the front door swung open. The intruder—a panicked look on his face—rushed out, pulling the door closed behind him. Rivka strode over, snapped the dead-bolt closed, and exhaled. What was that all about?

Turning the light on, she scanned the room. The closet door was open, but nothing else seemed amiss. She crossed the room. Inside the closet she found some extra pillows and blankets, a folded luggage rack, a blue plastic humidifier knocked onto its side, and an ironing board. Had the intruder been looking for a safe? That didn't make sense to her—the safe was in the main closet, closer to the entryway. And there was no way he had stolen anything from Cam or her since they hadn't even begun to unpack yet. She shrugged and slid the gun's safety back on. Another unsolved mystery to add to their list.

◈ ✚ ✡

During breakfast, Cam and Rivka discussed the strange mirror message and the even-stranger stranger sneaking around their room. They made no headway in solving either mystery. Pushing aside a growing sense of unease, Cam made the half-hour hike back to the River Arts District to meet with Lenny. The weather had turned, a cold breeze from the north dropping temperatures into the thirties. Hopefully, Astarte's flight would not be delayed.

He had made the strategic decision not to bring Rivka to the meeting. He didn't really trust Lenny, and the less he knew about Cam's personal life, the better. Rivka, not surprisingly, had been fine with it, saying she needed to pick up some things at the drugstore. Cam liked that she seemed to enjoy his company but not *need* it.

Or perhaps it had nothing to do with him; perhaps Menachem had some spy work for her to do. Cam wasn't naïve enough to think the Mossad boss had been completely forthcoming with what he knew about the Ark of the Covenant possibly being in America. It had, at first blush, seemed like a ridiculous possibility. But after what they learned in Portugal and Lalibela, and given the Mossad's interest, Cam was beginning to think there was a chance it could be.

He shook his head. Somehow what had begun as an investigation of the Lincoln family painting had mushroomed into a larger mystery involving the Melungeons, the Templars, the Portuguese, the Ethiopians, the Freemasons, and the Ark of the Covenant. Not to mention the Mossad. It was the story of his life—it seemed like every time he pulled on one of history's loose threads, the entire tapestry unraveled.

He sensed that the Cherokee tribe played a larger part in this somehow also, though he was not sure how. As if on cue, his phone dinged. A text from Astarte, telling him to check his email for information she had found on the Cherokee that might be important to his Melungeon research. He smiled—leave it to her to do research on the tribe before flying out to address them.

Blowing on his hand for warmth, he read through the email. She explained that most Cherokee lived in Oklahoma—they had been forced westward during the famous Trail of Tears march in 1838. But smaller bands remained in North Carolina and Tennessee, exercising sovereignty as independent nations. Astarte had especially focused on these bands, since they would be her audience.

What she found caused him to stop, despite the cold wind, and read carefully. She began with the bombshell revelation that the Tennessee Central Band of Cherokee tribal patch featured a Jewish Star along with assorted animal totems. Apparently, the tribe had done DNA work and concluded that they descended either from a lost tribe of Israel or early Jewish settlers. Cam pulled up an image on his phone and, smiling, shook his head. What a strange world we lived in.

Tennessee Central Band of Cherokee Tribal Patch

He read on, from a quote she had provided. "According to tribal member Dr. Donald Yates, President of DNA Consultants, there is compelling evidence that within the Cherokee nation of American Indians, mothers and other matrilineal forbearers bear bona fide Middle East Jewish genetic markers. 'The essence of my findings is that the Cherokee have had families of Jewish heritage in their midst since before Columbus, and that early Jewish traders married Cherokee women to cement their ties with the tribe,' Dr. Yates says."

Cam read the words a second time: *The Cherokee have had families of Jewish heritage in their midst since before Columbus.* He shook his head again. Was this another puzzle piece helping to understand the Melungeons? DNA tied the Melungeon to the Cherokee, which in turn tied them to Jews in the pre-Columbian time period. Did all this, again, provide evidence for early Portuguese/Templar visitation to America? One of his goals for tonight, with Astarte speaking at the Cherokee reservation in North Carolina, was to dig deeper on this subject.

Of course, none of this mattered if the Hopi doomsday prophecy turned out to be true. Cam had always been able to compartmentalize his thoughts and emotions and for the past week had basically ignored the possibility of the world erupting into a fiery ball of devastation. But that was just denial. If this prophecy were true, they'd need to make plans. That was another thing he hoped to learn tonight from the Cherokee—did they take this threat as seriously as the Hopi seemed to?

But, for now, he needed to share some news with Lenny. Just as their flight was landing last night, a fellow researcher who specialized in DNA work had emailed Cam. Cam had called in a favor and asked if she could look into Nancy Hanks Lincoln. The reply had been enough to get Cam to leave his warm bed with Rivka early this morning and come share the news with Lenny.

He arrived at Lenny's lime-green gallery. Anyone who knew Lenny's humorless personality would never think to look for him inside a pastel-colored row of storefronts. Well-played by him.

Lenny was waiting for him in the back room, the lights dim. "So, I bought some time with the family who owned the painting." His voice sounded off, like he had a cold.

"How?"

"I let them steal it back. But it was a fake."

Cam moved closer. "Holy shit." Lenny's eyes were black, his nose bandaged, his lip swollen. "Looks like you didn't *let* anyone do anything."

"Had to make it look good."

"Won't they figure it out?" Cam asked.

"Eventually, maybe. But probably not." Lenny shrugged. "I know what I'm doing."

"There's never been a doubt about that, Lenny," Cam replied, raising his eyebrows. "The question has always been, why are you doing it?"

Lenny offered a crooked smile. "Fair enough. But this one is pretty simple. I think this painting may be worth a fortune." He paused to breathe. "But to get there, I need to provide a credible history of Nancy Hanks Lincoln proving she's Black."

"That's why I'm here. I have some news. This is from a woman I know who does a lot of DNA research with the Mormon Church."

Lenny nodded. "I know the Mormons are at the cutting edge of genealogy research."

"Right. So she knows what she's doing. As I understand it, Nancy did not have any female children. But they tracked down the female descendants of her sisters and did DNA testing on them. That's how mitochondrial DNA gets passed down, through the women."

Cam read from the email.

Details of the early life of Lincoln's mother, Nancy Hanks Lincoln, are scarce. Her ancestral roots have been obscured by time and hotly debated among Lincoln scholars and genealogists for over a century and a half, spawning many conflicting theories. However, in 2015 a DNA study of the matrilineal kin of Lincoln's mother demonstrated that Lincoln's mitochondrial DNA belonged to the very rare haplogroup X1c. X1c had never been observed in the western hemisphere. Only two other cases had ever been observed in the world, one in southern Italy and the other in Tunisia.

"Southern Italy," Cam explained, "is only about sixty miles from Tunisia, at the narrowest part of the Mediterranean. Given Nancy's dark complexion and this rare haplogroup tying her to northern Africa, I think you could make a strong case that she was ethnically of African origin."

"Outstanding," Lenny replied simply.

"Like I told you the other day, we've been finding that many people from Appalachia are of Melungeon heritage. I'm guessing Nancy's one of them."

"And have you been able to narrow down exactly what *Melungeon* is?"

Cam nodded. "Best I can tell it's part Portuguese, part Jewish, part Cherokee." He paused. "And, of course, part northern African."

"Can I use this DNA information? Is it public?"

Cam nodded. "It was published already. I'll send you the link."

"Thanks, Cam. You've just made me a small fortune."

"Wait until you see my bill."

The corners of Lenny's mouth twitched. "Don't forget, I went to law school also. I know a bill is really just an invitation to negotiate."

◈ ✝ ✡

Cam stood on the street in front of the Null & Boyd art gallery waiting for his ride. He preferred not to take an Uber when he could walk, but he had much to do today before heading out to the airport to pick up Astarte.

As he rode back to the hotel, he thought about Lenny's painting. Nancy Hanks Lincoln's dark skin, combined with the DNA evidence, made a compelling case. But so what if Lincoln's mother was of African descent? Did it really matter? Cam shook his head. He was being naïve. It may not matter to him, but the truth was that it would matter to much of the country. America had never successfully dealt with its race issues and divisions. Learning that one of its iconic presidents had been part Black could have widespread and unpredictable consequences for the country.

Assuming, of course, there even was a country after the Blue Star explosion.

Exiting the Uber, Cam strode into the hotel lobby and, fretting over Rivka's report of a strange man in their room, stopped by housekeeping to see if they had sent a worker by for some reason earlier that morning. The woman shook her head. "This was before six? Our cleaning staff doesn't even arrive until seven." Cam furrowed his brow and thanked her. Another mystery. Add it to the list.

He checked his watch. Time to meet Rivka in the room and then head back to the airport to pick up Astarte. His parents would also be there, with Venus. The plan was to have a late lunch with Astarte, then head to the reservation for her presentation this evening. As he stepped into the elevator, a pang of sadness washed over him. Amanda would have loved to see her daughter, grown and poised, addressing a large crowd.

Her voice, which had been silent recently, no doubt trying to give him space alone with Rivka, chimed in as the door closed.

Don't kid yourself, Cameron. I'll be there with bells on.

✡ ✝ ✡

"Of course I want to come to the talk," Rivka said, grabbing her handbag off the bed.

"It means having another meal with my parents."

She took his arm. "I'm sure they'll be totally focused on their grand-daughter. It'll give me the chance to play footsies with you under the table."

The truth was, Rivka looked forward to it. Cam's parents were nice enough, and watching him interact with them gave her new insights into his personality—you could learn a lot about a man by the way his mother treated him, and even more by the way he treated her. The other truth was that Menachem was interested in this doomsday prophecy, so she really had no choice but to attend Astarte's presentation.

Walking the hotel hallway, Rivka studied the other guests. She was still bothered by this morning's intruder. Not so much by the invasion of privacy or even risk of danger—she was used to that. But she couldn't figure out what his game was. Not knowing made it hard to plan a defense.

Cam interrupted her thoughts. "I'm guessing Menachem is interested in this Blue Star prophecy."

She nodded. "Israel tends to benefit from these types of things." Repeating much of what Menachem had related to her on the plane ride out of the Baltics, she explained Israel's complicated relationship with America's Christian community. "Many Fundamentalist Christians believe that the second coming of Jesus is imminent, and that it will be portended by natural disasters signifying the end of days. Importantly for Israel, this can only happen while the Holy Land is being controlled by Jews." The Hopi prophecy could be advantageous to Israel in that American Christian groups will be even more committed to a strong Israeli state to ensure that proper conditions exist for the Second Coming."

He replied, "Advantageous, that is, assuming the Holy Land doesn't disappear beneath a flood of fire and seawater."

"Yes. There is that small detail."

◈ ✚ ✡

Venus was in dog heaven, cuddled in the back seat of the SUV with Astarte, her chin on the girl's thigh as Cam drove west toward the Cherokee reservation.

"I think someone missed you," Cam said, smiling into the rearview mirror.

"I should bring her back to Montana with me."

"Not a chance," Cam replied.

Astarte shifted forward. "Um," she said softly, glancing self-consciously at Rivka in the passenger seat, "I'm sort of nervous about tonight."

"You wouldn't be human if you weren't. It'll be a big crowd and the message you are delivering isn't exactly going to thrill them."

"Thanks," she replied sardonically. "That helps."

"I'm just saying, it's natural to be nervous. It's your body's way of telling you to get ready for action."

Her talk was scheduled for seven. They arrived a few minutes before six at the main complex of the Eastern Band of Cherokee Indians Reservation, a series of modern, low-slung buildings nestled in the foothills of western North Carolina, likely paid for from the profits of the luxury Harrah's Cherokee Casino. One of the tribal elder's daughters had agreed to watch Venus during the presentation, freeing up Cam to help Astarte set up the projector and her PowerPoint presentation. He glanced around the assembly hall, about the size of a high school auditorium. "They must be expecting a big crowd," he said, looking around.

"Great," Astarte replied with a sigh.

"Look. I've done a bunch of these. Just let your images carry the presentation, one at a time." He was glad to see her slides were rich with images and low on text. He had seen some dull presentations where the slides were packed with text, which the presenter read aloud.

"Matthias thinks I should focus on not trying to sell them on this."

"I agree. Be matter-of-fact. *Here's the prophecy, here's the evidence, here's what you might want to do about it.* Let people make up their own minds."

A local television station, along with a handful of print media, wanted to interview Astarte before the presentation, so Cam and Rivka got permission to wander around and view the exhibits in the otherwise-closed tribal museum.

"Are we looking for anything in particular?" Rivka asked, her voice echoing in the empty halls.

"Anything that connects the Cherokee to the Melungeons or the Templars or the Jews. We've found some connections, but my gut says there's more that we don't know about."

A few seconds passed, then Rivka pointed. "You mean like this?"

She had stopped in front of a display case exhibiting a round, black stone disc about the size of a catcher's mitt. Etched into the center of the disk, surrounded by snakes, was an engraved hand with the all-seeing eye in the middle of the palm. The display card explained that the disk, dating to pre-Columbus times, had been found in an Indian burial mound in Alabama, about 300 miles to the southwest. Cam snapped a picture.

Burial Mound Disk Featuring Hamsa Hand, Moundville, AL

"This is a Hamsa Hand," Rivka said. "Very common in Israel."

Cam nodded. He had run across this before in his research on the Phoenicians. "Not just Israel. All over the Middle East."

"A coincidence?" she asked.

He shook his head. "I don't think so. It's too particular an image, a hand with an all-seeing eye in the palm. If it were more basic or common, I could see it being invented independently both here and in the Middle East. But something like this gets shared from one culture to another."

"And the Cherokee lived in Alabama?" she asked.

Cam nodded. "They did."

"Then I agree with you. Either the Jews or Phoenicians brought it here, or the Cherokees brought it there."

Cam checked his watch. "Let's keep looking."

He stopped in front of an exhibit featuring the writings of Cherokee chief John Ross. The writings, part of a 2,200 page compilation on loan from a collection in Chicago, were written by Ross in the days before the Trail of Tears in 1837, apparently as a way to record the Cherokee history on the eve of what he feared (correctly) would be a devastating relocation. One letter in particular, detailing Cherokee traditions, caught Cam's eye. Scanning it, he suddenly froze. Squinting in the dim light, he reread a passage, this time aloud. "The Cherokee most sacred name of

God is 'Yi-ho-wa,' a name which no common person was ever allowed to speak."

He called Rivka over and showed the passage to her. "That's just like Judaism," she said. "*Jehovah* is the name of God. The Tetragrammaton—four letters, Yodh, Hey, Vav, Hey. In English, J-H-V-H. And, traditionally, nobody was allowed to utter it aloud."

Cam grinned. "Pretty amazing, huh? Why would the Cherokee have the same name for God as the Jews? Remember, this is 1837, *before* they were forced to convert to Christianity."

Smiling, she said, "Well, you know what they call us Jews. Members of the tribe."

They continued, circling through the collection. "Is that Elvis?" Rivka asked, pointing at a life-size cardboard cutout of the rock star.

Cam stepped closer and read aloud from an informational placard:

Few people know it, but Elvis Presley claimed to be Jewish and Cherokee. A DNA test run on a rare specimen of his in 2004 bore this out. Both of Elvis' assertions were based on the ancestry of his mother, Gladys Love Smith. Growing up in Memphis, Elvis went to summer camp through the Jewish community center. When his mother died, he took care to have her grave marked with a Star of David. He studied Judaism increasingly in later years and to the end of his life wore a chai necklace, a symbol of Jewish life. Published genealogies take Gladys' strict maternal line back to great-great grandmother Nancy Burdine, a professed Jewess born in Kentucky, whose mother was White Dove, a reputed full-blood. Through his mother's direct female line, Elvis was a Jewish Indian, an American Indian Jew.

"Didn't you also tell me Elvis was Melungeon?" Rivka replied.

Cam nodded. "Cherokee, Jewish, Melungeon," he counted off on his fingers. "We seem to keep running into all three of them together."

"Too much for a coincidence."

"Agreed." He checked his watch again. "Okay, we should get in there."

She took his arm and they circled back toward the assembly hall. An image on a display board, part of an exhibit entitled "Legends of the Cherokee," caught his eye. He did a double-take. *The Ark of the Covenant*. What was that doing here?

"Hold on," he said. He strode closer and read quickly. His eyes widened. "You won't believe this. This says that the Cherokee have the Ark." He read aloud:

Cherokee legend clearly describes the Ark of the Covenant accompanying the ancient Cherokee as they came across the Atlantic Ocean. Atop its four corners are found four winged personages. There are staves with brass handles located on the outside of the Ark, going through goldish/brass colored type rings. There is a cloud of mist that surrounds the Ark. On the exterior of the Ark one notices the decor of gold and silver. The Ark of the Covenant is protected in a cave and is guarded and cared for by specially selected men. No one is allowed to touch the Ark under penalty of death, except for the Chief Grand Council Medicine man.

"That's crazy," Rivka replied. "All the things it talks about are the same as in the Old Testament, the same as Jewish traditions. The winged angels on top. The poles through rings for carrying it. The gold decoration. The cloud of mist, which is the presence of God. Special guards, being the priestly family. Only the high priest being allowed to touch it." She exhaled. "Do you think the Cherokee really have it?"

"It says here that they had to move it when the Tennessee Valley Authority built all those dams and locks in the 1930s."

"Does it say where it is now?" she asked excitedly.

He leaned closer. "Something about guarded by snakes."

"Really?"

He grinned. "No, Indiana Jones. It doesn't say."

They found their way back to the assembly hall, Cam's mind racing. He had never taken seriously the possibility of the Ark of the Covenant being in America. But, Indiana Jones jokes aside, mounting evidence pointed in that direction. He pictured the Cherokee tribe in the early 1800s, its land stolen and its spirit crushed by the nascent United States.

Would they be inclined to share a treasured religious artifact like the Ark with their oppressors? Probably not. And would they have the where-withal to keep its existence a secret? The Indians—and the Cherokee in particular—were a proud, resilient people. Of course they would. Does that mean they did? No. But the door was opened to the possibility.

◈ ✟ ✡

Gertrude Little sat back in her wheelchair, directing her youngest son to the front row of the second section of the auditorium where spaces had been left for handicapped seating. She didn't actually need the chair, but using it assured both a prime seating location and a seat wide enough to accompany her girth.

"Good. Now go find me a Mountain Dew and some trail mix," she ordered. His brother—the smarter of the two, though that was not saying much—was waiting out in the parking lot, hopefully not screwing things up.

"The sign said no food or drinks."

She turned and fixed him with a hard stare. "These people are here to learn about the world coming to an end. Do you really think they're going to care about raisins on the floor?"

She glanced around. A good crowd, a couple hundred and growing. She wasn't surprised. Hard to find something more important to do on a Saturday night than figure out a way to save your family. Back in the day, she and Martin used to pack places like this. He with his magic act, she with her hypnosis, the crowd skeptical but wanting oh so badly to believe, to be taken to a land of marvel and miracles. They had a good gig going. Until Martin went and died from a heart attack at age forty-seven. She shook her head. *She* was the obese one, the one supposedly at risk. Now she was left to hustle on her own, burdened by sons cursed with her plain looks and Martin's simple mind. Would it have been too much to ask for at least one of them to have gotten her brains or his looks? She let out a long, tired breath. This treasure scheme had better pay off—she was running out of both money and ideas.

✠ ✚ ✡

While Cam gave a few last-minute pointers to Astarte, Rivka moved offstage and texted Menachem. *I know you said Tables of Testimony was new target. But turns out you may be right that Ark is in Appalachia. Maybe in hands of Cherokee tribe. How far can I go with this?*

He replied almost immediately. *If necessary, go all the way. If that doesn't work, go further.*

Smiling, she stuck her phone back into her pocket. Other than the fact he often kept her in the dark, she liked working for Menachem. He never left any doubt about what he wanted.

And she liked being with Cam. He wasn't as clear as Menachem about what he wanted, but that was fine with her. She didn't know, either. They could figure it out together.

A thought struck her: When was the last time she had been content both personally and professionally? She bit her lip. The answer, in fact, was never.

The lights dimmed for the beginning of Astarte's talk. Rivka took a seat near where Cam was running the projector. The first slide appeared, a fiery image of a galactic explosion. She sighed. Just her luck. She was finally happy with her life, and the world was about to come to an end.

✠ ✚ ✡

Baseball cap pulled low, tinted glassed covering his blackened eyes, and a medical mask covering his face, Lenny Null slipped in just as the lights dimmed. He didn't normally go to events like this. Too many people, any one of whom might recognize him. And he'd need to leave a few minutes early. But dark rooms were generally safe, especially now that masks had become acceptable in a post-COVID world. He did not want to miss this presentation.

He focused not on Astarte but on the audience, watching their body language, their reactions. It didn't matter what Astarte said, didn't even really matter if the prophecy she discussed was real or instead just the Native American equivalent of campfire ghost stories. What mattered was what people *believed*, because beliefs were what motivated behavior. And if knowledge was power, the kind of knowledge which allowed someone to predict future behavior was the trump card within the knowledge deck.

Involuntarily, Lenny rubbed his fingers together. He had become addicted to playing that card.

✡ ✝ ✡

Astarte took a deep breath, ignoring the rivulets of sweat running down the sides of her body from her armpits. Good thing she had worn a thick sweater. So many people, looking at her so intently. As if she—and she alone—had the answers which would save them, save their families.

Having the lights off helped. Not seeing the audience was even better than picturing them in their underpants. She exhaled again. Just her, alone in a room. All that rustling and breathing was mere white noise.

"This is Soohu," she began, clicking to the second slide. "She's a Hopi Elder. Her name, appropriately, means 'star.' She is the keeper of a Hopi prophecy. The Blue Star, or Kachina, prophecy." Like Dad said, put up the slide, talk about the slide, go to the next slide. Easy-peasy.

She was almost surprised when she got to her last slide, an image of the hills of Appalachia. She glanced up at the clock—she had been speaking for forty-five minutes. Her dad had told her not to go much longer—"We were all conditioned in high school to pay attention for fifty minutes; after that, people tune you out."

With a final deep breath, she concluded, "The good news, if there is any, is that the mountains of Appalachia offer both enough altitude and a temperate enough climate to be good candidates for underground shelter facilities. In fact, other than the southern Rockies, this area offers probably the best chance for survival in all of the United States."

That was it, then. She had just told a crowd of a few hundred Cherokee that doomsday was near. Almost dreading what would come next, she signaled for the lights to be turned on. Blinking, she said in a low voice, "I'd be happy to take your questions."

✧ ✝ ✡

As Astarte spoke, Cam turned in his seat and took a short video of the event on his phone, making sure to document the size of the impressive crowd. He could not have been prouder as he watched Astarte skillfully, and with grace, respond to questions from the audience. But it was a bittersweet emotion. The fact that so many of the Cherokee, including many of the tribal elders, took the Blue Star prophecy seriously drove home to Cam the seriousness of the danger. Even a moderate galactic explosion—not the cataclysm that was feared—could unleash floods and fire which would devastate much of the planet.

Astarte made that exact point. "Nobody knows yet how bad things might get. But the blue glow at the center of the galaxy is real. There's been an explosion. Something's coming." She shrugged. "The only question is whether it ends up being a cataclysm or merely an inconvenience."

"When will we have the answer to that?" a man's voice asked.

"I don't know. I'm not an astronomer, not a scientist. One of the reasons I'm speaking out is to get our national leaders to pay more attention to this. This needs to be studied. And we need to start preparing for the worst."

Cam found himself nodding in agreement. He recalled what his softball buddy had said about evidence in the ice core of Greenland seemingly confirming that a similar galactic explosion had brought about the end of the last Ice Age. And he thought about his first-floor apartment in the coastal city of Newburyport, only a few feet above sea level. He was proud of his daughter, no doubt. But she was starting to frighten him.

✧ ✝ ✡

As Rivka watched Astarte field questions, she sat back and tried to see the big picture in all this. Why had Menachem assigned her to this case? What was his true goal? As always, and as was customary Mossad practice, she was only given small pieces of information, a few pieces of the puzzle. But that didn't mean she couldn't try to figure out what was happening behind the curtain.

Originally, she had been told that the painting of Lincoln's mother was important. Menachem had explained that Israel was worried that America might swing too far to the left politically. Best she could tell, the Mossad feared that the revelation that Lincoln was part Black would further strengthen and embolden minority voters in the country, pushing the political needle further to the left, where opponents of Israel resided. Rivka wasn't sure she agreed with this analysis—an argument could also be made that Lincoln being Black would serve as evidence for those on the right who claimed that America was a color-blind society and that claims of racial discrimination had been overblown. But she wasn't paid to make these types of decisions. What she was paid to do, and what she feared she may be tasked with, was destroying paintings like this which threatened Israel's self-interest.

But she sensed the painting had become secondary. Menachem's focus had turned to the Tables of Testimony. And back, it seemed, to the Ark of the Covenant. Understandably so, especially in light of what she and Cam had just learned about the Cherokee possibly being in possession of the sacred Ark. She trusted she would not be tasked with *its* destruction, at least.

And there was a third matter in play as well, which was why she was here tonight. Prophecies of an Apocalypse brought on by natural disaster, as Menachem had explained to her and she had explained to Cameron, rallied the religious right to support Israel because the Second Coming of Jesus could only occur when Israel was in Jewish hands. Based on what she had seen tonight, the Native American community, at least, was taking the Blue Star prophecy seriously. Perhaps Israel should as well. Much of its population lived along the coastal plain.

So, three balls in the air, four if you counted the Ark and the Tables of Testimony as separate balls. Was there also a fifth she did not yet know about, perhaps involving the odd death of Nathan Paris? She let out a long breath. If they were going to ask you to juggle a bunch of balls, the least they could do was tell you which ones to focus on. As her grandfather used to say: When juggling, it's okay to drop a ball or two—just don't drop the glass one.

✠

Rivka on his arm, Cam carried Astarte's briefcase as they crossed the Reservation parking lot on a cold, windy night. Astarte followed with Venus.

Cam checked his phone. "Interesting. A message from my astronomer buddy. He's been watching the blue star, or blue glow, all week. He says it's not growing."

Astarte turned. "Really? That's great news." She smiled. "Even if it does make me look like Chicken Little."

"Hey," he said to Astarte as they piled into the SUV. "How about a drink at the hotel bar?" It was almost ten, Astarte having fielded questions for over an hour and chatted informally for another thirty minutes.

"You do remember I'm not of age, right?" she said from the back seat.

"But you're, like, seventy in chicken years."

"Very funny."

He put the vehicle in gear. "Besides, if you're old enough to save the planet, you're old enough for a glass of wine."

She grinned. "Or two."

"I thought your talk went very well," Rivka interjected.

"And she's a tough critic," Cam added, turning onto a two-lane county highway for the hour-long drive back to Asheville.

"Tough?" Rivka replied. "If I were tough, I'd be hanging out with a different guy."

Cam smiled to himself, aware that she had been careful not to use the *boyfriend* word.

"She's got you there, Dad."

Their bantering was interrupted by a pair of high beams bearing down on Cam. His skin tingled, his body sensing danger. He sped up, but the vehicle kept pace, less than a car length off his bumper. Slowing, he eased toward the shoulder. But the car stayed on his tail.

"We've got a problem," he announced, speeding up again. The road was dark, barren.

Rivka, who must have also sensed the danger, had already spun in her seat. "Man driving, another guy in passenger seat. Can't see the back. Pick-up truck, older model. I think Ford." She pulled her night vision monocular from her bag. "This won't do us any good with his headlights on." She patted the holster at her side. "But this will."

"Hold on there, cowboy." No way did Cam want this to escalate, especially with Astarte in the car. And it was entirely likely their pursuers were armed also.

"I know. But just in case."

"I just tried 911," Astarte said. "No cell coverage out here."

Cam continued at the speed limit. Suddenly, the pickup rammed them. "Shit," Cam said over the sound of grinding metal and broken glass. He gripped the steering wheel, regaining control of the SUV. "Assholes." He sped up.

"Okay, that's my cue," Rivka said. Gripping her revolver, she opened the sunroof, stood, and pushed her head and shoulders through. "Hold steady," she yelled, her streak of blue hair whipping in the wind. With two quick shots, she shattered the pickup's headlights. "Okay," she said, "let's see what they do now."

"You mean like shoot back?" Cam set his jaw and accelerated. "Astarte, stay down."

"Not too fast," Rivka said.

"Why not?" He wanted to press their advantage and just get away.

She stood again, this time with her monocular. Yelling over the wind, she said, "Because I want to see who our new friends are."

A few seconds passed, then Rivka fired again, this time taking out one of their tires. The pickup skidded onto the shoulder as Rivka dropped back in with a grin. "Okay, off we go. I've seen enough."

"Recognize them?"

"No. Driver is heavyset, wearing baseball cap. Guy in passenger seat is bald, beard, thick glasses, I think tall. A woman in the back seat."

Cam turned. "Wait." He pulled out his phone. "Scroll through my pictures. You'll see a bunch of a painting, a family portrait. In one, there's a guy standing nearby."

Rivka took the phone and zoomed in. "Could be the guy in passenger seat." She angled her head. "In fact, I'd say good chance."

Cam shook his head. "Really?" Lenny was always playing some game. But ramming Cam's SUV wasn't a game.

✡ ✠ ✡

Astarte sat at a round table in the hotel bar with her dad and Rivka, sipping a glass of white wine. The wine didn't so much make her feel like an adult. Nor did the act of socializing with her father's new girl-friend. But she couldn't shake the ringing of the gunshots in her ears. She had never fired a gun, much less seen one wielded as a weapon.

More to the point, why were people trying to run them off the road? Dad seemed to think it had something to do with a family painting, but that seemed odd to her. She sensed he was downplaying things. She knew the Ark of the Covenant was in play—that, clearly, raised the stakes high enough for someone to ram a bumper or two.

Dad bought Rivka a drink, and she thanked him with a quick squeeze of his hand. It jarred Astarte a bit, but not as much as she guessed it would have. Probably because Rivka was so different than her mom. If Dad had chosen someone similar, it would have been weird. It also helped that Rivka wasn't all clingy with him. And that she didn't try to mother Astarte. To be truthful, Astarte thought it was pretty cool that she was such a hard-ass. And good for Dad not to be intimidated by a woman who could probably kick his butt. And she might come in handy, given that—once again—Dad seemed to have picked up an enemy.

✡ ✠ ✡

Cam tried to appear relaxed as they sipped their drinks, not wanting to alarm Astarte. But the incident on the highway had unnerved him. He had never liked Lenny, much less trusted him. But he had not counted him as a threat or enemy. What angle could Lenny be playing, what did

Cam have that he wanted or needed? He stared off, his eyes settling on a mural along the far wall, a smiling family together sharing a meal...

The realization hit him like a thunderbolt. Cam had no evidence the Nancy Hanks Lincoln family portrait was authentic—he had just taken Lenny's word for it. What if Lenny had used the portrait to lure Cam to North Carolina, hoping that Cam would follow the Melungeon clues around Appalachia and find the Ark of the Covenant, rumored to be kept in these parts by the Cherokee? Just, in fact, as Cam was doing. It was exactly the type of strategy Lenny would employ—puppeteer an expert like Cam into doing the dirty work and then swoop in at the last minute to claim the prize. Cam didn't know all the details, or what game Lenny had been playing earlier tonight in the pickup truck, but he knew enough to perceive the gestalt of Lenny's scheme. Had Nathan Paris been part of the plan, killed off once his part had been played? What about the rifle-carrying boys in the woods? Also Levi and Esther and the clues hinting at their 'Jewishness'? Even keeping Shelby away from Asheville had been part of it; no way would she go along with a sting on her old friend. Cam took a deep breath. Lenny had been playing him the whole time, dropping breadcrumbs in the woods and waiting for Cam to waddle along like a dimwitted chicken pecking at corn kernels.

Face flushed and palms sweating, Cam fought to settle his breathing. For the first time since Rivka had arrived in Asheville six days earlier, Cam wanted to be alone—not alone exactly, but alone so he could talk to Amanda. "Be right back," he said, standing. "I need to hit the men's room."

He splashed water on his face and stared at himself in the mirror. He took a deep breath and spoke aloud.

"I didn't see the Lenny thing coming."

He's a master. But are you certain you have this right, certain he's playing you?

"Certain? No. But pretty damn close. Why else would he have been ramming us with that pickup truck? I don't know what he was doing, but I'm pretty sure it wasn't a love tap."

Fair enough. Lucky for you Rivka was there. Lenny hadn't planned on you having a night-vision Ninja."

"True. But you're better than her at figuring things out. What his game might be."

Nice of you to say, Cameron. But, truly, I'm not jealous. I know I can't have you myself, and I want you to be happy.

"This is just me hearing what I want to hear."

Of course it is. That's the problem with me existing only in your head. But, having said that, I think you're spot-on with your theory. Even if there's only, say, a five percent chance of you finding the bloody Ark, it's worth it to Lenny to take the chance, right? I mean, what a find it would be!

"Right. And no doubt Lenny would milk it for all its worth." Cam lifted his chin and began to walk away. Over his shoulder, he said to the mirror, "The Ark deserves better than that."

✡ ✚ ✡

After their second drink at the hotel bar, Cam yawned and asked for the check. "Long day today. And another tomorrow."

"I'll be up in a minute," Rivka said. "You two go ahead."

She went straight to the reception desk and booked her own room. She had been thinking about it all evening and decided it would more comfortable for everyone if she just stayed alone. Astarte wouldn't have to imagine a woman in her dad's bed, Cam wouldn't have to be embarrassed in front of his daughter, and Rivka wouldn't have to fight the urge to jump Cameron in the middle of the night while trying to stay quiet enough to keep from waking Astarte.

She went up to say goodnight and grab her things.

"That's silly," Astarte said. "You should stay with us."

"You are sweet to say so. But, truly, I think this is better. Besides, the Mossad is paying."

She dumped her bag on the bed in her new room a floor above Cam's but—recalling the intruder in Cam's room this morning—didn't settle in. Instead, using an army knife she kept in her bag, she unscrewed the hinges of the door of the medicine cabinet in her bathroom. Carrying the mirrored door and a pillow, she descended a flight of stairs. In the hallway a few doors down from Cam's room, she rested the mirrored door on the floor. Standing in the stairwell, peering through the window of the stairwell door, she experimented with the mirror until she had placed it in a location where she could view the reflection of the hallway outside of Cam's door from the stairwell. Then she dropped the pillow onto a stair, sat, and waited. Nobody would notice the mirror resting against the wall—and if they did, they'd assume a workman had left it there.

She settled in, playing games on her phone, and waited. At one point a tipsy, middle-aged couple stumbled by—Rivka smiled, shrugged and explained, "Fight with my boyfriend." Otherwise, things were silent. She was about to give up and head to bed, when at three in the morning the elevator dinged. She watched in the mirror as a young, husky man shuffled toward Cam's room. Standing just outside, he pulled what looked like a television remote control from his jacket pocket. He sent a short text, then received one in reply. Pointing the remote at Cam's door, he clicked. A few seconds passed, then she heard Venus begin to bark. The man smiled. He waited a few minutes, aimed the remote again, clicked, and ambled back to the elevator.

What the?

She had no idea what she had just witnessed. Had the man turned on the television in Cam's room? Some other appliance? But why would Venus react? Rushing down four flights of stairs, she bounded out of the stairwell just as the man pushed through the lobby's revolving door and climbed into an idling black SUV.

Frustrated and bewildered, Rivka took the stairs two at a time back to the fifth floor. But all that did was cause her heart to race along with her mind. She peered through the curtains at the starlit night. A few hours until dawn. She normally loved to watch the sunrise. But normally that was after getting some sleep.

CHAPTER 9

Cam awoke early Sunday morning to drive Astarte back to the airport in Charlotte. Fortunately, the damage to his SUV was just cosmetic. Rivka had texted in the middle of the night, saying she was having trouble sleeping and so would catch up with him for lunch. Just as well. He had another stop to make.

One hand on the steering wheel, he reached out and squeezed Astarte's knee. "Hey. I'm proud of you."

"Thanks, Dad. I just wish I didn't have to be such a … what's the opposite of a Pollyanna?"

"Debbie Downer."

"Yeah. That. People see me coming and they knock on wood or throw salt over their shoulder."

He smiled. "It's not that bad. Though I did see a black cat try to avoid crossing your path last night."

"Not funny." She shifted in her seat. "Did you see this morning's newspaper?" she asked, holding it up. "There's an article already. Front page. And an editorial, the lead one."

He smiled. "I didn't know your generation even knew what a real newspaper looked like."

"I've started fires before."

"I didn't see it yet. Can you read it to me?"

The article was fairly basic. But the editorial struck Cam as odd—it must have been written before the lecture even took place, as if the writer knew what was going to be said. The editorial complained that the tribe was looking out for itself only, preparing shelters in the mountains but not including its non-Indian neighbors in their plans.

"Pretty ironic," Astarte said. "Now people expect the Indians to save their asses."

"I was looking at a map. The problem is that most of the land at high elevation is national forest, so you really can't build on it. Except the Cherokee Reservation land—they can do what they want."

"So what if it's public land. The world is about to come to an end. Are they going to arrest people for trespassing?"

He chuckled. "I see your point. But it's not so easy just to build an underground shelter. You need utilities, roads, supplies, infrastructure. Not to mention the ground is frozen. It can be done, sure. But you're talking serious money and time."

"The Cherokee have already started."

"Good. They should. But they believe the prophecy. Until your talk last night, I don't think most people had any idea what was barreling down the highway at them. It's going to be really hard to get local governments to mobilize in time."

She bit her lip. "So am I wasting my time?"

"Not at all. You got a lot of publicity. Plus, like you said, the Cherokee have already started making preparations. The message is getting out there."

She yawned. "I'm wiped out. What was Venus barking about in the middle of night? She never does that."

Once again, last night, Cam had been awakened by Venus barking at the dark. Getting out of bed, he had seen the faint image of Amanda backlit on the curtain for a second or two before disappearing. And, once again, there was seemingly nothing for Venus to be barking at. The scary thing wasn't so much that Cam was seeing ghosts. The scary thing was that he was getting used to it.

But no way was he going to tell Astarte that her mom had been haunting him. "Venus probably just heard something in another room." He glanced over. "So what's your next stop?"

"They have me flying all over the country. Pretty much every weekend for the next couple of months."

She went through her schedule, and then Cam gave her a few suggestions on streamlining her presentation, and then she asked about Portugal, and then the trip was over and they were at the terminal. He gave her a hug and held on for an extra few seconds. "Love you so much, honey."

She held his eyes. "When you hug me like that, it makes me think you believe the prophecy and you'll never see me again."

He took her hand. "When you get to be a parent, you'll understand. Every time you say goodbye to your kid, you worry it'll be the last."

Back in the Cherokee, he dried his eyes and texted Lenny. It was around seven. *Can I swing by your office at nine?*

The reply came back a few seconds later. *Sure. What's up?*

Cam didn't want to spook him or let him know he suspected anything. *New development on Melungeon research.* He paused, then added. *You're going to like it.*

Just outside of Asheville, Cam ran into a Home Depot and purchased zip ties and duct tape. Using his phone, he then found a hunting supply store which opened early and sold stun guns. From there, he drove to Lenny's gallery.

He had chosen nine as a meeting time on purpose, knowing the gallery didn't open until ten. Lenny met him at the front door, unlocked it to let Cam in, then relocked it and escorted Cam through another locked door to his windowless office in the rear. Lenny had made sure that the gallery was private and secure. Cam would use that to his advantage.

"So," Lenny said, leaning against his desk, "what'd you learn?" His face looked no better than it had a day earlier.

Cam stepped forward, his phone in his left hand, his right hand holding the stun gun in his jacket pocket. "Check this out," he said, turning the phone.

As Lenny leaned in, Cam whipped the stun gun out, shoved it into Lenny's ribcage, and pulled the trigger. A loud sizzle erupted, accompanied by a flash of light. The sizzle was quickly drowned by Lenny's anguished scream. Lenny slumped to the floor, moaning, a metallic smell from the electric charge mixing with the acidic stench of Lenny having urinated on himself. Cam turned away and took a deep breath. *Well, this is fun.*

Holding his breath, he turned back. Within seconds, he had bound Lenny's hands and feet with zip ties and duct-taped his mouth.

"Okay," Cam said, rolling Lenny to a sitting position on the floor against an empty wall and taking his phone. "Now we talk."

Eyes wide, Lenny met Cam's glare. He seemed confused. Betrayed, even. But not angry or defiant, which was what Cam expected. He pushed on. "I know what you're doing, Lenny. I figured out your game."

Keeping his fingers away from Lenny's teeth, Cam yanked off the duct tape.

"What the fuck, Cam?" He worked his jaw. Blood dripped from the cut on his swollen lip. "What are you talking about?"

Cam had thought about different ways to get Lenny to talk, had even considered buying a butane torch at Home Depot. But it was one thing to subdue a man, another entirely to torture him. "This is pretty simple, Lenny. Tell me the truth, or I tell the world where you're hiding. You know I don't have the stomach to beat it out of you, but others won't be so shy. Let's start with last night. Why'd you ram us?"

Lenny, again, seemed more confused than angry. It was throwing Cam off a bit. "Ram you? Cam, seriously, I'm totally clueless."

Cam moved closer, brandishing the stun gun. "Maybe this will refresh your memory. Around ten o'clock."

"My memory doesn't need refreshing. Shelby and I were watching a movie together. Not together, obviously. But at the same time. Call her."

Cam chewed his lip. Lenny was too smart not to have an alibi. But also too smart to use Shelby for it, given that she might raise a stink about lying to an old friend.

Cam tried a different tack. "Look, I get it. The Ark of the Covenant is a big prize."

"The Ark?" He shook his head. "Cam, this is crazy. I don't know anything about the Ark of the Covenant."

"You know it's worth a fortune."

"Well, sure, I guess so. But that doesn't mean I know what you're talking about." He shifted. "Check my phone, the call log. You'll see a call to Shelby that lasted from, like, nine-thirty to almost midnight. Like I said, we were watching a movie together."

Cam had played a lot of poker. And he had read the body language of many a juror. As much as he hated to admit it to himself, his instincts told him that Lenny was telling the truth. But he also knew that Lenny was a professional con man. He scrolled through the phone log. There it was, just as Lenny said. One hundred forty-four minutes, encompassing the time around ten o'clock when the pickup truck rammed them. He recalled Astarte's comment that there was no cell coverage on the county highway last night—if Lenny had been in the pickup, the call would have dropped. Or had Lenny somehow anticipated that contingency as well? Cam tossed the phone aside and began to pace.

What the hell? Had he been wrong about Lenny? If so, who had rammed them? Or was Lenny simply playing him?

In the end, he knew he had only one option. He was in over his head. He reached for his own phone. "Rivka, I need your help on something."

✦ ✝ ✡

Rivka stood over the bald, bearded, beaten and bound art gallery owner, not sure whether she should be flattered that Cam called her or peeved that he hadn't brought her with him to begin with. She opted for the former, subscribing to the old mantra that it was always best to be an optimist because there would be plenty of time to cry later.

"Is that the guy you saw in the pickup?" Cam asked.

She angled her head. "Could be. But night vision monoculars aren't exactly high-definition. And I don't remember all the bruises."

"He says it wasn't him."

She kicked at Lenny's foot. "Of course he does."

"Okay, what's the next step?"

"You leave," she whispered.

"Leave?"

She nodded. "This might get ugly. I don't want you to think of me that way." Hard to feel romantic when you just watched your lady friend put battery cables to a man's scrotum.

Cam blinked, looking visibly distressed. She was glad of it—no man should be comfortable with torture. And if Cam was distressed, she could imagine how Lenny felt. She avoided making eye contact with their bound captive.

"Okay," Cam said. "I get it. But don't, you know, hurt him."

She shook her head. "That's not how this works, Cameron. Not if you want to know the truth." She made sure she said it loud enough for Lenny to hear.

"Guys, this is crazy," Lenny interjected. "I wasn't in any pickup truck, and I sure as hell didn't ram anyone."

Cam ignored him. "Can't you use a truth serum or something?"

Rivka hesitated. "I could, yes. I have some sodium pentothal. But it's not as reliable. Especially if he's a pro."

"He's a professional con man and art thief. Not a professional spy. I don't think he's trained to resist truth serum."

She shrugged. "Okay. We can try it your way first."

From her bag, she removed a syringe and a vial. All Mossad agents were trained in field operations like this. But there was always risk when injecting drugs into human veins. "Listen carefully, Mr. Null. This is what I do. I *will* have the truth. I think you know that. I'd rather not injure you ... or worse ... to get it. But that is entirely up to you."

She injected him in the buttocks, the stench of urine making the task doubly unpleasant. "It'll take six or seven minutes to begin working. Then we'll only have about ten minutes before it starts to wear off," she said to Cam. She didn't want to risk an overdose. "So pick your questions carefully."

Cam nodded and scribbled a list of inquiries.

"It's best if you do yes or no questions," she added.

Lenny's eyes began to dilate and his head to bob. "Okay," Rivka said. "I think he's ready." She leaned closer and whispered, "Start with questions you already know the answer to, just to test him."

Seated in a chair opposite him, Cam did so, working through six or seven items from their shared past, all of which Lenny answered truthfully. Cam leaned forward. "Where were you last night?"

"Lecture," Lenny mumbled. "Cherokee Reservation."

Rivka shot Cam a look. He whispered to her. "To be fair, he had told me he might attend." He addressed Lenny again. "Why were you there?"

His lips moved into a swollen smile. "Chaos. Chaos is best place to find opportunity."

Cam nodded. He turned back to Rivka. "Sounds like Lenny. Why not make a few bucks as the world is coming to an end?" To Lenny, he said, "Were you in the pickup truck that rammed us?"

"No," Lenny mumbled. "I left early."

Cam looked at Rivka. She shrugged. If not him, who?

"Did you kill Nathan Paris?"

"Who?"

"Never mind. Is the painting of Nancy Hanks Lincoln a fake?"

Lenny's head swung back and forth, as if weighing his answer. "Yes. I mean no. I mean both."

Cam asked again, got the same answer. He looked at Rivka for guidance.

"I think he's telling the truth. It's not the kind of lies people tell with these drugs. All it does is invite more questions, so why bother." She pursed her lips. "Is it possible there are two paintings?"

"Oh," Cam replied. "That's it, Rivka. You're right. Lenny made a fake copy and let the original owners steal it back."

"Okay, good," she said. "That means the drugs are working. He's telling the truth." She pointed to her watch. "Move on, running out of time."

Cam turned back to Lenny. "Are you looking for the Ark of the Covenant?"

"Yes."

"I knew it," Cam whispered to Rivka.

"Hold on," she said. Turning to Lenny, she asked, "How *long* have you been looking for the Ark?"

"Since Cam told me about it this morning." He smiled dreamily. "Ark would be worth a fortune."

Cam's eyes widened. Rivka guessed he was wondering if he had been wrong about Lenny. He pressed on. "Where do you think the Ark is?"

"I don't know."

"No guesses or ideas?"

"Book I read said Ethiopia."

"Not here in America?"

Lenny smiled again. "Maybe in basement of Smithsonian Museum, like in movie."

✦ ✝ ✡

On one knee, Cam cut Lenny's ties and stammered an apology. They weren't really friends, so there was no relationship to repair. Other than their working one. "I'm really sorry. I thought you were playing me."

Lenny merely stared up at him, still not fully recovered from the sodium pentothal. But Cam had begun to notice that his stare was starting to turn into a glare.

Cam stood and rubbed his face, half-expecting to find egg on his hands after doing so. He owed Lenny more than an apology. Turns out the worst thing Lenny was guilty of was, well, pissing on himself. And even that was Cam's fault. Lenny had not lied to Cam, had not forged the painting, had not killed Paris, had not rammed them with a pickup truck, had not schemed to find the Ark of the Covenant.

Using a chair, Lenny pulled himself up. "I have a change of clothes in the bathroom," he muttered, shuffling away.

Rivka had gone back to the hotel, leaving Cam to clean up his own mess. So what next? Was it time to head back to Massachusetts? A weekend trip had turned into a week. At some point, he needed to get back to his law practice. Especially because Lenny might not be so willing to pay Cam's fee in light of this morning's little adventure with a stun gun and truth serum. Not that Cam blamed him.

Would Rivka follow him north? And did he want her to? He wasn't ready to make that decision yet, just as he wasn't quite ready to leave North Carolina. Answers, if any, were here. Not to mention, possibly, the Ark.

✧ ✝ ✡

Lenny looked at his bruised and swollen face in the graying mirror of his closet-sized office bathroom. "Well, that was no fun," he said grimly. But fun was not how he kept score. And, in light of the fact that, an hour ago, he was faced with the threat of Cam outing him to the world and a Mossad agent pulling out his fingernails, he felt pretty fortunate.

He filled the sink with hot water, removed his urine-soaked pants and briefs, dropped them in, and added some liquid soap. He'd deal with them later. They were a small price to pay for the chance to see his opponent's cards.

The Mossad, huh? Lenny hadn't seen that coming. But there was no doubt that the tall, striking woman was an operative—civilians didn't carry sodium pentothal around with them. More to the point, civilians didn't size people up with the same cold, appraising stare she had fixed on him. Cam had even used her name, Rivka, a Hebrew name. If she was not Mossad, she should be.

The Mossad being here opened the door to the Ark of the Covenant actually being in play. He blinked. Had the world's greatest historical treasure been in his backyard all this time and he been oblivious to it? He shook his head. What an irony that would be.

He wiped himself down with a wet towel and stepped into clean clothes. He still felt a little loopy, but it seemed to be passing. Not that he was in a rush. No doubt Thorne was in the next room, beating himself up, filled with remorse and guilt, trying to figure out a way to make it up to Lenny. Lenny popped a Life Saver in his mouth, sat on the toilet, and checked his phone for messages and the latest news. As Napoleon famously said, never interrupt your enemy when he is busy defeating himself.

✧ ✝ ✡

Shaking his head, Cam strolled back to his SUV parked outside Lenny's gallery. Cam had racked his brain for a way to make things right with Lenny, only to have Lenny simply shrug it off. "No big deal. You didn't trust me. Given my past, that's understandable. So you did what you had to do. Nothing personal, I get it."

Maybe Cam would get paid after all. Or maybe Lenny was simply biding his time, knowing that revenge was a dish best served cold. That was the thing with Lenny—there was always a play behind the play. Maybe this, maybe that. Cam sighed. Maybe, in fact, he should head back to Massachusetts.

But he knew he wouldn't. The game was afoot, and the playing field was here, in and around Asheville. As were the answers to who killed Nathan Paris. If it wasn't Lenny, then who? Paris had been studying the Freemasons, stalking them even, hell-bent on revenge. Had the Masons made a preemptive strike, especially in light of Paris sharing his research with Cam? Did that mean Cam was a target also?

He started the Cherokee and headed back toward the hotel. He didn't subscribe to the all the conspiracy theories when it came to the Freemasons—some people believed the group was trying to take over the Western democracies and impose a new world order. On the other hand, Cam didn't doubt that some Masons were capable of doing evil. In that sense, Masonic lodges were similar to any other group in America. Some of its members were heroic and some villainous, with the vast majority somewhere in the middle.

Perhaps one of the villainous ones murdered Paris.

✦ ✚ ✡

Cam stepped back into his hotel suite just before lunchtime. Rivka met him there, her bags already unpacked. She bounded over and kissed him on the mouth. "Hope you don't mind, I invited myself back. I checked out of my room."

He smiled. "Of course not. Couch is free."

She didn't miss a beat. "Um, negative. You owe me for this morning. And I *will* collect."

"Now?" he asked, raising an eyebrow.

"Normally I'd say yes. But we need to talk."

He removed his jacket and dropped onto the couch. "Uh oh."

She took a seat at the kitchen table. "The reason I slept in this morning is because I was up late." She explained the man outside of Cam's room with what looked like a channel clicker. "I don't know what he was doing. But he was doing *something*."

"What time was that?"

"About three."

"That was the same time Venus woke up and started barking." He left out the Amanda ghost part. He wasn't sure at what point in a relationship one was supposed to admit to seeing spirits. But he did know the conversation was complicated by the fact that the ghost in question was his ex-wife.

"Maybe she heard him."

Cam angled his head. "Maybe. But she was looking the other way, not toward the hallway."

"Sorry I couldn't catch him."

"What would you have done with him if you had?"

"Kicked his ass."

He nodded, believing her. "Could it be the same people who rammed us?"

"Good guess. And for some reason, they disguised one of their people to look like Lenny." She shifted. "Or maybe it was just dark and they happen to look alike."

He explained his suspicions about Nathan Paris' death. "If Lenny didn't do it, I'm thinking the Freemasons."

"Okay."

"We haven't looked at them. I'm wondering if there's a connection between them and the Melungeons."

"Makes sense. The Melungeons seem to be at the center of this web, the hub of the wheel. Everything connects back to them."

He stood and grabbed his coat. "All right, then. Maybe it's time to dig deeper into the local Freemasons."

As he turned, she sprung from her chair and shoved him back down onto the couch. "The Masons have been around for hundreds of years. They'll still be there in an hour, I promise."

☩ ✚ ✡

Cam and Rivka strolled out of the hotel into the bright sunshine, her arm
in his, both of them leaning into a brisk wind. Three hours, not just one,
had passed. The sex ate up an hour, and then Cam and Rivka needed to
eat, and then sex came back for seconds. Now, finally, they began their
stroll toward the Masonic temple where Cam had first met Nathan Paris.

"What are you hoping to find?" she asked.

He had called ahead to arrange a tour. "Not sure. One thing I want to
look into is the connection between Masons and Melungeons. I've been
playing connect-the-dots a lot—making assumptions, drawing infer-
ences. One of them is connecting Nathan Paris' research with ours. He
thinks the Freemasons descend from the old Jewish priestly families and
therefore might have custody of the old Temple treasures, including the
Ark. And we think the Melungeons might descend from Jewish families
who made their way to Portugal during medieval times and then crossed
the Atlantic with the Templars—again, maybe with the Ark. Well, we
can't both be right, unless—"

Rivka interjected. "Unless the old priestly families *are* the
Melungeons."

He smiled. He guessed that many people overlooked Rivka's intellect
in light of her imposing physical stature and her attractiveness. They did
so at their peril. "Right. If so, we should find a strong connection around
here between the Freemasons and the Melungeon families."

"How? You going to look through the membership list for Melungeon names?" She pursed her lips. "Not sure they'll let you do that."

"Not *let* me, no. But one thing about Masonic lodges. They love their
history. They always display old pictures of the brothers on the walls,
with all their names listed."

"Okay, it's a plan. You distract them, I'll take pictures of the
pictures."

"Um, I think you have a better chance of distracting them than I do."

Smiling, she unbuttoned the top button on her blouse. "There you go
again, using me for my body."

"You didn't complain back at the hotel."

"Back at the hotel, you weren't pimping me out."

But, like a pro, she said it with a shrug and a smile.

Not that it mattered. When they arrived at the temple and rang the bell, they were met with a scowling, hulking middle-aged man dressed in a tuxedo. He stepped onto the landing and closed the door behind him. "I apologize, Mr. Thorne, but it turns out we will not be able to offer you a tour of the temple."

Cam studied the man. What had changed? "But I just arranged it."

The Mason eyed Rivka and swallowed, but held firm. "Again, I apologize."

"Can we just come into the foyer?"

The man shook his head, arms crossed in front of his chest. Clearly a decision had been made. Cam guessed someone had figured out, probably through connections with the police, that Cam had been friendly with Nathan Paris. Which meant they probably didn't want Cam sniffing around. Which meant they might have something to hide. Which meant they might be responsible for Paris' death. Which meant he might have been on the right track.

Of course, it might also be that they simply didn't like Paris because of the threats he had made against them and were punishing Cam by association.

Cam and Rivka descended the temple's stone steps, Rivka examining something on her phone. The Freemason eyed them, then punched at the alarm pad and reentered the lodge building. "Now what?" Rivka asked, putting her phone away.

They walked in silence for a few seconds. "I have an idea," Cam said. "Professor Campbell-Klein gave me a list of cities and towns that historically have had large Melungeon populations. Should be easy enough to cross-reference them against locations of older Masonic lodges."

They found a coffee shop and began working on their phones. Cam gave Rivka the list of cities and towns. "Find out if there is a Masonic lodge in town, then track down when it was founded. I'm going to do some Google searches."

Fifteen minutes later, sipping hot chocolate, he found something. "So

I did a search for Melungeons and Freemasonry. Check out what this book says." He read the passage from his phone. "Virtually every town where the Melungeons settled also simultaneously had established a Freemason lodge."

She nodded. "I'm finding the same thing. I found a list of the oldest Masonic lodges in the Southern states, then cross-referenced it against the cities and towns the professor gave us. It's almost a perfect match."

"And it reminds me of something odd I read about the history of Newport, Rhode Island. The oldest synagogue in the country is there, Touro Synagogue. It was founded by a group of fifteen Jewish families who had worked their way to America from Portugal, via Holland. One of the first things they did when they settled here in 1658 was perform Masonic rituals." Cam found the Masonic history article on the internet. "Here's the exact quote:"

In the spring of 1658 Mordecai Campannell, Moses Pockeckoe, Levi, and others, in all fifteen families, arrived at Newport from Holland. They brought with them the three first degrees of Masonry, and worked them in the house of Campannell; and continued to do so, they and their successors, to the year 1742.

"The odd thing about that," Cam added, "is that Freemasonry wasn't officially founded until 1717."

"Someone should have told the guys up in Newport."

"This goes back to what Paris said, about them practicing in secret all the way back to Roman times. And did you notice the name 'Levi'? I think these guys were part of the priestly families. Paris was right."

She nodded. "Good catch."

"The Newport guys weren't Melungeon. Or maybe they were, I guess. But the point is, they came from the same area. Sephardic Jews from Portugal. With a long history and tradition of Masonic rituals."

Cam felt the familiar tingling on his skin. He sat back in his chair. "This can't be a coincidence. There's really no reason for the Melungeons to form Masonic lodges other than if it's part of their family history, their heritage. Like up in Newport. I mean, most Masonic lodges in the U.S. were founded by establishment types, community leaders, old money. Like the Founding Fathers. The Melungeon were poor, isolated, mostly uneducated. They'd be the last group you'd think would form lodges."

"But they did. I agree, there must be a reason."

⚜ ✚ ✡

Lenny hung the 'Closed' sign on his gallery door, locked the deadbolt, set the alarm, and strolled in the midday sun to his car parked in the lot across the street. Normally he stayed open until 5:00 on Sundays. But normally he wasn't zapped by a stun gun and shot up with truth serum.

It was too cold to open the top of his BMW Series 8 convertible, but he did so anyway. He'd crank the heat and pull up his jacket collar and shiver if necessary. He needed to clear his head.

Speeding out of town, he climbed, the elevation dropping the temperature even further. The cold slapped at him, cut through him. But also gave him clarity—there was a reason they called it *cold* reality.

First, it was no longer safe to stay here. Thorne was no longer an ally. Perhaps not an enemy, at least not yet. But no longer could Lenny trust him not to reveal Lenny's true identity.

Which meant that Lenny would need to accelerate his plans. He had hoped to have another few weeks. But hope was not a plan. One hand holding his phone, he dictated a quick text to his realtor. *I'm ready to hit the market now. Asking price $5.25 million. Must close quickly.* He was into his mountain complex for less than half that. But that was before the Blue Star prophecy. And before the editorial he somehow arranged to get published in this morning's newspaper. Already comments were coming in, complaining about the Native Americans keeping the mountain retreats for themselves at the expense of the non-Indians. Lenny was acutely aware that there was no better way to fuel demand than to make people believe there was a shortage of supply. It had only been one day, but, suddenly, as a result of Astarte's lecture, mountain land with an underground bunker was starting to become a necessity rather than a luxury.

Finally, he would need to think more about this Ark of the Covenant development. He was not used to surprises of this magnitude—up until now, everything had pretty much gone according to plan. The problem with an artifact like that was, like a Rembrandt or a da Vinci, it was too well-known to fence easily. No reputable dealer or buyer would touch it. And whoever ended up buying it would not be able to display it. No doubt there would be some Arab oil money interested in it, if for no other reason than to lord it over Israel. But even they would face political pressure to return it for display in Jerusalem or Rome. And, most importantly of all, Israel would no doubt exact revenge on anyone involved with absconding with the Ark. He had spent an hour with the Mossad this morning. That was enough.

Downshifting, he accelerated through a tight turn, feeling the thrill of the roadster responding to his commands even as his eyes watered and his fingers turned numb. Who was he kidding? He fed off the adrenaline, craved it.

If it turned out the Ark really was in play, he'd be a player.

✠ ✡

When they got back to the hotel, Rivka made an excuse about needing something from the gift shop. "I'll be up in a few minutes," she said.

Finding a quiet corner of the lobby, she phoned Menachem, not caring that it was ten o'clock at night in Israel.

"Talk to me."

"We got stopped at the door of the Masonic temple. They sense something."

"I was afraid of that."

"But I got the alarm code, recorded the guy punching in the alarm code as I walked away."

"Don't forget who taught you that trick."

She chuckled. "How can I? You won't let me."

"We can't wait any longer on this, Rivka. The Tables of Testimony inscription is even more important than the Ark, as I said. And I'm afraid the Masons may be on the verge of moving it." His voice hardened. "You're going to have to go in."

"Okay. But they have cameras."

"Wear a disguise." He paused. "Has Thorne mentioned the Tables of Testimony?"

"Just once, in passing. My sense is he doesn't really know much about it." Which made him only slightly less ignorant than the rest of the world.

"I think we have to assume eventually he'll figure it out. He's too sharp, too knowledgeable, too curious."

"Agreed."

"If he gets in the way, you'll have no choice." Menachem paused. "Can you do it?"

She knew she had to answer yes. Otherwise, he'd pull her from the mission and assign someone who would not hesitate to put a bullet in Cam's head. "Of course."

"I'm not sure I believe you."

"Look, Menachem. I'm okay with you criticizing me when I screw up. But I haven't done anything wrong yet and you are already condemning me for it."

"That's my job. Understanding my agents' limitations and weaknesses. Being proactive *before* you screw up."

"I've earned the benefit of the doubt, I think."

She heard his tongue clicking against his teeth, as he often did when thinking. "Okay. We'll leave things as is for now. But you need to get into that lodge. Soon. And Thorne can't find out."

"Understood. What if the tablet is not there?"

"It's there. It's been there since the building was built a hundred years ago. Hell, that's what they built the building *for*. Get in, find the Tables of Testimony, get out. Then straight to the airport. Got it?"

He made it sound simple. "Yes, boss." She guessed it would be anything but.

☩ ✡

Waiting for Rivka to return to their hotel suite, Cam opened his laptop and began to make some lists. He had developed the habit back in law school as a way to help organize his thoughts. It was one thing to know something. But seeing it laid out on paper or a computer screen somehow allowed him to internalize it in a different way, like viewing directions on a map.

These lists were meant to help him determine his next step. He had come to Asheville to examine a painting. That seemingly simple task had quickly mushroomed into a mystery involving the Freemasons, the Melungeons and the Ark of the Covenant. But Cam had hit a dead end. He didn't have a next move, a way to solve the mystery. In fact, even calling it a mystery implied some kind of secret at the heart of everything which may not even exist. It was entirely possible, he had to admit, that Lincoln and the Melungeons and the Cherokee and the Freemasons had nothing to do with the Ark of the Covenant. Sure, there may be an interesting hidden history here, involving remnants of the Jewish priestly families crossing the Atlantic in medieval times with members of the outlawed Knights Templar and taking refuge in Appalachia—perhaps even with some of the Temple treasures in tow. But that was a long way from the Ark of the Covenant being stuck in some cave or crypt somewhere close by.

He shared his thoughts with Rivka when she entered. "I think I'm done here. Short of actually finding the Ark of the Covenant—which I seriously doubt will happen—there's not much left of this mystery. I think Paris is probably right—Freemasonry is a continuation of the old Jewish priestly families and their secrets. And I think that's why there's so many connections between the Melungeons and the Jews and the Masons." He shrugged. "But, like Paris said, I'm not sure many people really care."

She gave him a funny look, almost as if she was disappointed. "Wait, you're leaving?" Was she worried that this treasure hunt was all that was keeping them together, and that once it ended they would end also?

He took her hand, the words spilling from his mouth even before he was aware he had made the decision. "Why don't you come back to Boston with me for a few days?"

✡ ✝ ✡

Rivka stood there, mouth agape, Cam waiting for a reply to his invitation to join him in Boston. "Sure," she felt like saying, "that'd be great. I just need to go AWOL from the Mossad. What's the weather like this time of year?"

Instead, she made a split-second decision, squeezed his hand and smiled. "That's sweet. But I have a feeling you're going to want to stay down here for a couple more days. I just got an email from Tel Aviv. More information."

"Which you're going to share with me?"

She feigned surprise. "Don't I always?"

"Um, no."

"How about this." She leaned forward and kissed him softly. "I'll share if you promise not to leave."

He laughed. "Sounds like sexual blackmail."

"That's the best kind."

"And the Mossad's okay with this?"

She turned serious. "No. In fact, I could get into big trouble. But I trust you." She pulled up a chair next to him at the table. "Besides, compared to the Golden Menorah secret, which I'm pretty sure you've kept, this is nothing."

Nothing, that was, except possibly a big mistake. What was she doing, convincing him to stay? It would be easier, and better, if he drove back to Boston and out of harm's way. Menachem had made it clear what she must do if he interfered with her theft of the Tables of Testimony. But she had grown to rely on his input, his ability to decipher and analyze new pieces of information. And, more to the point, she had grown reliant on his company. Simply put, she didn't want him to leave. It was a selfish decision. She hoped it would not turn out also to be a foolhardy one.

Sighing, she turned her laptop toward him and began to click through the information Tel Aviv had sent her. She'd share the info with Cam, get his input, then figure out a way to keep him from interfering with the theft. "Here's the thing," she said. "There's more to the Abraham Lincoln story."

"More? You mean, him being Black is not enough?"

She leaned closer. "Apparently, he was also Jewish. Just like the other Melungeons we've been studying."

Cam's eyes widened. "No way."

"That's the real reason I'm here, on this case. That stuff Menachem told me about Israel caring about racism in America was all bullshit. What we care about is that your most famous president, or second-most famous president, was Jewish." She clicked on an image.

Text from February 19, 1863 Edition of *Ha-Magid* Newspaper

"What's that?" Cam asked.

"A newspaper from 1863 in Prussia called *Ha-Magid*. It specialized in news of Jews around the world. I assume you'd like me to translate it for you?"

"Please. My Hebrew pretty much begins and ends with *shalom*."

She did so:

The ruler Abraham Lincoln, head of government of the Lands of the North in America, during a recent visit of the learned rabbis, Messrs. Wise and Lilienthal from Cincinnati, and attorney Martin Bijur from Louisville, who had come to vent their spleen upon General Grant and ask him to reverse the evil decree issued by the general upon all the Jews in the territory of Tennessee, told them in the course of conversation, after promising to reverse the decree, that he (the president) sprang from the belly of Judah, and his forefathers were

Jews; and these emissaries indeed report that the facial features of the
president are evidence of his descent from the loins of the Hebrews.

"Hold on," Cam said, leaning forward. "Lincoln said his forefathers were Jews?"

"Yup. He 'sprang from the belly of Judah.'" She smiled. "Literally, the translation is 'bowels of Judah,' not 'belly,' but you get the picture." She sat back. "Out Lincoln came."

"Wow," Cam said, shaking his head. "I get why the Mossad is interested. That would be big news if Lincoln really was Jewish."

"Honestly, I'm not sure how it would play. It's similar to him being Black. People will spin it as they see fit."

"But, in the end, it's important. It's a good cudgel to hit the racists and anti-Semites over the head with."

"I agree. That's always a good thing."

"So, what else?"

"Rabbi Wise, who was quoted in the article above, said the following: 'Abraham Lincoln believed himself to be bone from our bone and flesh from our flesh. He supposed himself to be a descendant of Hebrew parentage. He said so in my presence. And, indeed, he preserved numerous features of the Hebrew race, both in countenance and character.'"

"So, he looks Jewish."

She spun her laptop. "What do you think?" She showed an image of Lincoln taken from an angle and without his trademark beard.

Abraham Lincoln

"Could be," Cam agreed.

"There's more." She counted the points off on her fingers. "The Abraham name itself is Jewish. His great-grandfather, along with his paternal cousin and uncle, were all named Mordecai. He was the only president not to belong to a church, which was a big deal back in his day. The town in England where his family came from, Lincoln, had a large Jewish population. And his ancestors were metallurgists, a common Jewish profession."

Cam nodded. "That's good evidence. Especially not belonging to a church. And the Mordecai name—Abraham could be Christian, but Mordecai is almost always Jewish."

She glanced at her computer. "It says here that when Lincoln died, Jewish communities all across the country sat *shiva* and mourned him. They knew." She smiled. "My grandmother is like that. She always knows another Jew just from meeting them. She says she has a special Jewish radar."

Cam sat back and looked up at the ceiling for a few seconds. "It makes sense. If Lincoln's mom was Melungeon, that means she was part Jewish herself. And so she married another Melungeon who was also part Jewish. The professor told us that—these families kept marrying into each other, generation after generation. The family trees look more like vines, winding back around themselves."

"This is all a bit silly, actually," she said. "I mean, if you go back far enough, we're all related. This shouldn't matter so much."

"I agree. But, unfortunately, it still does. Maybe proving the great Abraham Lincoln was part Black and part Jewish will help make people realize that race doesn't really matter."

"So you'll stay and help me? In exchange for sexual favors?"

He nodded, his face serious, and spoke slowly. "But to be clear: I'm not doing it for myself, I'm doing it for my country."

✡ ✝ ✡

Cam fell into an easy rhythm, the mid-afternoon sun on his cheek as he jogged downtown on the streets surrounding the art gallery in the old Woolworth department store building. He was perfectly comfortable in shorts and a hooded sweatshirt in the forty-degree temperature, while the locals trudged by him in heavy parkas, hats and mittens. As in most things in life, perspective was everything.

Which was why he had agreed to stay in Asheville with Rivka. This Lincoln thing was important to her, to Israel. Cam didn't really get why, but that was probably because he wasn't Israeli. Or perhaps it was because there was more at play here than they were telling him. It wouldn't be the first time that Rivka and the Mossad had told him a half-truth.

To be frank, it was also important to America. As he and Rikva had discussed, America had a lot of racial issues to deal with. Having a national hero who was multi-ethnic would provide a role model for millions of non-European Americans. But there would be pushback, no doubt, especially if the evidence was flimsy. Which was the other reason Cam agreed to stay. He was a historian. In addition to being curious about the truth surrounding the sixteenth president, he also wanted to make sure the research behind any bombshell revelations was solid.

◈ ✚ ✡

Taking advantage of Cameron being out on a run, Rivka paced the aisles of a Walmart, grabbing items she needed for tonight's break-in. This was her last errand of the morning, having already rented a car and done some advanced scouting. It felt odd to be doing things behind Cameron's back, almost as if she was cheating on him. In a way, she was. With a sigh, she tossed a black ski mask into her carriage next to some spray paint, bungee cords, a tarp, and a bright yellow skateboard.

She refocused on her task. Menachem had told her to wear a disguise, but the truth was it really didn't matter. She'd be on a private jet back to Israel before anyone would have a chance to look at security footage. And, even if she screwed up and they identified her while she was still in the states, the Israeli Embassy would step in and smooth things over. She smiled wryly. The truth was, if she did screw up, she'd rather take her chances in the American penal system than face Menachem's wrath.

She glanced at the skateboard. Would she even need it? How heavy was this tablet? Maybe she could just slip it into her duffel bag. On the other hand, rock weighed 150 pounds per cubic foot, so anything larger than, say, a toaster oven and she'd need to wheel it out. Again, more information from Menachem would have been nice. But, to be fair, it was entirely possible nobody had a clue how large the tablet actually was. It was apparent that they knew little about it. Not even what was inscribed on it—if they knew what it said, they wouldn't be so desperate to acquire it and she could spend the night curled up against Cameron's back rather than skulking around behind it.

She made her way toward the register. Was it possible these Cosmic Equations really did impart ancient, lost knowledge? She let her mind wander and wonder. She thought about the legends of the ancient world, things most modern people dismissed as myths and exaggerations. Did flying carpets really exist? Was that how—through levitation—the great Pyramids had been built? Had a Philosopher's Stone, allowing base metals to be converted to gold, really been discovered? If so, did that explain the mountains of gold allegedly 'mined' during King Solomon's time? And what about the mysterious manna used by Moses to feed his otherwise-starving people in the desert? Could such a substance have been produced through some archaic scientific formula? No doubt there were other examples she had not thought of. The point was, any of these three—the abilities to levitate, to convert metal to gold, and to create food from desert sand—would be incalculably valuable in the modern world.

She glanced at the yellow skateboard and pictured herself rolling a stone tablet which could change the world through the dark streets of Asheville, perhaps being pursued by aproned, sleepy-eyed, middle-aged Freemasons alerted to the theft. She shook her head and smiled. Life for her had become many things. Boring was not one of them.

☆ ✝ ✡

Gertrude Little stood behind the Mossad agent in the checkout line at Walmart. She resisted the urge to ram her carriage into the back of the legs of the Amazon-like operative. Tall and fit and smart and beautiful—

how unfair was that? And with an exciting job to boot? Not to mention arrogant enough to add a blue streak to her hair, as if the rules of proper society didn't apply to her.

Of course, the too-cool-for-school agent would ignore the obese, plain-looking woman behind her in line. That was the thing about being fat: People pretty much always underestimated you, assuming that being overweight was a product of being lazy and having no willpower. Gertrude glanced at the junk food piled into her own carriage. Well, they got the willpower part right.

Her eyes narrowed. But not the lazy.

Holding her phone as if chatting into it, Gertrude snapped pictures of the items in the Mossad agent's carriage. A ski mask? Really? After their visit to the Masonic temple earlier today, it was obvious she was planning a break-in. Which would make sense if the Table of Shewbread really was being kept there, as Paris suspected. But good luck on the getaway—even a modest-sized table made from hard acacia wood and overlaid with gold would weigh at least a couple of hundred pounds. They would need to break in, find the table, drag it out, and dump it into some getaway vehicle before the alarms sounded. Better them than her.

Glancing again at the carriage, Gertrude smiled and nodded. *The skateboard.* That was it, of course—they planned to wheel the table out. She shrugged. The details didn't matter.

Gertrude had learned an important lesson as a young girl playing tag. Too slow-footed to catch any of the other children, she had learned instead to anticipate their moves, to hide in waiting and then pounce as they approached.

It was a strategy that worked with adults as well.

✦ ✝ ✡

Cam and Rivka sat at a corner table in a stone-floored tapas restaurant tucked into a brick warehouse building in the old downtown area of Asheville. He raised a glass of wine. "Cheers. Tapas is as close as I could come to the meal we didn't get in Lisbon."

She closed her eyes. "That meal is gone forever, I'm afraid. Such a tragedy."

Chuckling, he reflected on his first few meetings with her. He had noticed her exotic beauty and toned figure, of course. And her intelligence and loyalty to her country. Her toughness, both mental and physical. But, as she became more comfortable with him, he came to appreciate her dry, sardonic sense of humor. He wondered what other surprises were in store.

In fact, her question was a bit of a surprise. "What do you think about the Tables of Testimony tablet?"

"What do I *think* about it?"

"Yes. You know, what is it? Where did it disappear to?"

"Honestly, I haven't give it much thought lately. I've been sort of busy, in case you hadn't noticed."

"You really need to work on your multitasking, Cameron," she said with a smile as she sipped her wine. "I've been wondering about it. You mentioned it the first night I was here as one of the items in the Ark that had been lost. And you've made it clear that you don't really think the Ark is in play. So, I thought, could it be the Tables of Testimony that made its way across the Atlantic?"

He leaned forward. "You know, that makes some sense. Like you said, I have trouble believing the actual Ark of the Covenant is here. I think, if anything, it's a replica. But why make a copy of the Ark?"

She didn't miss a beat. "To put something sacred in."

The waitress came by to tell them their meals would be out shortly. Cam ordered another glass of wine, while Rivka stuck to seltzer water. "I've been drinking too much," she explained. "A girl needs to keep her wits about her if she's going to help recover a sacred artifact."

He let her lead the conversation. "So," she continued, "what do you think the Tables of Testimony is? What's carved on it?"

"All I know is that it supposedly contained the Cosmic Equations— the divine laws of number, measure and weight."

"And what does that sound like to you?" she asked, her head angled.

He smiled. Obviously, she had given the artifact some thought. "I see where you're going with this. You're right, it sounds like Freemasonry.

Bernard de Clairvoux, who wrote the rules for the Templars, defined God as 'length, width, height and depth.' In other words, geometry." He sat back. "Some people think that the 'G' symbol used in Freemasonry stands for 'Geometry,' not 'God,' which would explain their compass and square symbolism also."

"Good. Freemasonry. That was my reaction, too." She took a deep breath and leaned closer. "So, what if the big secret at the center of Freemasonry was that they had the Tables of Testimony, the Cosmic Equations?"

Cam felt himself nodding even before she had finished. "That ties in with what Paris thought, also. The priestly families would have taken the Tables of Testimony with them from Jerusalem when they fled, then built secret societies like the Templars and Freemasons to keep the Cosmic Equations a secret." He paused. "And one more thing. Under Masonic tradition, the Tables of Testimony survived the Great Flood inside a pair of massive pillars called the Pillars of Enoch. Well, every Masonic lodge I've ever been in features two ceiling-high pillars. And Enoch is a big part of Masonic teachings. In fact, the Masons credit Josephus with teaching them about the Pillars of Enoch. Remember, Josephus was the guy Paris believed led the priestly families out of Jerusalem and founded Freemasonry." He smiled. "The pieces all fit together. It would make perfect sense if the Tables of Testimony ended up with the Masons."

"So why keep it all secret?"

"Survival," Cam replied. "The Church felt threatened by any science they couldn't spin to support their own narrative. They wanted people to rely on faith and prayer. Science challenged their supremacy. Which meant any person, or group, who championed science was a threat. Just ask Galileo."

Before Rivka could respond, their meals came. Each took a couple bites while the food was warm, but then Rivka waved her fork in the air.

"Getting back to what's in these equations, here's where I'm not sure I'm on the right track. I think it might go beyond just geometry. I mean, knowledge of geometry would explain those amazing Gothic cathedrals like Notre Dame and Chartres that the Templars built, seemingly out of the blue. But if you're going to call something the Cosmic Equations, they should relate to, well, the cosmos. Not just building amazing cathedrals."

"Continue. This is good stuff." He was correct earlier when he wondered what other surprises Rivka might have in store for him.

"I started thinking about flying carpets, and how they built the Pyramids, and where all of King Solomon's gold came from, and what really was the manna the Israelites ate in the desert. Not to mention all the incredible technology from Atlantis." She continued to wave her fork. "What if these things weren't just legends? What if we used to be able to levitate and make gold from base metals and make food from sand, but then the knowledge was lost?"

His skin tingled. "You think the Cosmic Equations reveal all that?"

She sat back and let out a long breath. "I don't know, Cameron. I'm in over my head with all this. You're supposed to be the expert. It just seems to me, like you said, all the pieces fit together."

He held her eyes. "You know, I read once that the word 'levitation' derived from 'Levite,' the priestly families. That would be telling." He shook his head. "So let's say you're right. Where is it?"

She blinked twice, which he had noticed she rarely did, then quickly sipped her seltzer. "Like I said, that's your department." She smiled. "I just save your ass while you're out looking."

He smiled back, sensing she was hiding something. But, then again, she was a spy. She was probably always hiding something. "Well, as you said earlier, maybe it made its way to America. Maybe that's what the Freemasons and Templars and priestly families have been hiding and protecting for thousands of years." He paused, not wanting to be overdramatic but sensing they were on the verge of uncovering something truly monumental. "Maybe the Cosmic Equations really are the secret at the center of Freemasonry."

❖ ✠ ✡

Rivka held Cam's arm—which, he had to admit, he was getting used to —as they sauntered home in the brisk night air from the tapas restaurant.

Rivka hummed a Beatles tune as they walked. They had reached the stage where silence was not uncomfortable.

Ever since taking a class in college, Cam had been interested in the intersection between mathematics and nature. He sensed that this interest was itself about to intersect with his Templar research. "Have you ever heard of the Golden Ratio," he asked.

"Do you mean two parts alcohol, one part mixer?"

"No," he said, chuckling.

"Right, sorry," she replied. "That's the Cosmic Equation."

He laughed again and stopped walking. "What I mean is this. In nature, many things exist in a ratio of 1.618 to 1." Using his forefinger and thumb, he measured the width of Rivka's eye. "If this is a measure of one..." He then did the same to her mouth. "This would measure 1.618. And the same is true with other parts of your face." He put his hand horizontal, beneath her nose. "If the part of your face below your nostrils is 1, the part above is 1.618."

"Is that true for everyone?" she asked.

"Attractive people, yes. For some reason, we are wired to find that ratio—the Golden Ratio—pleasing to our eye. When the ratio is out of whack, we see that as unattractive."

"How very shallow of us."

"Says the person with the perfect facial ratios."

She smiled and kissed him lightly. "That was sweet of you to say."

Walking again, he continued. "It continues through the entire body. If you divide the human body at the bellybutton, the bottom half to top half ratio is, again, 1.618 to 1."

"Except for people who have unattractive bodies."

"Exactly."

She leaned into him. "You can show me back in the room."

He smiled. "You might not want me once you see my math nerd side."

"Try me."

"Okay. It's not just the human body. This Golden Ratio exists all through nature. An egg, for example—the length is 1.618, the width is 1. Flowers, plants, even the spiral of a tornado."

Her brow furrowed. "I don't get the tornado thing. A tornado is just a swirl."

"Okay, here's the math nerd stuff. It's based on something called the Fibonacci Sequence."

"I've heard of it."

"Basically, it's a line of numbers. You add the previous two numbers together to get the next one." He quickly found an example on his phone. "Like this."

0 1 1 2 3 5 8 13 21 34 55 89 144 233

Fibonacci Sequence

Cam continued. "Okay, so here's the interesting thing. Take the last two numbers, 233 and 144." He grinned. "Guess what their ratio is?"

"The Golden Ratio?"

"Exactly. 1.618 to 1. You can go to infinity with this, and the ratio holds. This was what I was saying about the intersection between mathematics and nature."

"You say nature." She paused. "Some people would say God."

He nodded. "Yes, they would."

They reached the hotel. Cam borrowed a pen and some scrap paper at the front desk. They sat on a couch in the lobby. "Okay, so here's the tornado connection." He pulled up an image on his phone. "Basic tornado."

Tornado Spiral

"Got it," she replied.

He began to draw. "If we take the Fibonacci Sequence and draw squares using the numbers as the length of sides, and then we draw arcing lines connecting the squares together, corner to corner, we get a spiral shape." He showed her how the first rectangle was 1x2, the next 2x3, the next 3x5, the next 5x8, etc. He then drew the arcing lines. "Here. This is what we get."

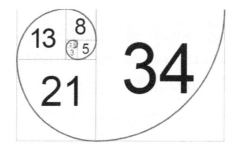

Fibonacci Spiral

"It looks like a snail." Her eyes widened. "And, yes, the wind patterns from a tornado."

He sat back. "You mentioned God earlier." He pulled an image up on his phone. "You ever seen this staircase?"

Golden Ratio Staircase, The Vatican

"No," she answered. "But it's pretty obvious what it is."

He smiled. "It's inside the Vatican, believe it or not. Like you said, the intersection of mathematics and God."

"And you think this is all part of the Cosmic Equations, all part of the Tables of Testimony?"

"I do. There may be more to it than just the Golden Ratio and Fibonacci Sequence, but this has to be part of it."

"Then why has it been kept hidden?"

"Despite this staircase, the Church has always been skeptical about science and mathematics. They live in a world of faith, not reason. If the world can be explained by equations, there's no need for God."

"And you think that's why the Tables of Testimony have been kept secret."

"During medieval times, especially, it would have been a death sentence to talk about stuff like this. So the Templars and Freemasons would have kept their mouths shut. As for now..." He shrugged. "Who knows? I'm sure the Masons have their reasons."

"Or we're wrong and the Masons have nothing to do with the Tables of Testimony."

Cam shook his head. "I don't think so. I'm pretty sure these guys were locked in on this."

"Why do I get the feeling you're going to go all nerd on me again?"

"I know you find it irresistible."

She stood. "What I find irresistible is the need to use the lady's room. Let's go up, you can walk Venus, and then you can regale me with more of your egghead brilliance." She smiled. "You can think of it as foreplay."

✧ ✚ ✡

Rivka splashed water on her face and stared at her reflection in the bathroom mirror. "Could you be any more pitiful?" she asked herself. Replaying the dinner and walk home in her mind, she could count at least half a dozen times when she practically threw herself at Cameron. *"Think of it as foreplay,"* she parroted back to herself in a sing-song voice. *"You can show me back in the room."* It was one thing to be playful and flirtatious. But she sounded like a drunken sorority girl on spring break.

The truth was, she knew that tonight could be her last night with Cameron. She was about to sneak off, steal an artifact they were supposed to be hunting together, and jump on a plane with it. All without so much as a goodbye. He'd be pissed. More to the point, he'd be hurt.

And that was the best-case scenario. It was also possible she'd get caught, in which case he'd likely find himself accused as an accessory. Talk about him being pissed.

All the more reason for her to try to squeeze every ounce of joy she could out of tonight. This math geek side of him was something new. With a pang, she realized she found it endearing. Which, she realized, was bad news. After a week together, she was supposed to be getting tired of him, impatient with his foibles and quirks.

Ugh. She had it bad. Maybe it wasn't such a bad idea for her to skulk away in the dark of night.

✠

"Okay," Cam said, taking Venus off her leash as he entered the hotel room. "Round two of Cam the math nerd. Ready?"

He watched as the dog trotted over to greet Rivka, still in black jeans and a light blue sweater. Did Venus like her because dogs truly were good judges of character, or was it because she always shared whatever she was eating?

"Ready," Rivka said, flopping onto the couch. "Let's geek out."

"So you asked if we're certain the Templars knew about the Tables of Testimony. And I said yes. This is why." He showed her an image on his phone. "This is Notre Dame Cathedral in Paris. You made the point at dinner about how the Templars built amazing cathedrals all across Europe. But check this out."

Notre Dame Cathedral and Golden Ratio

He explained, "We're back to the Golden Ratio. The long segments are 1.618, the short ones are 1. You can see how all the architectural features, both vertical and horizontal, are spaced according to this ratio. By the way, modern architectural firms use the Golden Ratio as a default even today. I've known all about this stuff for years, but never made the connection to the Tables of Testimony." He smiled wryly. "Probably because I'd never heard of them before."

She leaned in, her scent fresh and floral, studying the image.

He added, "Same with Chartres and other cathedrals. All use the Golden Ratio. I doubt it was random. I think they learned about the

Golden Ratio, and other architectural secrets like those amazing flying buttresses, while in Jerusalem."

She nodded. "The story holds together. They dig under the Temple of Solomon, find something amazing, and return to Europe and become incredibly powerful." She shrugged. "That something could have been the Cosmic Equations."

"There are other clues, also. The stained glass in these cathedrals, for example. Somehow, it glows even at twilight. Nobody's ever been able to figure out the formula for how to do it."

He continued. "And here's another thing. Ever wonder why Jewish people win so many Nobel Prizes? Only 0.2 percent of the people in the world are Jewish, but Jews win over 22 percent of all the Nobels. That's like, 100 times more than they should." He paused. "I have no evidence for this, but it seems to be that one possibility is that secret knowledge—the Cosmic Equations—has been passed down through the generations of the Jewish priestly families."

She nodded. "If nothing else, it would help explain the Jewish emphasis on education and science."

He sat back. "So here's where it gets a bit crazy. I did a quick Google search while I was walking Venus. There's not much information on the Cosmic Equations, but what is there is pretty eye-opening. One guy wrote:

> It unifies and correlates all of the following phenomena: all the fundamental phenomena in biology such as cell and physiological rhythms; cyclical events in botany, including vegetative cycles; cycles in zoology such as counts of head of livestock and number of fish caught; meteorological cycles of the weather; the physics of the movements of the Sun and the Earth; the ebb and flow of human emotion as seen in financial market activities; levels of population; cycles of criminal behavior; and earthquakes and other epic natural disasters.

"Basically," he continued, "if this guy is right, the Cosmic Equations explain everything."

"*The Cosmos*," she observed.

"Yup. Everything about it. Weather cycles. Food shortages. Financial markets. Natural disasters. It's crazy." He shifted on the sofa. "I wonder if it can help us predict the Blue Star prophecy."

"I was thinking the same thing," she replied excitedly. "If what you just read is accurate, it should be able to. No wonder my government wants it."

"Every government would want it. Some would use it for good—for example, to warn people of natural disasters like the Blue Star explosion. Others," he shrugged, "probably not so much."

Cam stared out the window. "You know," he continued, "this would explain a lot of the stories—the miracles—in the Old Testament. Moses knowing when to cross the Red Sea. Joseph predicting seven years of famine and seven years of plenty. The ten plagues."

"And also why the Jews thought of themselves as God's so-called 'chosen people.'"

There was still much they didn't know yet. "I'm guessing the Cosmic Equations are not all written out neat and pretty. That's why much of the knowledge—stuff like levitation and converting metals to gold—has been lost. Someone's going to have to decipher and translate it. But whoever ends up with these tablets, with these Cosmic Equations, well, like they say—"

Rivka finished his thought. "Yup. Knowledge is power."

◈ ✝ ✡

Rivka quietly turned the lights off before joining Cam in bed.

"What, are you feeling shy all of a sudden?" Cam said, wrapping her in his arms.

"Sometimes I find the darkness comforting. Like a blanket."

He kissed her. "I like to look at you, but okay."

She relaxed into him. "Thanks, Cameron."

They made love slowly, Rivka on top, Cam willing to allow her to set the pace and the mood. She would have liked it to go on forever, their lovemaking somehow to transport them to another dimension. The darkness helped—for a few brief, blissful moments, she imagined a lifetime of this, that this was her destiny. But, as much as Cam was a prince, she was no princess, and this was no fairy tale.

A few minutes, or perhaps many hours, passed—she had lost the ability to judge. Naked and spent, she burrowed into Cam's body much as he, without her even realizing it, had burrowed his way into her heart. Gently, she lifted his face toward hers and placed her mouth against his. He kissed her languidly, humming lightly, their mouths and noses sharing the same air, until she felt him drift off.

He began to snore lightly, his breathing regular. Turning her face away after a final kiss, she allowed the tears to come. Silently she wept, both for the loss she was about to suffer and the pain she was about to inflict.

CHAPTER 10

Cam feigned sleep, listening as Rivka quietly slipped out the door. He was not surprised. He knew 'goodbye sex' when he saw it. Or felt it.

What he didn't know was why.

Striding to the window, he watched the hotel exit. There. Out she went, turning right. Half a block up, at the next corner, she took a left. Toward the Masonic temple.

Dressing quickly, and leaving the sliding door ajar and water and food out for Venus, he jogged to his SUV. He circled his way around the temple to approach from the rear, parked a block away, and crept closer. In the distance, periodically illuminated by street lights, he saw Rivka and her tall strides approaching, dressed in dark clothing and carrying a duffel bag.

There was little doubt what she was doing. But what should *he* do? One thing was certain: He wasn't going to stand by and let her run off with the Tables of Testimony. They had tracked it together, unraveled the mystery together. If they were going to steal it, they should steal it together.

Hiding in the bushes next to Paris' boulder across the street from the Masonic temple, he waited as Rivka approached. "You forgot something. Or someone."

She froze but did not look his way. "Cameron."

"Not even a goodbye?"

She shook her head, her eyes squeezed shut. "I couldn't."

He sensed her misery. It didn't make it okay, but in some ways it made her actions more noble. She was choosing country over self. Or, more accurately, country over him.

He stepped onto the sidewalk. "Well, now you don't have to."

Her head turned slowly. "What do you mean?"

"I mean that you're stuck with me. At least until we steal this tablet."

"I need to do this alone."

"Sorry. We do it together, or I call the police." He paused. "Or, I suppose you can try to stop me." He spread his arms.

"No. I won't ... *can't* ... hurt you."

"Okay, then. It's settled. So, what's the plan?"

She let out a long breath and began to walk again. He fell in beside her. "I know the alarm code. Once we're inside, we know where the tablet is hidden—your friend Paris told you, and you told me. Inside one of the pillars."

"So you're going in with *my* information, without me?"

She ignored the question. "According to our experts, the tablet is blue —like lapis lazuli—and is about the size of a tombstone. I have a skateboard to roll it on, if it's too heavy to carry."

"And you plan to just waltz out with it?"

"No. I have a plan for that also."

"You do realize I asked what the plan was and you gave me a bunch of details but basically told me nothing?"

She offered a tentative smile. "Yes."

"You really should have gone to law school."

That brought a full smile. "You're sweet for not being angry."

He felt hurt, and sad, and a bit foolish. But she was right—not really angry.

She gestured toward the temple. "It's not a particularly elaborate security system."

"I'm guessing because they didn't want to draw unnecessary attention. If you treat someplace like Fort Knox, you're basically telling people there's gold inside."

"And inviting them to try to steal it." She slipped on a ski mask. "In this case, the security is inside. The tablet is well-hidden."

He pulled his shirt up over his mouth and his baseball cap low on his forehead as they strode across the street toward the entrance.

"Just so you know," she said, "the Mossad can't protect you. And this is a felony."

He slowed and contemplated her words, playing it out in his mind. Would the Freemasons bring charges if he and Rivka were caught? Doing so would mean acknowledging that they had been hiding an ancient Biblical artifact, depriving the world of invaluable knowledge and technology which could have saved millions of lives. He guessed they'd rather keep things quiet.

Still, it'd be best not to get caught at all. "Felony? I thought you said you had a plan," he said.

"I do."

"Is it a good one?"

"Let's just say, I don't have to outrun the cops, I just have to outrun you."

He laughed aloud. "Touché."

Twenty feet from the entrance, she said, "Wait here. I'm going to disable the alarm."

"How do I know you won't go ahead without me?"

"You don't."

She jogged ahead and punched at the keypad, then pushed through the door. He could make out her profile, can of spray paint in hand, pointed upward at what he guessed was the security camera. She waved him forward.

"Why disable the camera if you're masked?"

"You're not. And I don't want the authorities to know what we stole. The Freemasons might prefer to sweep this all under the rug." She closed the door behind them, locking it. "If the police come, that'll delay them."

"You have another escape route?"

She nodded and led him across the foyer to a pair of ornate, dark-wooded doors. "This is the main lodge room." She tried the knob, then quickly dropped to a knee with a metal tool in her hand. In seconds, she picked the lock. "Come on," she said, again locking the door behind them. "Pull that over," she ordered, pointing to a heavy wooden chair. Tilting the chair onto its back legs, he wedged it under the doorknob as she spray-painted another camera.

Police sirens sounded in the distance. "It is possible they have a motion detector?" Cam asked.

"Not just possible. Likely."

She jogged to the far side of the rectangular, high-ceilinged room, Cam following. He had been in enough Masonic lodges to know the basic layout: Lodge Master's chair on a platform in the east, symbolic of the rising sun; altar with a collection of various religions' Bibles in the center of the room; a bare wall along the north side of the room, north historically being associated with darkness.

Rivka stopped in front of two gilded, ornately carved pillars which dominated a corner of the room next to the Master's raised chair. Cam knew that the two pillars were inspired by architectural columns prominent in King Solomon's Temple. And, of course, they tied back to the Pillars of Enoch, used to preserve the Tables of Testimony during the Great Flood. It really was an ideal place to hide the tablet today.

Rivka studied the pillars, running her hands over their surfaces and examining them with a powerful flashlight. "Help me, Cameron. There should be some kind of hidden door in one of these pillars. Unfortunately, your guy Paris told us where it was, but not how to get inside."

On his knees, Cam studied the pillars, tapping them and listening for hollow areas or other anomalies over the sound of approaching sirens.

Neither had any luck. Rivka stood and backed up, shining her light on the silver Hebrew letters ringing the top of the columns. "*Jakin* and *Voaz*," she said aloud.

"Actually, it's *Jachin* and *Boaz*," Cam replied, pronouncing the 'ch' as in *challah*.

She focused her light. "No, it's not. That's definitely a *vet*, not a *bet*.

There's no dot inside." She moved the light. "And same with the other letter. This time there is a dot. So a hard 'k' sound."

"Well, then those are mistakes."

She looked around. "These people, the Freemasons, don't seem the type to make mistakes like that. I mean, they're all about their ritual and symbolism." She chewed her lip. "I wonder."

He looked up. "Well, wonder quickly."

She dragged a chair over between the pillars and stood on it, peering at the silver inscription on each of the pillars. "I think I can see smudges, fingerprints," she said. She smiled knowingly down at him. "But only on the two letters that have mistakes."

"Eyes that see," Cam said. "Good job."

"Perhaps."

Tucking her flashlight into her waistband, she reached out, spread-eagled, using her index fingers to push simultaneously on the two Hebrew letters with the mistakes. A muffled tumbling sound rumbled from within the Jachin pillar, and a second later a hidden door sprung open. "Voila," she said triumphantly, jumping off the chair.

Cam nodded. "Makes sense to hide it in that pillar. Jachin symbolizes wisdom."

She peered inside the column with her light. "It's here, inside a golden display case." She tucked a shoulder into the cavity, wriggled her body, and emerged with a brilliant blue stone the size of a bed pillow. "Help me," she grunted. "It's heavy. But close the door first. And put the chair back." He nodded, understanding that she did not want to leave any clues that they had been focused on the pillars.

The beep-beep-beep of the front door alarm code echoed from the foyer of the temple. "Shit," Cam said, taking one end of the tablet. He could see strange script and a series of shapes, including what looked like the Fibonacci spiral, carved into the bright blue tablet-shaped stone. "Now would be a good time for that escape plan."

"Wait," she said, removing her phone from a pocket. "I need to get pictures."

"Now?"

Her flash lit the room. "The inscription is crucial. And if we get caught…"

He nodded, waiting as she texted the images out.

"Okay." She lifted one end. "Follow me."

Rivka, walking backward, led the way toward a door at the rear of the lodge. She kicked it open and together they wrestled the tablet through to a landing at the top of a set of stairs. "Down we go," she said, as Cam pushed the door closed with his foot.

The loud crack of wood splintering announced the arrival of the police inside the lodge room. Through the crack at the bottom of the door, Cam could see light beams sweeping the room.

The instant they reached the bottom of the stairs, Rivka laid the tablet down, wrapped it in a black tarp, and removed a skateboard from her bag. Together they lifted the tablet onto the board, where she secured it with bungee cords.

"Now where to?" Cam asked.

"The boiler room."

Cam looked around, noticed a red steel door. "That way," he said, pushing the skateboard as Rivka strode ahead.

He found her inside, peering at the wall behind an old oil furnace. "Here," she said. She slid aside a faux brick panel, virtually indistinguishable from the real brick. "Push it through."

On his knees, Cam shoved the skateboard over a lip on the floor and into a dank, dark tunnel of some kind. Rivka followed him in and slid the panel closed behind them.

"Okay," she said. Her light reflected off cobwebs and water-streaked rock walls. "This is an old escape tunnel, dating back to when the temple was built during World War I."

"How'd you know about it?"

"It was one of the pieces of information Paris fed us years ago. Useless, until now. Thankfully, it's all digitized."

Cam nodded. "The Masons often built escape tunnels. Never know when people might decide you're the agents of Satan." In fact, Hitler murdered thousands of Freemasons not long after these tunnels had been built. And, of course, he and Rivka had seen similar escape tunnels both in Sintra and Ethiopia.

The tunnel sloped slightly downward, making Cam's job easier. Suddenly, perhaps fifty feet in, he froze. "Did you hear that?"

She shook her head and extinguished her light. "Remember, I have bad hearing."

"I think I heard voices in the furnace room." He looked back. "Who else knows about this tunnel?"

"I'm assuming other senior members of the lodge. But I'm also assuming the only people back there are police. I doubt the lodge members are here already."

"Fair assumption." He paused. "Maybe they followed our footprints. That furnace room was pretty dirty."

"Which means eventually they'll come after us. Keep moving."

"Where does this lead?"

"It's dried up now, but there used to be an old stream west of the temple that leads to the main river. My guess is that there were boats standing by to ferry the Masons away from danger."

A few seconds later, the tunnel arced to the right. At the turn, a short door had been set into the tunnel wall a couple of feet off the ground, a thick deadbolt securing it from intruders from the outside. "This is us," Rivka said, spraying the lock with WD-40 and then wrenching it open, being careful to keep her light muffled. "You go through first, and I'll lift the tablet up to you. You'll be in a basement. I have a car waiting in the alley."

Cam climbed through, finding himself in a dark, dank room with a cement floor and a furnace humming close by. Turning, he kneeled to receive the tablet. "I think we've come in a circle," he joked. "I'm back in the Masonic temple."

But the joke was on him. The door swung close. He heard the iron lock set and, a second later, Rivka's voice. "I'm very sorry, Cameron." She paused. "Truly."

Blinking back her tears, Rivka pushed on through the tunnel. She knew, from the information Paris had supplied, that this spur of the tunnel passed under another block of buildings beyond where she had ditched Cameron. A second exit door—this one unlocked—awaited her, along with a rental car she had parked in the alley nearby. There would not be enough time for Cameron to find his way out of his basement and to her alley before she made her escape.

It was heavier going here, the tunnel now ascending slightly. Her back ached from being stooped, and the air was growing thick. She froze. Beams of light shined on the walls behind her, at the arc. Still faint, but they were getting closer.

She had no choice.

Unzipping her bag, she removed a brick of Semtex the size of a candy bar. Working quickly, she wedged the plastic explosive into a gap in the tunnel ceiling, attached a timer, and rushed away, pushing the skateboard ahead of her. Ten seconds later, she crouched, turned her body, and curled into a ball. "Three, two, one," she counted. The explosion rocked the tunnel, sending a dark cloud of dust and debris rolling toward her. She didn't wait for it.

Pushing ahead, she listened for signs of pursuit behind her. She had used a minimal amount of Semtex, just enough to collapse the tunnel ceiling and make it unpassable. And she had made sure to set it off before her pursuers had reached the turn. It was one thing to steal an artifact. Another entirely to kill a police officer.

Ahead, the tunnel ended. Another door, almost identical to the first, in another basement, this one with a direct exit to an alley. She exhaled. Sure would be nice to have Cameron to help lift the tablet up and through.

Sure would be nice to have Cameron, period.

Cradling the tablet like a baby, and using her legs to lift, she managed to wrestle the artifact through the opening and rest it on the cement floor. She pulled herself up next to it and spotted the glow of an exit door. All she needed to do was roll the tablet out the door, hoist it into the car, and make a quick drive to the airport—and this whole chapter in her life would be behind her. For better or worse.

Crouching with the artifact, Rivka pushed open the basement door. A burst of cold air met her, followed immediately by the flash of a bright light, blinding her.

A woman's voice. "That's far enough, honey." The cocking sound of a couple of shotguns put an exclamation point to her words. "You have two choices. You can go scurry back into that basement, or we can put a couple holes into you. You decide."

Damn. Her mind raced, considering her options. She had none. Outmanned, outgunned and outmaneuvered. Gritting her teeth, still blinded, she backed slowly away.

"And, honey, close that door behind you. Tight."

� ✝ ✡

Menachem watched from behind a parked van, his night-vision binoculars focused on the black SUV.

"Should we go in?" a baby-faced operative asked, his face glistening with sweat despite the cool night air.

"No. Let it play out." Who was this? And how had they anticipated Rivka's move? Menachem shook his head. *He* was the one who was supposed to be playing Rivka. Apparently, there was a new participant in the game. Possibly Paris' killer.

He hated operations like this. Too many actors, too many variables, too many things which could go wrong. These missions were planned— "scripted," they called it—in office buildings in Tel Aviv, by people who had not been in the field in decades, people who forgot that the real world was not a chessboard. Sometimes, while the black pieces fought the white, red pieces rushed in and created chaos. Like now. Menachem's mind raced, seeing the possibilities. With chaos came opportunity.

"They've got the artifact," the young agent said, straining to move forward like a dog on a leash. "They're getting away. Should I follow?"

In this secluded alley, it would be impossible to follow without being seen—even with headlights off, cars displayed brake lights and dome lights. Menachem did not want to spook them. And the highway was less than a block away—they would be gone to the wind by the time the agent was able surreptitiously to pursue. Menachem shook his head and made a note of the license plate. "They are going away. That is different from *getting* away."

✦ ✝ ✡

Cam jogged through the back alleys of downtown Asheville in the general direction of where the Masonic temple tunnel ran, his anger fueling him. Not that he expected to find anything after needing ten minutes to free himself from the office building basement where Rivka had left him. Other, perhaps, than Rivka's fresh tire tracks.

He cursed. This time, he was pissed. Rivka had slammed the freaking door in his face.

Just stop. Amanda's voice.

"What do you mean?" He spoke aloud, as he usually did to Amanda.

Do you think she wanted to ditch you? Wanted to drag that block of stone around on her own? Of course not. She did it because she was trying to protect you.

"I'm a big boy."

Well, you're not thinking like one. What was your plan, to get on the plane with her and go to Israel? Maybe request asylum? What about Astarte? And what makes you think the Mossad would even let you board?

"Why would I have to go anywhere?"

Cameron, you're not thinking. As it stands now, there's nothing tying you to the theft. Rivka spray-painted the security cameras. But how long do you think it would take for the Mossad to pin this whole crime on you? Why should they take the heat when they have a perfect pigeon like you?

He thought about Menachem. Amanda was right. He would not hesitate to sacrifice Cam. Rivka had been trying to protect him. From himself, in fact.

What were you thinking, anyway? You've never stolen anything in your life.

"It seemed almost like a mission for me. One that I couldn't turn down."

Couldn't turn down?

"Even you—or your ghost—was telling me to 'find the treasure, find the treasure.' Every time I turned around. 'Find the treasure.'"

Think about it, Cameron. Do you really believe in ghosts?

He stopped. "You think I've been played? Someone's been messing with me, trying to get me to obsess over this artifact?"

What do you think?

"Shit," he replied.

Figure it out. Piece it together. Tell a story that uses every clue, every piece of evidence.

"Okay. Someone wants me to go looking for a treasure. They figure I'm the only one who can find it, which probably means it's related to the Templars. Or maybe it's the treasure I already found, the Golden Menorah. Either way, they figure I'm more likely to go on this quest if you, or your ghost, is spurring me on. But I don't believe in ghosts, so they need to grease the skids first." He paused, thinking. "So they hire these singers, put them in places they know I'll be. And they all sing this same song, with lyrics that could be interpreted as you haunting me, imploring me to find answers, find the treasure. *I am gone but in your dreams I live; I mean no harm but answers I must give.* Somehow they get the song to play in my bedroom. Maybe they even set up the apartment rental in Newburyport and planted the recording behind the wall or something." He paused. "Heck, maybe even the real estate agent was in on it. That whole thing with the guy wanting to rent our house, then having the condo become available—it all seemed a bit odd to me at the time."

Good. Go on.

"I don't know, Amanda. It sounds too elaborate."

Can you otherwise explain it?

"No. I guess not."

And, though it may sound elaborate, think about what's at stake. Indescribable treasures. The Golden Menorah. The Ark of the Covenant.

Now, this Tables of Testimony. When the stakes are this bloody high, what's wrong with being a bit elaborate?

He sighed. "Okay. In addition to the songs, maybe they send me subliminal messages in my sleep—again, to get me to go looking for the treasure."

Good.

"So then, I guess, they follow me down here. Do the same thing with the recording in the hotel room. And even in my car, somehow." He paused. "But not in Portugal or on the plane—that would have been too hard to arrange. And somehow they project your image onto the curtain, again in my hotel room. And also get Venus to react to your ghost." He shook his head. "I don't know, this is getting farfetched…"

No. Continue. How would they get Venus to react?

He mulled it over. "A high frequency, something only she could hear." He lifted his chin. "Wait, that's what Rivka saw in the hallway, a guy with a remote control of some kind. Something was inside the room, emitting a sound that bothered Venus." He recalled Rivka mentioned a humidifier being disturbed. *Of course.* "Modern humidifiers use ultrasonic technology to reduce noise. Noise to humans, that is."

And the note on the mirror?

"That's easy. We did that as kids, using soap. When the mirror fogs, the moisture doesn't adhere to the soap residue."

Good. What else is there to explain?

He spoke more quickly. "The death of Paris. They knew he was sharing info with me. They questioned him, found out what I was researching and what treasures might be on my radar screen. Then they killed him to cover their tracks."

Perhaps through hypnosis?

"Yes. If they're adept at using dreams and ghosts and other kinds of manipulations, they probably also use hypnosis. That's how they got Paris to step in front of that bus."

So, who's our suspect?

"Someone who followed me down from Boston. Someone with a background in psychology—maybe even an illusionist or magician."

Excellent, Cameron. I believe my work is done here. But not yours.

He continued, jogging through a dark alley, looking for signs of recent activity. Amanda was correct. He couldn't let this go.

There, ahead. A basement door ajar, near where he guessed the tunnel ran. He turned on the flashlight on his phone and crouched. Engine oil, the pavement warm. But no Rivka. And no tablet. Which was really no surprise.

He kicked at an empty soda bottle, sending it clattering into a brick wall. He was still pissed. But, guided by Amanda, his anger had turned away from Rivka and toward whoever murdered his new friend. He gritted his teeth. Rivka may be gone from his life, and with her the Tables of Testimony. But he could still avenge the death of Nathan Paris.

⚏ ✠ ✡

"What in the world?" Dr. Gertrude Little breathed as she pulled the tarp off the wedge of turquoise-colored rock plopped next to her in the back seat of their Honda SUV. One son drove, the other kept watch. She would have to trust them not to get lost or run a red light and get pulled over. Her attention was totally focused on the artifact.

"What is it, Ma? Gold?"

"No," she said quietly. "Not gold," though there were yellow flecks of something in the stone. Her plan had worked perfectly, the artifact delivered right into her waiting arms. Not perfectly, actually. She was expecting gold and instead got, what? Lapis lazuli? She didn't think sapphire or turquoise could be this large.

"Silver, then?"

Focused on the strange script, she didn't reply. With a tentative hand, she touched the stone, ran her fingers along the edges of the inscription. Smooth and worn, as if very old. What was that old writing called? Cuneiform? Was it from the Middle East? Is that why the Israeli woman had stolen it? Gertrude shook her head. Whatever it was, it wasn't gold. She was expecting the Table of Shewbread, which she had estimated contained about forty pounds of gold overlay—at today's prices, just over a million dollars. She assumed a museum or a collector would pay many times that for a famous Old Testament artifact. Worst-case scenario, if it was too hot to fence, she would have simply melted it down.

But what was she supposed to do with an inscribed blue block, no matter how old it might be? She didn't run in that crowd, didn't know antiquities dealers and collectors.

"Shit," she said aloud.

"What's wrong, Ma?"

"Just shut up and drive." The frustrating thing was, she couldn't even blame this on her dimwitted sons.

CHAPTER 11

Cam had eventually retrieved his SUV and drove back to the hotel, parking his SUV in the purple light of predawn. He greeted Venus, then began to undress for a hot shower. He planned to catch a few hours of sleep before heading over to the police station to see if he get could get the detective on the Paris case to buy into his theory of a murdering magician.

A tentative knock on the door caught him naked, waiting for the water to heat. He wrapped a towel around his waist and went to the door. "Yes?"

"It's me. Rivka. Can I come in?"

He blinked once before unbolting the door. She stepped in tentatively.

"I assumed you'd be over the Atlantic by now." His heart raced, but he kept his tone curt. Maybe he wasn't completely over his anger after all. Or maybe it was just his bruised ego.

"Me too. But things went sideways."

He lifted his chin. "Are you okay?"

"Other than my pride, yes."

"Let me grab a robe." They had spent much of the night together naked. But the slammed door had come between them.

Rivka called to him from the living room as he retrieved the robe. "You don't have any wine, do you?"

Interesting how she didn't feel comfortable looking for herself, in a room she shared with him until a few hours ago.

"Sure," he replied.

"I know it's almost dawn. But it's also been a long night."

He poured them each a glass. He thought about sticking to water, not wanting to make this a social occasion. But that would be punishing himself as much as her.

"So," he said. "You going to tell me what happened? Nothing personal, but don't bother unless it's the truth."

Her shoulders sagged. After rubbing her nose with the back of her hand, she swallowed and replied, "I guess I deserved that. But it hurt."

He didn't reply.

She took a sip of wine. "After you ... left ... I set off a small explosion to block the tunnel so the police couldn't catch me. There was another exit further into the tunnel. I had a car waiting. But when I opened the door, someone was waiting. They took the tablet."

"Who was it?"

"They had a bright light in my eyes, so I didn't get a good look. But I think it might have been the woman in the back seat of the pickup truck that rammed us. Same build, heavy-set. With long, straight hair."

Cam told her what he had deduced. "I think they followed me down from Boston, using the songs to convince me to look for a treasure." He left out the part about Amanda's ghost. "Then, of course, to steal it. Like we did. And I think they killed Paris."

Rivka nodded. "Any clues?"

"Just that they seem skilled in illusion and hypnosis." He shrugged. "So maybe a magician or someone with a psych background. Or both."

"Wait," she said. "Didn't you video Astarte's presentation? If that woman was in the pickup truck, maybe she was at the lecture also."

Cam nodded. "Good idea." He connected his phone to the hotel room television. "I scanned the crowd just before she started. Let's see if I got anything."

They sat on the floor and peered at the screen. "There," Rivka said, pointing. "That woman, in the wheelchair. With the soda bottle. Could be her."

Cam zoomed in. "Mountain Dew."

"Wait, Cameron." She grabbed his arm. "Remember that commotion in the airport? A woman spilled soda on a girl's bag?"

"Yes. And I think it was Mountain Dew."

Her eyes widened. "And I think it was the same woman."

"And I saw a Mountain Dew bottle stuck in storm drain right after Paris was killed." He paused. "And I think I kicked a Mountain Dew bottle in the alley tonight, where they ambushed you. That's a lot of Mountain Dew."

Rivka nodded. "A mountain of it."

✡ ✝ ✡

While Cam showered, Rivka phoned Menachem. She had already called him from outside the tunnel to give him a brief update.

"I don't understand why you didn't get better pictures."

"Was I supposed to do that while the police were chasing us or while I was being ambushed?"

"Yes."

She knew he was right. The artifact itself was, of course, valuable from a historical and religious perspective. But its primary value was scientific—what knowledge could be gleaned from the ancient inscription? For that, they needed clear, high-resolution images. Not rushed shots in poor lighting. But, like she said, time hadn't been on her side. And easy for Menachem to micromanage from thousands of miles away. Hell, he should have been here, with her, given the importance of the artifact.

She changed the subject. "I have some good news. We might have a suspect." She summarized the Mountain Dew evidence.

"You say 'we.' Is Thorne back in the picture?"

"Yes." She hoped she was right about this. It was the silver lining to losing the artifact. She was here, with Cameron, rather than on a plane over the Atlantic.

"Good. But I'm still sending a team. I should not have let you do this alone."

Damn right. She should have had backup, someone watching the tunnel exits. But she bit back a retort. They both had made mistakes.

"Rivka," he continued, "we need to get this back. The pictures are not enough. Our experts think the stone needs to be put under ultraviolet light to fully reveal its secrets. Or heated, so the gold inside begins to glow. Much of it may not be visible to the naked eye."

"I understand."

"One more thing. You mentioned the Cherokee might have the Ark of the Covenant. As important as these Cosmic Equations may turn out to be, are you certain the Ark of the Covenant is not in play? If one is in or around Asheville, why not the other?"

"Cameron thinks, and I agree, that whatever ark is here is a replica, built to house the Tables of Testimony. The Old Testament gives specific instruction as to how to build the Ark, so it would have been fairly simple to do. That's what people saw with the Cherokee, the replica."

"And the connection between the Cherokee and the Masons? Explain it to me again?" He paused. "So I can explain it to the bureaucrats."

"The connection is the Sephardic Jews who came over here with the Templars from Portugal in the 1400s. They settled in Appalachia and married into the Cherokee tribe. Some of them were North African. The result of that intermarrying was the Melungeon people. The Melungeons guarded the Tables of Testimony, just like the priestly families before them. They were the earliest Freemasons in Appalachia. It was the obvious way to continue their legacy."

"So all of this tracks back to the priestly families, the Levites."

"Right. They left Jerusalem with the Temple treasures and formed Freemasonry as a way to preserve their heritage and their secrets. They eventually made their way across Europe to Portugal. Everything in Europe seems to intersect in Portugal, just like everything in America seems to intersect in Appalachia."

"Okay. Thanks for the history lesson." He paused. "Now go find that tablet."

"I shouldn't wait for the backup team?"

"Let me put it this way. Had it been me who lost the artifact, well, I wouldn't be wasting my time on the telephone."

✡ ✝ ✡

Seated with the Mossad agent in the back room of his art gallery in the River District of Asheville, Lenny picked at a bagel. Nose broken, he had to eat in small bites so he could breathe. He watched as Menachem hung up the phone and pursed his lips.

"Did she buy it?" Lenny asked.

"I think so. She's very bright. But she thinks I'm still in Israel, that she's alone on this mission."

"That's why you asked her about the Ark of the Covenant and for the history lesson."

"Yes. She needs to think I am only partly engaged."

"This is a narrow needle we're trying to thread here," Lenny said.

"I know. But it's worth it." Menachem's dark eyes held Lenny's. If Lenny could read thoughts, he'd guess Menachem was thinking: *If it weren't, I wouldn't be caught dead working with a maggot like you. A competent and skilled maggot, but a maggot nonetheless.* The truth was, the Mossad needed a middleman in the arts and antiquities community, and Lenny was the obvious choice. Especially when he told Menachem he already knew—from the rantings of his gallery partner, Boyd—about a secret treasure hidden in the temple. It didn't hurt that Cam, who Menachem apparently respected, was already working with Lenny.

"Is it time for me to reel the doctor in?"

Menachem nodded. "Yes. If we wait, Rivka might find her. I thought we would have more time."

"As you said, your agent is skilled. So is Thorne."

"Make the call."

Lenny did so. "Dr. Little," he said in his deepest, most assertive voice. "You and I have not had the pleasure of meeting. My name is Lenny Null. I am a dealer in fine arts and antiquities. I believe I may be of service to you."

A pause. "How did you get this number?"

"It matters not, I assure you. What matters is that I have a buyer for your recent acquisition."

"I don't know what you're talking about."

"Please, doctor, do not insult me. I've been doing this a long time. Very little shocks me. I care not how you came to … *acquire* … the artifact. You have it. My client wants it." Lenny cleared his throat. "He is willing to pay three million euros for it, just over three-and-a-half million dollars. But it must be today."

"Why today?"

"Suffice it to say that the people you *acquired* it from are on your trail. My client fears that, if we wait, the artifact may be repossessed." He paused. "Something about Mountain Dew bottles."

Menachem smiled at the sharp intake of breath.

But the doctor quickly rallied. "It's worth a lot more than that. And we can handle ourselves."

"Very well," Lenny replied. "Name your price."

They went back and forth, eventually settling on five million dollars, to be wired to an offshore account, a million now and the balance upon delivery. Lenny felt pretty good about it. Menachem had been willing to go much higher.

Lenny suggested his gallery at eleven o'clock, three hours from now. "You will feel safe here, in a reputable establishment," he said. "I will make sure there is a parking spot for you right out front."

Menachem nodded as Lenny hung up. "Well played."

"Not my first rodeo."

"I'll need wire instructions for your fee as well."

Lenny nodded. He had asked around. The Mossad *always* paid. Of course, they might circle back and assassinate you later.

Assuming he lived, it will have been a good play. A few million profit on the real estate side. Another half-million from the Mossad. Sure, it cost him a beating. And Shelby would be pissed for him double-crossing Cam. But Cam was a big boy. And Lenny really hadn't screwed him—he would be well-compensated for his week of work.

But first things first. They needed to consummate this transaction with the good doctor. Or, more accurately, the bad doctor.

Lenny had one more call to make. "Now?" he said to Menachem.

"Yes."

"Even though we don't have it yet?"

"The Freemasons are probably going crazy. Best we calm things down."

Nodding, Lenny dialed a number Menachem had given him. The call was answered on the first ring.

"Yes."

"Is this the Worshipful Master?"

"It is."

"Things are proceeding. You should have your artifact back later today. As we agreed, no police."

The whistle of a long breath being let out. No doubt the lodge master understood he would not be so 'worshipful' if the Mason's priceless artifact was stolen on his watch. "Thank you."

"You can thank me by wiring the funds we agreed upon."

Another quarter million, a finder's fee. Menachem had merely shrugged when Lenny suggested it. Apparently, he had other things to worry about.

◈ ✟ ✡

Cam did his best to zoom in and brighten the image of the Mountain Dew woman on his laptop, then used the hotel printer to spit out a few color copies. From the lobby, dressed in a zip-up sweatshirt and jeans, he strolled into the warm winter sun with Venus, jumped into his Cherokee, and made the short drive over to the two-story, brick police station. Fortunately, the female detective Cam had met a few days ago was on duty.

"I'm back," he said with a smile. He thought it best not to mention he had flown to Portugal and Ethiopia since their last conversation.

"Sorry," she said. Hispanic, heavy-set, in her thirties. "I've got no updates for you."

The fact that she didn't arrest him for last night's theft was a good sign—they must not know of his involvement. He planned to keep it that way. He waved the photo. "Can we talk? I think I have something."

She led them to a small conference room. He slid the image across a table. "My daughter gave a lecture at the Eastern Cherokee reservation Saturday night. On the way home, a pickup truck rammed us. I happened to video the lecture, and when I looked through it I recognized this woman as being in the passenger seat of the truck. She was drinking a Mountain Dew at the lecture. And I saw an empty Mountain Dew bottle stuck in the storm drain next to where Paris was killed."

"That's it? Lots of people drink Mountain Dew."

"Actually, not that many. It makes up only six percent of the soda sold in the country. And only half the people drink soda regularly. So it's really only three percent. A one-in-thirty chance." He sat back. "Plus, she was at my daughter's lecture. Not to mention, she rammed us. That's a lot of coincidence."

The detective's eyes narrowed. "Okay. I'm listening."

"Also, someone's been screwing with me, trying to make me believe in ghosts." He described the Amanda 'ghost' projections and the use of the humidifier. "And people said Paris was in a trance. I'm thinking maybe this woman has a background in hypnosis. Maybe a magician or illusionist."

"Are you saying someone hypnotized Mr. Paris and told him to step into traffic?"

"Scientific studies have shown that some people are very susceptible to hypnosis."

She shook her head. "I'm sorry. I've been doing this a long time, and that's one of the craziest case theories I've ever heard." She stood. "I'll put this woman's picture in the system." As she walked away, under her breath, she concluded, "And if I find her, maybe I'll hire her to come to my daughter's birthday party."

✠

Menachem left the art studio and drove along the river, turning into a cluster of old warehouse buildings forgotten by the recent downtown gentrification. He parked, entered an alarm code, and pushed open a steel door. Navigating his way down a long hallway, he entered a brightly lit, white-walled room which looked like it belonged in a medical office. A pair of men stood on either side of a table, chisels in hand, hunched over a block of blue stone.

Nobody greeted Menachem.

"You have two hours."

One of the men nodded. "We could use two weeks."

"And I could use a ten-inch schlong. But I'll make do with what God gave me."

Menachem paced the room. The craftsmen were right. They needed more time. They had done a commendable job with the artifact's size, color and shape—the ruined blocks of lapis lazuli flown in from Afghanistan and now scattered around the room testified to that. But the inscriptions were far from perfect, based as they were on Rivka's imperfect photos. And there really was no way to make the inscriptions feel smooth and weathered to the touch. He sighed. They'd just have to hope that the Master of the lodge, who had probably only viewed the artifact at most a handful of times, would see a tablet-shaped block of blue stone with strange engravings and assume it was the same one stolen from his lodge overnight. After all, how many blocks of inscribed lapis lazuli could there be lying around in North Carolina? Later, if anyone figured out a switch had been made, well, it would be too late.

✦ ✟ ✡

Pacing back and forth through the connecting door of their adjoining motel rooms on the outskirts of Asheville, Gertrude Little barked commands. "Pack up. We leave in ten minutes."

"Where we going?"

"Anyplace but here. They're on to us."

Her younger son pushed back. "But what about the five million?"

"We've got a million already." She had just checked her bank account, confirming it. "Whatever this thing is, if it's worth five million today, it'll be worth five million, or more, tomorrow. But no way am I risking walking into a trap."

She had made a show about negotiating the price. But all she really cared about was the deposit. A million would allow them to lay low for a while, give her a chance to figure out what this artifact was really worth.

"Come on, boys," she barked. "We've got a tiger by the tail. The worst thing we can do now is to let go."

✡ ✝ ✡

Cam pushed through the police station door, his mind already on his next move. The police clearly weren't going to make this a priority. And, even if they found something, he knew better than to expect them to share investigation information with him, just as he knew better than to trust Rivka. But he had one piece of information neither of them had: He knew exactly where the Tables of Testimony tablet was. While in the temple with Rivka, he had surreptitiously removed the Tile tracking device Astarte had given him from his keyring and clipped it onto one of the eyeholes on the tarp, hiding it under a seam. As long as the tablet stayed wrapped in the tarp, he could track it on his phone.

Currently, at a motel on the outskirts of the city.

He thought about enlisting Rivka's help. Whoever stole the object wouldn't give it up without a fight. But what good would that do him? She'd insist on taking it back to Israel. And Cam had other plans for it.

He climbed into his Cherokee, greeted Venus, and mounted his phone on the dashboard. The Tile app flashed—the tablet was on the move, heading north on Route 26. "Shit," he hissed. He had hoped for more time. He had his laptop with him, and of course Venus—was there anything else left in the hotel room that he couldn't live without? Rivka's face popped into his head, but he blinked it away and put the SUV into gear.

Driving quickly, he found his way to the interstate. "Easy," he said to himself. No reason to overdo it. They wouldn't be speeding, not with a stolen artifact in their vehicle. He'd catch them, eventually.

Twenty-five minutes later, as they approached the Tennessee border, he spotted a black Honda SUV with Massachusetts plates in the right lane. Pulling alongside on their left, he allowed himself a quick glance— burly guy driving, heavy-set woman who looked like the Mountain Dew lady in the passenger seat, another guy in the back seat. "Bingo," he said, quickly dropping back before they recognized his SUV with the telltale rear-end damage.

Now what? He was like the dog who had caught the mail truck. He put himself in their shoes. They had left in a hurry, probably spooked. Now, safely away, they had probably begun to relax. Soon they'd need a break—food, bathroom, gas, whatever. When they did so, they'd park in a crowded area and leave one person with the vehicle at all times. But that was better odds than he had now.

Rivka rang his cell, but he ignored the call. Maneuvering his way back into the right lane, he settled in behind his quarry. Lucky for him he had a full tank of gas.

� ✝ ✡

Menachem paced around Lenny's gallery, his scowling countenance scaring away a small group of tourists. "Call again," he hissed.

"She's not coming," Lenny replied. The doctor was twenty minutes late and hadn't answered her cell. "They're on the run."

"Idiots."

"Well, they have a million dollars, at least."

Menachem made a quick call. "Reverse the wire. Just do it." He turned back to Lenny. "Like I said, idiots."

Lenny raised an eyebrow. "You can do that?"

"Legally, no. But unless they've emptied the account, which I doubt very much given that they are on the run, our bank will pressure the receiving bank to return the funds. One of the advantages of having the reputation that we have."

"A well-earned one."

"Yes, well, our reputation apparently was not enough to stop this doctor from screwing us."

"What's the next step?"

Menachem stared off into space. "We go ahead with handing the fake tablet over to the Masons. One fewer ball in the air. And, of course, we go after the doctor."

He dialed Rivka, moving to the back of the gallery for privacy. He had already informed Rivka that the doctor was willing to make a deal, leaving out any explanation of how they had connected with her so quickly. "Do you know the location of the Mountain Dew woman? She double-crossed us."

"No. Cameron is at the police station, sharing her picture with them. I'm waiting for him to check in."

"Well, she still has the tablet. So we need to find her before the police do."

✦ ✝ ✡

Still cruising in the right lane behind the Honda SUV, Cam answered the call from Rivka. Hand-held, not speaker. "I'm still at the police station." He hated lying to her, but, well, she sort of had it coming. "The detective was tied up."

"Apparently, Mountain Dew Momma is on the run. Double-crossed Menachem."

"Really?"

"I'm guessing he's going to ask us to go after her. Or ask me, at least."

"You know, I think I'm done. Let the police handle it. Or Menachem. Time for me to go home." He paused. "We can talk about it more when I get back to the hotel."

That pretty much summed up things. Rivka would do what Menachem ordered, while Cam would try to do what was right. The two, it seemed, were rarely the same thing.

The Honda's right blinker flashed. Cam eased back, said goodbye to Rivka, and followed them off the highway exit ramp to an Exxon station with a Subway sandwich shop attached. The police and the Mossad were both in pursuit, and it would likely be hours before they stopped again. If Cam was going to pull this off, this was his chance.

The Honda came to a stop in the gas pump line, three cars deep. The Mountain Dew woman and one of the men stepped out, likely to get food or use the restroom. The driver waited, edging forward in the line. Cam saw his chance.

Circling around the pumps, Cam pulled his Cherokee to a stop next to a couple of parked trucks. "Wait here, girl," he said to Venus, locking the door. He jogged back to the pumps and spotted the Honda. The station was self-serve, but, pulling his hat low, Cam shuffled over and began to pump as if he was an employee. The Honda pulled forward.

"Fill her up." The driver handed Cam a credit card.

Cam began to edge away, then stopped. "Move it up a bit," he called.

As the Honda's engine restarted, Cam slid the windshield squeegee under the rear tire. The vehicle rolled. "Shit," he yelled, hopping forward. "You ran over my foot!"

The man opened his door and stepped out. "Damn. Sorry. I thought you were out of the way."

Cam rested an arm on the driver's shoulder. "I think you broke my toes." He leaned harder against his mark. "Help me over to that stool," he groaned, cursing.

Ten feet from the Honda, Cam pivoted, stuck out his foot and shoved the man in the back, sending him tumbling to the pavement. "Hey," he shouted.

Spinning, Cam took three quick strides and slid into the driver's seat of the still-running Honda. In a second he was in gear, racing toward his own SUV parked just ahead.

"Help," the man yelled, getting to his feet. "He's stealing my car!"

Cam screeched to a stop next to his Cherokee. Reaching into the backseat, he grabbed his laptop and clasped Venus' leash to her collar. As he opened the passenger side door of the Honda and let Venus jump in, he glanced back in time to see a man sprinting toward him. *Must be the other passenger.* Burly, but moving fast.

Cam scurried around the front of the Honda, reaching the driver's side just before his pursuer. He swung the door open and began to slide in, only to feel a strong hand grab him by the arm and yank him outward. *Shit.* Spinning, he ducked a wild punch and countered it with a short cross to the man's jaw, knocking him sideways. Looking up, he saw the first pursuer now racing over. He might fend off one, but not both. He needed to end this quickly.

Again he lunged for the Honda door. Again the man grabbed him, this time by the hair. And again Cam countered, this time throwing his elbow into the assailant's neck. Gasping, the burly man dropped to a knee.

For the third time, Cam leapt for the door. This time he made it inside, but as he did so the man rolled forward, seized the bottom of the door, and swung it closed, catching Cam's left hand inside the doorframe.

The pain crashed down on him, firing up his arm, almost causing him to black out. Screaming, he shoved the door open and yanked back his mangled hand. Barely able to see through tears of anguish, he put the car in drive and floored it, hoping to race away. Suddenly, one of the parked tractor-trailers pulled out. *Shit.* He had no choice but to slow, waiting for the lumbering truck to accelerate. Glancing in the rearview mirror, Cam gulped as the original driver gave chase, gaining, ready to grab at the rear bumper. Cam sped up and then, at the last second, slammed the brakes just as the man lunged, causing him to smash face first into the rear hatch. Venus offered a sharp bark at the sound of the thump as the man slumped to the ground.

Finally free of pursuers, Cam sped toward the highway on-ramp, fighting to fill his lungs. Driving with his knees, he unzipped his sweat-shirt, yanked the sleeve over his crushed, bleeding hand, and wrapped the fabric tight around his fingers. Biting back the pain, he elevated his hand, resting his elbow on the lip where the door and window met.

His fingers throbbed, the blood coursing through the wound. What he needed was ice and ibuprofen. Maybe x-rays and some stitches. What he had was an old sweatshirt.

For a mile, he continually checked the rearview mirror. Nothing in pursuit. Maybe he could risk a stop soon. In the meantime, he'd just have to tough it out. As his eyes lowered, he caught sight of the black tarp on the back seat. The corner of a blue stone peeked out at him, almost like a wink.

Amanda's voice. *Bloody well done, Cameron.*

"Yeah. Bloody is the operative word. And now we can add assault and carjacking to my list of felonies."

✧ ✟ ✡

Racing north on the interstate, Cam knew he didn't have much time. Presumably the Honda SUV he had commandeered had LoJack or other tracking technology. He was tempted—sorely so based on the throbbing in his hand—to take the next exit. But one exit beyond that brought him into Tennessee. And police would not cross a state line unless in hot pursuit. It would give him a few extra minutes.

Ten miles across the border, using his phone to guide him, he exited at the town of Erwin. There wasn't much to it, other than an auto body shop which rented U-Hauls. Not having keys to restart the push-button-ignition Honda, he left it idling within sight. He forced a smile at the young woman behind the counter, hiding his hand. "I'm kind of in a rush." He slid two fifty-dollar bills, a credit card, and his driver's license across the counter. "Any chance you can get me out of here in ten minutes with a U-Haul pickup truck with a full tank of gas? And also a bag of ice?"

She smiled back. "I don't see why not."

He pushed across another fifty. "And maybe don't put the paperwork on this through until tomorrow?"

He pulled around behind the building and waited, eyeing the street. Would the Mountain Dew woman and her sons risk calling the police, given that they were in receipt of stolen property? He shrugged. It made no sense to guess. Either the police would come roaring down the street or they wouldn't.

Fifteen long minutes later, the rental was ready. He bummed some Advil off the clerk with another smile, opened the gate of the Honda, backed the pickup against it, and, one-armed, wrestled the tarp-covered artifact from one vehicle to the other.

Twenty miles north, back on the interstate, he approached an intersection with Route 81. Going north, the major highway tracked the

Appalachian mountain range and would eventually bring him close to home. But he turned south instead. Home would have to wait.

✦ ✝ ✡

Cam drove west on Route 40 through Tennessee, into the setting sun. He expected to hit Memphis at twilight. Then he'd need to make a decision. Fortunately, he kept an emergency supply of insulin and syringes, along with a glucometer, in his laptop carry bag.

In Knoxville, two hours into his drive, he had withdrawn ten grand from his savings account at a Bank of America drive-thru and purchased a used Chevy Malibu sedan, taking title in the name of a trust he had set up years ago which was not traceable back to him. The car was not really his taste, but he wanted something reliable which would blend in. And he opted for a sedan rather than an SUV because of the trunk. If he happened to get pulled over by the police, he didn't want the tablet to be visible in any way. After transferring the artifact to his new car, he had left the U-Haul pickup in the used car lot, telling them he'd return for it later. He sighed. This adventure was starting to cost him. Not that it would matter if the world came to an end.

For now, ignoring the pain in his hand, he let his mind work—filtering, processing, making connections, drawing conclusions.

One thing was certain: At some point, Rivka and Menachem would figure out that he had the Tables of Testimony. And they'd come after him.

Something he had read kept popping into his head. The ancient writers, in discussing the various Pillars of Enoch legends, had all agreed on one thing: The population would perish by flood and fire. This was remarkably similar to the Hopi Blue Star prophecy. He thought of all the other ways to destroy humankind—starvation, disease, earthquake, meteorite strike, war, drought, freeze. None of these was mentioned. Yet flood and fire kept repeating themselves.

His phone rang. Rivka, for the fourth time. He didn't answer, but called her back—he owed her that much—using a prepaid cell phone he had purchased along with other supplies at a Walgreens drive-thru in

Knoxville. No reason to risk the Mossad or FBI tracking his cell calls. To be extra-careful his texts wouldn't be traced, he had downloaded an app to his phone which cloaked his GPS location.

"You're tough to reach," she said.

"Sorry. I've been … busy."

"I bet you have. Were you successful?"

"Yes."

"Good. I'm glad."

"Are you coming after me?"

"What do you think?"

He chuckled. "I think I was smart to get a head start."

"By the way, they arrested the Mountain Dew lady. She tried to downplay the carjacking, but that just made it look like she was trying to hide something. They searched her hotel room, found some incriminating evidence."

"Great. I wasn't sure the police took me seriously."

"They didn't. But a call from the FBI got their attention."

"Let me guess. Menachem pulled some strings. Trying to get the police to chase down the artifact for him."

"Bingo. And it worked. But you—and the artifact—were already gone, like smoke in the wind."

"Is he mad at you?"

"How can he be? This is all his fault. He played it too cute. Played *me* too cute. Turns out he was there, at the tunnel exit, when they stole the artifact from me. He could have stopped them. But the Mountain Dew lady gave him a chance to keep the Mossad's involvement secret. His plan was to give the Masons a fake tablet, a fake block of inscribed lapis lazuli. He figured they wouldn't notice the difference, at least not until he had whisked the real one back to Israel. Ideally, his plan was to steal the tablet with nobody realizing it was gone. That way Israel wouldn't be under pressure to share its secrets with the world. And if someone did realize it was a fake, Menachem could just blame it on the Mountain Dew lady. As far as anyone knew, the Mossad had nothing to do with any of it."

"Good plan. Classic Mossad. Keep the Cosmic Equations for Israel."

"Until Mountain Dew lady got greedy. Even that would have been fine, but then you came along."

"That's me, always the turd in the punchbowl."

"Not your fault. Like I said, Menachem played it too cute. In a way, I'm actually glad it blew up in his face. Maybe next time he'll be straight with me."

"I seriously doubt that, Rivka."

Cam mulled over what she had just told him. "One thing I don't get. Obviously the Mossad had its eye on this artifact for a while. Why rush? Why send you in so quickly?"

"The Masons were getting nervous after Paris' murder. Menachem was worried they were going to move it. And then the Blue Star prophecy added to that—why leave the artifact in the flood zone? Once we learned from you exactly where it was, he decided it was time to go in. Before that, we would have just been flailing around inside the lodge."

"Glad I could be of use," he said with a sniff.

She ignored his acerbity. "Hey, I'm watching the sunset." Her voice softened. "Thinking of you, missing you." She sighed. "Can you see it?"

He laughed. "If I could, I sure wouldn't admit to it." She didn't need any clues as to where he might be.

"Well, can't blame a girl for trying."

He paused. "Hey, one rule."

"What?"

"Leave Astarte out of this, okay?"

"Yes, Cameron. Of course."

"Thanks. Otherwise, give it your best shot."

"Loser buys dinner when it's all over?"

He blinked. "Assuming we're both still alive, sure. I'd like that."

"Goodbye, Cameron. And I really do miss you."

After hanging up with Rivka, Cam phoned Astarte with the prepaid cell phone to give her an update. "Remember how I was trying to play things safe? Well, I just stole a priceless, sacred artifact from the Mossad."

"Did you ever consider just taking up golf or something?"

He laughed. "I bashed my hand pretty good. I couldn't even hold a club."

"Seriously, what are you going to do with the artifact?"

"Not sure yet. I have a couple of ideas I'm working on." He described the Tables of Testimony to her. "It seems to me, it belongs to everyone, right? I mean, from what I read, it's basically a reboot for humankind after things like the Blue Star explosion. Scientific equations, formulas, stuff like that."

"Maybe give it to the United Nations?"

"That's one possibility. But too bad Manhattan is basically at sea level. Like I said, I'm still mulling it over."

"A museum?"

"Another good suggestion." He shifted. His back was starting to stiffen from sitting corkscrewed in his seat so he could keep his hand elevated. "Listen, you might want to lay low for a couple of days." He trusted Rivka, but not Menachem. "Maybe go visit Matthias' family or something."

"You think they might use me to get to you?"

"Yes."

"Okay. The semester is just starting, so I won't be missing much. I can attend class on-line."

"Great. Be safe. Love you."

Now just over an hour east of Memphis, Cam found an old rock-and-roll station, turned the volume up, and let the music drown out the trauma of his day. It was not the time for planning. It was the time for big-picture thinking.

He tackled the biggest question of all first: Who inscribed the Tables of Testimony? The first possibility, of course, was that they were written by the Finger of God and given to Moses, as the Book of Exodus recounted. The problem with this option was that the Pillars of Enoch were part of the Great Flood narrative, which predated Moses and the events of the Book of Exodus by many centuries. In other words, the Tables of Testimony—which were secreted within the Pillars—were already in existence by the time Moses came along. A second possibility was that the tablet had been inscribed by some advanced, pre-Flood culture, intended to be a guide for the survivors of a future calamity. This, of course, was consistent with the legends surrounding the Pillars of Enoch. One possibility was that the ancient, advanced culture was Atlantis. A third possibility was that ancient aliens had visited earth and shared their advanced technology. Finally, it was possible that alchemists and scientists living in a post-Flood world had carved the tablet as a way to record and maintain accumulated scientific knowledge.

He went round and round on this question for half an hour, in the end leaning toward the Pillars of Enoch option: Some advanced society, possibly Atlantis, existed in pre-Flood days, and this society—expecting some cataclysm—inscribed the Tables of Testimony for the benefit of future generations. Somehow, it found its way into the possession of the ancient Israelites; perhaps Moses and his gang had spirited it out of Egypt much as Cam had stolen it from the Freemasons and the Mossad.

But this was just an inkling. He could be wrong. And then, as the refrain from R.E.M.'s, "It's the End of the World As We Know It," blasted, it hit him: *It didn't matter*. Whoever carved it—be it God or aliens or an advanced culture or ancient scientists—was a lot smarter than Cam was. They had decided that this knowledge was essential, crucial to mankind's survival, especially after a calamity. Who was Cam, a lawyer-turned-historian, to argue? Hell, other than the Fibonacci spiral, he didn't even know what was on the tablet. And, if he did, he probably wouldn't understand most of it.

He turned the music down. Did reaching this conclusion help him determine his next step? It did insofar as it confirmed his gut feeling that the artifact belonged to humankind in general, not one specific group. Which meant he wasn't going to turn around and hand it over to Menachem.

But he knew that already.

Night fell as Cam crossed the Mississippi River west of Memphis, the 'M' shape—for Memphis—of the Hernando de Soto Bridge impressively illuminated as a kind of urban art.

On the other side, a text dinged. Shelby, asking him to call her.

"Hello, stranger," he said by way of greeting.

"Hi, Cam. I'm sorry I never made it down to Asheville. It's not so easy to sneak down. Are you still there?"

He hesitated. "Yes." He didn't know who he could trust.

"Anyway, I know this is going to sound strange." She paused. "But is Br—, I mean Lenny, okay?"

"What do you mean?"

"He's been acting weird. Very quiet. Secretive. I can usually tell when he's up to something."

Cam didn't know if, or how, Lenny might be involved in the Tables of Testimony theft. But when it came to Lenny, nothing would surprise Cam. He played dumb. "Last I saw him was yesterday. He seemed normal." Except for the small matter of being drugged by Rivka. "What do you mean by secretive?"

"Well, for example, he put his property up for sale. Totally out of the blue. He loved that house. I'm guessing he showed it to you?"

"No."

"Really? It's his pride and joy. High in the hills, with a whole underground living area. Lots of security, of course. And very isolated." As if thinking aloud, she added, "It's almost like he's going on the run again."

Cam blinked. "He didn't mention anything to me. Sorry."

After hanging up, Cam let his thoughts drift. What had Lenny said, about his gallery partner being a former Masonic lodge Master? And having dementia? Had Lenny somehow learned about the Tables of Testimony? And decided to make a play for them? Alternatively, what was he doing at Astarte's lecture? Under truth serum, he said something about chaos creating opportunity. But Rivka hadn't asked him if he himself had created the chaos. Lenny was a master of the real estate play. Had he been manipulating Astarte and the Native American community as a way to cash in on his mountain compound? Cam shook his head. It sure was a happy coincidence that Lenny's compound happened to boast the two attributes—elevation and underground living—essential to surviving the Blue Star explosion. But Cam didn't believe in coincidences, happy or otherwise.

Twenty miles into Arkansas, he pulled onto the shoulder and found the name of a real estate broker in Asheville. Back on the highway, he dialed. "Hi. I'm looking for a property in the mountains around Asheville. Something with underground living."

"You saw the news, huh?"

"Yes. I'm willing to spend for it."

"Well, a compound just came on the market yesterday. Very high, very secluded, with a large underground complex. Asking price is just over five million. But I should tell you, there's already offers coming in."

Cam hung up. Of course there was.

He didn't even put his phone down. He took a deep breath and made another call. "Astarte, honey, we need to talk."

Astarte paced her dorm room, ranting.

"Easy," said Matthias. "You don't know for sure."

"Not for sure, but think about it. This woman Soohu shows up out of the blue with this whole world-is-ending story. Says nobody will listen to her. But of course I do. When we ask the Hopi about her, they don't know anything. Supposedly, she's part of some splinter group. We take her word for the Blue Star prophecy, and on the science, but my dad's buddy says the blue glow isn't really expanding at all. Then a known scam artist, who was at my lecture, makes, like, a three million dollar profit two days after my lecture. After I get everyone all riled up to run for the hills."

Matthias smiled. "When you put it like that…"

"Argh! I can't believe how stupid I've been."

"Astarte, come on, this is good news. Maybe the world's not going to come to an end after all."

She let out a long breath. "Of course. You're right. It *is* good news. I just feel like a fool. I believed the whole story."

"Most of the story happens to be true. The Blue Star prophecy is real."

"Right. The prophecy is real. Kachina is real. But Soohu is fake."

"Fake?"

"Yes, fake. I don't know. Maybe an actress. Or maybe really Hopi, but hired by the con man. Her research is definitely fake."

He put out his hand. "Slow down. We don't know that. Even your dad's friend said he saw a blue glow."

"Yes. A small one. So maybe there'll be a small explosion." She shook her head. "If you happen to live in the middle of the Milky Way, you're in trouble. For the rest of us, who knows?"

✦ ✝ ✡

Rivka began carefully to fold Cameron's clothes and personal items and set them in his overnight bag. As far as she could tell, the only thing he took with him when he left was his laptop. At least that meant he hadn't planned on leaving. On leaving *her*.

She looked around. The contents of the room said a lot about the man she had come to feel so much affection for. A picture of his daughter on the end table next to the bed. A five-dollar bill—his daily tip for the chambermaid—tucked under the desk lamp. A pair of running shoes, a nod to his commitment to fitness. The fact that he had rehung his wet towel over the door rather than expect a fresh one every morning. A bag of dog treats for Venus. A refrigerator magnet he had purchased for his mother, who collected them. A book on the history of religion. They testified to a man committed to his family, a man of compassion and intellect and generous spirit.

With a long sigh, she finished packing. She closed the bag, hoisted it off the bed, and carried it down to the front desk. "Cameron had an emergency," she said, "so we'll be checking out. Can you see that this bag gets shipped to his home address? You can add the cost to the room tab."

Carrying her own bag, she exited the hotel, shoulders slumped. A cold wind buffeted her. She could have stayed in the room—Menachem had asked her to stick around in Asheville for another couple of days.

But why torture herself with memories and recollections? The Cameron chapter in her life was probably over. It struck her that it had been one of the few joyful chapters in the dreary book which had become her life.

⬦ ✚ ✡

Cam was tempted to take the next exit, reverse course, and drive the five hundred miles back to Asheville. But Lenny would likely be long gone, on his way to his next scam. Cam had called Shelby back, asked what she knew. Nothing, of course. But, she conceded, the ploy was classic Lenny, just the kind of thing he would come up with. Elaborate and convoluted, but also effective. And, of course, with a monster payday.

Cam cursed. He had Lenny under truth serum and still got fleeced. They had asked Lenny about the Lincoln painting being real or fake but never thought to ask anything about the Blue Star prophecy. Why would they? It had nothing to do with Lenny. Except that it did. The painting was just a way to get Cam to come to Asheville. He, in turn, was just bait to get Astarte to fly in and give her presentation, a presentation sure to send mountain real estate values, especially properties with underground living areas, skyrocketing. She could have spoken at any of a half dozen reservations around the country, but only one gave her the chance to spend time with her dad. Cam had to admit, it was a subtle but effective play.

So, what next?

Here he was, driving one-handed across the heartland of the country with an ancient, sacred artifact in his trunk and a well-behaved but antsy Labrador in the back seat. And he needed a bathroom.

As he approached Little Rock, his cell phone rang again. *Lenny.* Today was full of surprises.

He reached to answer but stopped at the sound of Amanda's voice.

Why bother?

"What do you mean?"

He's only calling because Shelby told him he had to. He'll make up some excuse, ask for forgiveness, explain how nobody really was hurt in all of this.

"Tell that to my hand. But I see your point."

So why give him the satisfaction? Why waste even a minute listening to him?

With a smile, Cam reached out and pushed the red 'end call' button. It didn't really change anything. But it made him feel a little better at a time when there was not much joy in his life.

"So," he continued, "you haven't weighed in on all this yet."

What's to say? I agree with you. It looks like Lenny puppeteered the whole thing. I'm not sure why he needed to bother with the whole Lincoln's mother charade, but whatever. He probably even paid to get that editorial printed in the newspaper, just to create a little extra demand.

"Supply and demand. All that mountain land, which nobody really wanted, suddenly becomes Boardwalk and Park Place."

And Lenny already owns them.

"I'm just sorry Astarte got caught up in it."

Cam waited, but Amanda didn't have anything to say in response to that.

CHAPTER 12

Cam awoke in the front seat of the Chevy to the sound of Venus growling. Even before he sat up and blinked away the sleep, his hand barked in pain. He tried to ignore it. The rest area parking lot was well lit, even at four in the morning; Cam spotted a couple of sketchy guys shuffling his way. He had no desire to make new friends. Hitting the ignition button, he put the car in drive and accelerated away.

He had driven last night until midnight, until his eyes grew heavy and his mind dull. Still heading west. In the end, it was the only destination which made any sense.

Now back on the highway, just east of Oklahoma City, he rubbed Venus' neck. "We'll stop soon, grab some breakfast, let you walk," he said.

A text dinged. Lenny. *We really need to talk.*

Cam ignored it. "Fuck him."

Yawning in the pre-dawn darkness, he passed a billboard advertising an all-night truck stop ten miles ahead. He wanted a shower, a doctor to look at his hand, and a hot meal. He'd have to settle for a wet napkin, more Advil, and a couple of breakfast sandwiches from a canteen truck. He couldn't risk leaving the artifact alone in a parking lot. Hell, he couldn't even risk pulling off to the side of the road and removing the tarp to examine it.

As he drove, something Amanda said last night continued to echo in his head. She had asked why Lenny needed to bother with the Lincoln's mother charade. Was it truly a charade? If so, what purpose did it serve? If not, how did it fit into Lenny's play? Cam didn't doubt that Lenny really had been beaten up by the painting's owners—there was no way to fake those injuries. But if Lenny was running a multi-million-dollar real estate scam, why bother with the painting? Sure, he may have needed it to lure Cam down to Asheville. But, after that, why take the beating? It made no sense.

In other words, there was one piece of the puzzle which didn't seem to fit.

❖ ✠ ✡

Cam continued to follow Interstate 40 west, his fingers swollen and stiff. He guessed he had at least a few broken bones, but thankfully the bleeding had stopped and none of the fractured bones had punctured the skin. By mid-morning, he approached Amarillo, Texas, in the notch of the state south of the Oklahoma panhandle. Cam knew the city was famous for its steaks. Not that he could hold a steak knife. He settled for two burgers—one for him, one for Venus—at a Wendy's.

Oddly, he also felt inclined to offer some kind of sustenance to the blue tablet, as if it were a living entity which required nurturing and care. And it surely deserved a better fate than being wrapped in an industrial tarp and shoved into the dark trunk of an old Chevy. This was, after all, the inscription which might save humankind.

In its earlier days, it was probably carried in a litter, perhaps within the Ark of the Covenant or similar vestibule by devoted members of a priestly family. Later, it would have been lovingly transported across Europe in a caravan, escorted by an armed entourage. Even during its long journey across the Atlantic, it likely would have occupied a place of honor, perhaps in the captain's berth. And, of course, it had rested inside a golden display case in a sacred pillar in the Masonic temple for the past hundred years.

Now, it was being jostled in a trunk, rubbing against a spare tire and the remains of some old bark mulch, being transported by someone with no training in ritual or sacrament. Cam slowed and moved to the right lane, leaving plenty of room between himself and the car ahead.

His mind continued to wander. What stories the tablet could tell. What things it had witnessed. How it had been loved, cherished, treasured. How many lives had it saved over the millennia? How many people had died protecting it or, alternatively, trying to acquire it? And now, here he was, unceremoniously dragging it across the nation's heartland. He felt weighed down, almost paralyzed by the responsibility. What in the past had been the responsibility of an entire family of priests now had become his burden alone...

Amanda interrupted his musings. *Let's not get carried away here. It's a blue rock. An important one, yes. But just a rock.*

He chuckled. "Fair point."

Let's focus on things we can control. Did you figure out why that puzzle piece doesn't fit?

"No. Did you?"

You know that's not how this works.

He sighed. "In law school, I had a really good Evidence class professor. He used to say that you need to give value to every piece of evidence. If any piece didn't fit your case theory, then the theory was probably wrong or incomplete."

Okay. So maybe you're wrong.

"About what?"

Could be something minor you're overlooking. Or, well, it could be that you're wrong about bloody everything.

He rubbed his face with his sleeve. "Great. Thanks."

He phoned Astarte. "Everything okay?" he asked.

"If you mean, has the Mossad come to kidnap me, the answer is everything is okay. We are someplace safe. If you mean, do I feel any better about what an idiot I've been, the answer is no, everything is definitely not okay."

"They fooled us both."

"No. They fooled me, and then you went along with it." She sighed. "Anyway, where are you?"

"I'd rather not say. Just in case."

"Probably a good idea. Glad you're being careful."

"Not sure it matters. No matter what I end up doing with this artifact, I'm going to be pissing someone off."

He continued west, the land flat and barren in all directions. Hours later, approaching Albuquerque, the foothills of the Rockies rose to break up the horizon. He stopped for lunch and gas, then, as he approached the Arizona border, exited Interstate 40 and continued on a state highway, Route 264. Yawning, he checked the time. He didn't want to do this in the dark. He plugged an address into the car's GPS. Almost four hours still to go. It would be close.

⚒ ✞ ✡

Cam turned off the flat, straight, two-lane highway he had been on for the better part of twenty minutes. In the middle of miles of nothingness, a cluster of a dozen simple ranch homes and trailers sat grouped among the tumbleweeds on either side of a gravel road spurring off the highway. No farmland, no livestock, no trees. It was as if someone had relegated the residents to the most undesirable land.

He parked in front of number four, a beige ranch, surprised to see a blue sedan in the dirt driveway. From what Astarte told him, Soohu didn't own a car. But, of course, Soohu may not even really be Soohu. He had driven 1,800 miles to answer that very question.

Cam stepped from his car in the day's fading light and walked tentatively up the drive. The front screen door of the ranch house opened outward. A moth fluttered around the light mounted next to the door. A tall man stepped out, head down. He looked up. "Hello, Cam."

Cam froze. "Lenny?" he mumbled, shocked. *What the—?* He didn't know what else to say.

"Like I said, we need to talk."

The door swung open again. A short, stocky, middle-aged woman with warm eyes and leathery skin stepped forward. "Please, Mr. Thorne, come in. Your daughter offered me kind hospitality. Doing the same for you is the least I can do."

Cam still hadn't moved. What was going on here? He had suspected that Lenny and Soohu knew each other, but hadn't expected them to be so brazen about it. He stalled for time. "You're the last person I expected to see," he said to Lenny.

"When you wouldn't take my call, I jumped on a plane."

"How'd you know where I was going?"

Lenny shrugged. His eyes were still blackened, his nose disfigured. "I figured you connected the dots and made the assumption that this whole thing was a real estate play by me. But you couldn't be sure. You had to come out and confront Soohu for yourself." He pursed his lips. "It's what I would have done."

"Good guess. But I'm not buying that you're here just because. Obviously, you've been working together."

Soohu shook her head. "I don't know what's going on with you two. But Mr. Null and I just met an hour ago."

Lenny added, "Soohu wasn't hard to track down. Astarte used her name in her lecture."

Cam blinked. "Why should I believe you?"

Lenny held out his arms. "Look. I'm good, but I'm not *that* good. I can't produce a blue glow in the Milky Way. This cosmic explosion is real. I just happened to get lucky on the real estate. I'm an art thief on the run. And a loner. You can't be surprised I ended up in the mountains with an underground bunker."

"And you flew across the country just to tell me that."

Lenny shook his head. "No. I flew out here to convince you the prophecy is real. You need to believe me. Astarte needs to keep lecturing." He stepped forward. "Look, I'm an SOB, but I'm not a killer. I don't want millions of deaths on my conscience."

"I'm supposed to believe that Astarte and I being in Asheville, where you happen to own mountain property with an underground bunker, is just a coincidence?"

He held Cam's eyes. "It wasn't a coincidence. You're right, I was playing you. My real target was the Masonic treasure, which you now have. I was trying to put it into play. I knew the lodge had something valuable, based on what my partner Boyd kept babbling about. And I had my own family stories. My last name is Portuguese." Cam nodded. *Arrujo*. Bruce/Lenny continued. "My grandfather's family was from this area. I'm pretty sure he was Melungeon. Which means *I'm* Melungeon."

Now, finally, some truth. But it was a different truth than Cam expected.

Lenny continued. "He moved up to Boston after World War II. But we used to come back to Appalachia in the summers. Lots of my relatives are Freemasons."

"I guess I shouldn't be surprised."

"Anyway," Lenny continued. "I'm in hiding, so I can't exactly visit my relatives and ask about Masonic treasures. I needed someone to shake this Masonic treasure loose, whatever it was."

"Me."

"Yup. When I saw the painting, I knew that would lure you down. I didn't show it to you the first day because I wanted to keep you in Asheville as long as I could, give you time to get involved in the Melungeon mystery."

"So the painting's legit?"

Lenny pointed at his face. "I think my nose proves it."

"I'd take a broken nose for three million bucks."

"I don't see how one has anything to do with the other. Like I said, the real estate play just dropped into my lap. What was I supposed to do, walk away?"

"Um, yes."

"Why? It wouldn't have changed anything. Some billionaire overpaid for a mountain retreat. Who cares?"

"Well, for one thing, selling wasn't too smart, if you ask me. Where you going to live when the Blue Star explodes?"

"Here."

"Here?"

"Yes. With the Hopi, in the cliff dwellings. Soohu and I were just talking about it."

"And why in the world would they let you stay with them?"

"Because I'm going to give them the three million dollars." He waited until Cam met his eyes. "To bring in experts from around the world to study and decipher the Tables of Testimony."

Cam nodded. Shelby had told him that, with Lenny, it wasn't about the money itself. It was only about winning the Monopoly game.

Soohu spoke up. "Our legends tell us about a carved stone like this. It contains the secrets of the universe." She lifted her chin. "We are hopeful it will allow us to predict the upcoming calamity."

Cam glanced back at his car. "You guys realize there's one thing missing in your plan, right?"

Lenny offered a rare smile. "An hour ago, it was missing. Not anymore."

◆ ✚ ✡

Cam had agreed to come into the house, provided he had a seat by the kitchen window from which he could see the Chevy, which he had moved up next to the ranch. Soohu had happily welcomed Venus, who pranced around the kitchen, joyous at being out of the car.

After administering first aid to Cam's hand, Soohu served baked beans and cornbread. She sensed the need to carry the conversation, Lenny being naturally taciturn and Cam still not sure he trusted the con artist. After dinner, she stood. "Come. Outside. I want to show you something."

She led them to a shed behind the ranch, not far from where Cam had parked. Using a crank mounted on the side of the home connected to a cable running to the top of the shed, she raised the shed's hinged roof. Inside, she removed a plastic cover to reveal what looked to be a powerful telescope sitting on a tripod. She hit the power button on a desktop computer, causing the monitor to display the night sky. "You can see, Mr. Thorne, that I am not a woman of wealth. This telescope set-up is worth almost as much as my home. I hope this convinces you of my sincerity."

Cam nodded. Even if they had suspected Cam would drive out to confront Soohu, there was no way to get a computerized telescope hooked up and running so quickly.

"It is here that I first noticed the blue glow," she said. "I check it every night."

"My friend is an astronomer. He says the glow is not growing," Cam replied.

"Yes. I see the same thing. A promising sign. But I am not convinced we are out of danger yet. Like a volcano or an earthquake, there are often dormant periods before a cataclysm. Kachina is as unpredictable as she is deadly."

Cam stepped out of the shed and stared up at the stars. He breathed in the desert air, listened to the distant wail of a coyote. He was skeptical that the Cosmic Equations on the Tables of Testimony would be of use in predicting the cycles of the Blue Star. It was possible, but, while many things in nature followed a pattern, some were random. This felt like one of them.

Yet that's not why he drove 1,800 miles to meet Soohu. Yes, he wanted to confront her and determine definitively if Lenny had played him. But it was more than that. Deep down, he sensed there was a chance that Lenny had *not* played him and that the Hopi elder really was trying to save humankind.

He wandered back into the shed just as Soohu, dwarfed by her telescope, finished positioning the instrument to display the Blue Star glow on the computer monitor. "Any bigger?" he asked.

"No," she replied with a sigh of relief. "The same."

He took a deep breath. "Let's say this does hit. Realistically, what are the chances for survival?"

"As a race, high. But individually, very low. Only the people in the mountain shelters will have a chance. And the world that they will inherit will be vastly different than the one we live in. The Gobekli Tepe site in Turkey, which dates back to just after the cataclysmic event which ended the last Ice Age, about twelve thousand years ago, offers a crystal ball. The earliest carvings at the site were intricate and sophisticated, carved by skilled craftspeople who, apparently, survived the cataclysm. But, as the generations unfolded, the level of craftsmanship rapidly declined.

The artisans died. The tools wore out. Knowledge of how to perform metallurgy and make new tools was lost. Life became hard, too hard to bother with luxuries like art. Near the end, the carvings became almost childlike in their simplicity. Hopi legends tell us the same thing happened here in North America." She frowned. "I think we can expect the same thing again. People, generally, are not nearly as skilled as they were, say, at the time the Colonists arrived. Things we take for granted—such as electricity and clean water and a dependable food supply—will disappear."

Standing between the two men in the small shed, her eyes shifted from Cam to Lenny and back to Cam again. "Be truthful. What skills do either of you possess that would be of use in a post-cataclysmic world? Can you make weapons to hunt? Can you grow your own food? Can you produce electricity? And, if so, can you design a motor that runs off it?"

They both shook their heads.

"Within a generation or two," she continued, "it is quite possible life will revert back to a hunter-gatherer level of sophistication. We will, in essence, need to start over again."

"Just like after the Flood," Cam whispered, feeling guilty for thinking ill of the tribal elder.

Soohu nodded. "That's why you brought the stone to us." Reaching out and touching Cam's arm, she continued. "Or, perhaps you don't even know why you brought it to us. But, at an instinctive level, you were drawn here. You sensed we would need it. Humankind would need it. Not now, perhaps. But someday."

Cam nodded. He didn't know if what she said was accurate. He had driven to Arizona for a multitude of reasons. But he had, indeed, felt drawn.

"So you'll take the stone, bring it up to the cave dwellings?" he asked. That's where it belonged. In the future, it would allow humankind to hit the reset button.

She nodded. "Just as we have done with other similar carvings in the past. It is my understanding this tablet has been guarded by the Old Testament priestly families—the descendants of Aaron—for thousands of years."

Cam nodded. "Yes. First in Jerusalem, then in Europe, then here. According to ancient legend, the stone at one point was hidden in something called the Pillars of Enoch. That's how it survived the Great Flood."

She folded her hands over her chest and bowed her head. "We have no such pillars, only secure cave dwellings. But another wave of flood and fire is imminent. It is our sacred duty to do everything we can to ensure that this ancient tablet—what you call the Tables of Testimony— survives this calamity as it has survived the previous ones."

CHAPTER 13

Cam sat alone at a table in the rear of the Sea Level restaurant in downtown Newburyport, watching chunks of ice float down the Merrimac River as dusk closed in on a warmish January afternoon. He picked at his fried clams. A week had passed since he drove cross-country to deliver the Tables of Testimony to the Hopi tribe for safekeeping. In that time, nothing of any substance had occurred, no loose ends had been tied.

He knew that couldn't last. The Mossad was not a fan of loose ends.

The scraping of a chair across the floor deck announced an arrival. He didn't need to turn his eyes away from the river to guess who it was. "Hello, Rivka."

She stood behind the chair. "I thought I might find you here." In fact, their first real date had been at an outdoor table only a few feet away. "May I sit?"

"Do I need to fear for my safety?"

"Don't be silly. If we wanted to harm you, it would have been done by now."

He made a gesture toward the seat. "You're not pissed I stole the tablet?"

"Me? No. Menachem, yes." As she sat, her clean, floral scent wafted over him. "But he's always pissed about something. And even he doesn't blame you. You beat us fair and square."

Cam shook his head. "It's not a game. We're trying to save humankind."

She touched his arm. "I know." She swallowed. "I'd like to think we, my country, would have done the right thing with the artifact if we had succeeded in taking it." After a shrug, she continued. "But I don't know that for certain. In the end, I think this is the best outcome." She smiled sadly. "Not for me. But for society."

"Why not for you?"

"Because you feel like I betrayed you."

"You did."

She nodded. "I told you from the beginning. I will put nothing over my loyalty to Israel. Even my own happiness."

Still looking at the river, he nodded. "I understand." Neither spoke for a few seconds. "Back to Menachem," Cam said. "Will he go after the tablet?"

"I don't think so. It's one thing to send a cat burglar into a Masonic lodge at night. But I assume whoever has the tablet is keeping it in a secure location. I can't see the Mossad violating U.S. sovereignty with an attack force. We get billions of dollars in aid from America every year, not to mention military support. As important as the Tables of Testimony is, I don't see us risking an international incident and putting all that in jeopardy."

Cam nodded. "I agree." He sat back and turned up his palms. "So, what happens next?"

"I have another assignment, in South America. I leave in four days." She leaned closer. "I thought, maybe, we could spend some time together. In Asheville, you invited me to come visit, remember?"

It seemed like a lifetime ago. "I do. That was right before you chose loyalty to Israel over loyalty to me."

"When there is that choice to make, that's the way it will always go, Cameron. But, here, now, there is no conflict." She spread her arms. "There's just us."

"It's more complicated than that."

"Only if you let it be." Her dark eyes held his. "If you accept that I will put you before anything in my life except my country, it is pretty simple."

Cam blinked. *Before anything in my life except my country.* It may not be the whole loaf, but it was pretty damn close. More, in fact, than Cam was ready to offer in return—Astarte would always come first in his life, not to mention that Amanda still possessed a part of his heart which would forever be closed to other women.

Before he could reply, Rivka pressed on. "You make me happy Cameron. Even more than that, you bring out the best in me. You can kick me out of your life, but I'm not going without a fight."

"You were ready to get on a plane back to Israel." He paused. "Without a fight, I might add."

"Yes. But not permanently. Once the mission was over, of course I would have returned."

He nodded. He knew he could never fully trust her given her allegiance to her job—her words, in addition to her actions, had made that clear. But, as she had pointed out, it was a simple question: Did he enjoy her company? Was his life richer with her in it? At this point in his life, that was enough.

"Okay," he said. "Since you've come all this way, and because you've made it clear you're not leaving..." He paused to smile. "I supposed it would be best to order a glass of wine." He motioned to the waitress.

Rivka arched an eyebrow. "May I order one also, or is it just for you?"

With a sigh and a chuckle, he reached over and took her hand. "Venus will be happy to see you."

"How did you get her home?"

"I couldn't see putting her on a plane, so we drove back. Just arrived yesterday. I hope never to be in a car again."

"Notice I didn't ask *where* you drove back from."

"Notice I didn't tell you."

"I can guess. Assuming I'm right, it was the right decision."

"There are still some loose ends. With us, I mean, not with my decision."

"I'll tie them up for you if I can," she said. "I owe you that much, at least."

The waitress brought their drinks. Cam held up his glass to toast, but did not offer any words. He and Rivka seemed often to be in this situation, being pulled apart and then having to figure out if and how best to come back together.

"I'm wondering about the Nancy Hanks Lincoln painting," Cam said. "Bruce—or I should say, Lenny—insists it's authentic. But I'm not so sure. He said so under truth serum, but he himself could be wrong."

"Why are you suspicious?"

"It's all just too convenient, me being in Asheville at the same time Menachem was trying to steal a Templar-related artifact."

She sipped her wine and stared out at the river. Nodding, she turned back. "I think you're right to be suspicious. It didn't occur to me at the time, but Menachem encouraged me to go spend time with you in North Carolina. I don't know for certain, but it would make sense that he planted that painting, hoping Lenny would reach out to you for help. Apparently, he wanted both of us in Asheville."

"What about those guys who beat up Lenny, supposedly from the family trying to get the painting back?"

"That could have been Menachem also, trying to make it look good. You know, make Lenny believe the painting was valuable."

"But you don't know for certain."

She shook her head. "I could ask if you want."

"Would you believe the answer?"

She laughed lightly. "No."

"Me neither. But it's important. If the painting is authentic, then one of our greatest presidents was part Black and part Jewish."

"You know, even if Menachem was behind the painting, it still could be authentic."

Cam chewed his lip. "You're right. The Nancy Hanks DNA stands on its own, without the painting. And it shows pretty clearly that she was Melungeon."

"Well, there you have it. The painting might not matter. You've got science."

"Belt and suspenders. It'd be nice to have both."

"Where's the painting now?"

"Lenny has it still. He's going to sell it and use the proceeds to help people survive the calamity."

"Sounds like he found religion."

Cam sniffed. "Don't be fooled. He just wants to save humankind so there'll still be people around for him to scam."

"I thought you were going to tell me his girlfriend made him do it."

"That too. In fact, that was probably his major motivation. Shelby was pretty pissed when she learned he was scamming me."

"Which, to be fair, he really wasn't." Rivka shifted. "Speaking of finding religion, what are we going to do about this whole end of the world thing?" She smiled. "Other than order more wine."

He let out a long breath. "Honestly, I don't know. My friend the astronomer was able to convince some government types to take this seriously. So that's good news. But if the Blue Star starts expanding, I'm not sure there's much we can do." He pointed toward the southern sky. "On dark nights, near dawn, I can see the Milky Way. I keep looking for a blue glow in the center. Sometimes my eyes play tricks on me. It's terrifying."

She touched his hand. "It puts the whole Lincoln background question into perspective. Doesn't matter what race or ethnicity you are if the floods and fire come."

He sat up. "You said you'd help me tie up loose ends. I know you took pictures of the Tables of Testimony inscription. What did it say?"

"You saw the Fibonacci spiral, right? And there were some other formulas and equations and a script I didn't recognize. They actually took my phone and erased the images." She shrugged. "I'm afraid I'm not much help."

"I did more research on the Fibonacci sequence," Cam said. "It goes back at least to 400 BC, in India."

"If it was on the Tables of Testimony, it goes back a lot further than that. Back before the Great Flood."

Cam started to reply, then caught himself. What he wanted to say was: "One of the things the Hopi are thinking of doing is building a modernized version of the Pillars of Enoch to keep the tablet in. Soohu said that it worked during the last Flood, so why not try it again. Also, many of the Hopi are Christian now. So it helps to blend the old legends with the Bible. Makes them more believable."

But he didn't want to give the tablet's location away. Instead, he said, "The people who have the tablet are taking steps to make sure it survives any cosmic explosion. Survives the *next* flood."

"Good." She chewed her lip. "But hopefully it won't ever come to that. Like I told you, we have these doomsday predictions all the time in Israel. Not to mention that we are under constant attack, with half the Arab world vowing to destroy us and the other half cheering them on. As a child, I was awakened in the middle of the night literally hundreds of times by air-raid sirens. And we constantly live in the dark shadow of the Holocaust. It's amazing we aren't all traumatized." She shrugged. "You just have to live your life. Otherwise, it can paralyze you."

Cam nodded. "Historically, we've had the opposite problem here. We're isolated, most Americans blissfully unaware of all the suffering in the world. We think we're immune from the planet's problems, though COVID and global warming have started to change that."

"Not knowing what tomorrow will bring can be liberating, in some ways." With a coy smile, she slowly ran her foot up his leg. "Like they say, *carpe diem*, seize the day. Eat, drink, laugh, dance. Make love." She paused. "You never know when it will be your last chance."

✧✚✡

Cam lay next to Rivka, listening to her soft, rhythmic breathing. He had no idea what time it was, nor did he care. Their lovemaking had been different than in Asheville. There, it had been first about exploration and learning about each other and then, later, about passion. This was more desperate. This was two people who thought they had lost each other searching for a way to reconnect.

Eyes still closed, she rolled into him. "That was nice," she purred.

"Like you said, seize the day."

"Well, you seized the night. What was that thing you did?"

"What thing?"

"You know. Where you start at my breasts, then move down, then around back, then to my mouth."

He smiled. "That, my dear, was the Fibonacci sequence."

She guffawed. "You really are a math geek!"

"If it's good enough to carve onto a sacred stone, it's good enough for me."

"So that's what we've been trying to preserve for future humankind?"

"Yup. That's the cosmic equation."

She kissed him. "Well, I suppose the universe did move a bit."

He lifted himself onto one elbow. "What you said earlier, about Israelis always living in fear of death. How do you do it? How do you get past the anxiety?"

"You don't get past it. You just get used to it. I remember getting braces as a kid. At first, I was constantly aware of them. Then, after a few weeks, I didn't think about them anymore. It's sort of the same thing. It moves to the back of your mind."

"I can't stop worrying about Astarte."

"Of course not. That's your job." She shifted. "But I asked my dad that once, when I joined the army. He had already lost one daughter. He said that, at some point, he came to realize how small our lives were. We're just a speck of sand in the universe, our lives spanning no more than a blink of an eye. We are nothing, really."

Cam began to interrupt. "That's depressing—"

"Wait, let me finish. Then he said that the one thing that added significance to our lives was that our souls would live on forever, nourished by the love we gave and the love we received. Our souls transcend space and time. Basically, love makes us immortal."

"And that made him stop worrying?"

"Not stop. But it gave him perspective. No matter what happened, his love for me and my love for him would be eternal." She smiled. "Same as you and Astarte." She lowered her voice. "And Amanda."

Cam contemplated her words. "When I was driving with the tablet, I thought about the people who carved it. Why had they done it? They had to know it wouldn't save themselves. At best, it would be helpful to some future generation, long after they were dead. Yet they did. And then other people preserved it, century after century."

"Same thing, I think. Love. They probably imagined it would be their children or grandchildren who would find it. Soohu is spreading the word out of love—she wants future generations to survive. Astarte is doing the same thing." Rivka shrugged. "In the end, that's all we can do. We are born, we love, and then we die."

Cam nodded. "That helps a bit, thanks." Rolling over, he grabbed his phone. "I want to find something I read once." A few seconds passed. "Here it is. Listen to this, from Marc Chagall, the painter." He read slowly. *"In our life there is a single color, as on an artist's palette, which provides the meaning of life and art. It is the color of love."*

"Nice."

"It put things in perspective, I think. That's what these whole past few weeks have been about—life and art. The Nancy Hanks Lincoln painting and mystery about her skin color started it. And then the question about life—the survival of humankind—became paramount with the Blue Star prophecy. Art and life. Life and art. Like Chagall said, it all comes down to love."

Eyes shining, she touched his cheek and smiled, then pulled him down to her. "Show me what you mean, Cameron."

The End

DEAR READER

I love to get reader feedback, both to help me continue to write about things that you (hopefully) enjoy and also to improve on the things you don't. Please feel free to reach out to me at dsbrody@comcast.net, and/or also to leave a review at Amazon or Goodreads.

If you enjoyed *The Pillars of Enoch,* you may want to read the other books featuring Cameron and Astarte in my "Templars in America" series, all of which have been Kindle Top 10 Bestsellers in their categories (see below). And if you enjoy legal thrillers, please check out the three legal thrillers in my "Boston Law" series, *Unlawful Deeds, Blood of the Tribe,* and *The Wrong Abraham:* https://www.amazon.-com/gp/product/B0753CRT9D

"Templars in America" Series

Cabal of the Westford Knight
Templars at the Newport Tower (2009)
https://www.amazon.com/dp/B00GWTZYLS
Set in Boston and Newport, RI, inspired by artifacts evidencing that Scottish explorers and Templar Knights traveled to New England in 1398.

Thief on the Cross
Templar Secrets in America (2011)
https://www.amazon.com/dp/B006OQIXCG
Set in the Catskill Mountains of New York, sparked by an ancient Templar codex calling into question fundamental teachings of the Catholic Church.

Powdered Gold
Templars and the American Ark of the Covenant (2013)
https://www.amazon.com/dp/B00GWTYJ5K
Set in Arizona, exploring the secrets and mysteries of both the Ark of the Covenant and a manna-like powdered substance.

The Oath of Nimrod
Giants, MK-Ultra and the Smithsonian Cover-up (2014)
https://www.amazon.com/dp/B00NW13QTG
Set in Massachusetts and Washington, DC, triggered by the mystery of hundreds of giant human skeletons found buried across North America.

The Isaac Question
Templars and the Secret of the Old Testament (2015)
https://www.amazon.com/dp/B016E3X2QK
Set in Massachusetts and Scotland, focusing on ancient stone chambers, the mysterious Druids and a stunning reinterpretation of the Biblical Isaac story.

Echoes of Atlantis
Crones, Templars and the Lost Continent (2016)
https://www.amazon.com/dp/B01MXJ0BNX
Set in New England, focusing on artifacts and other evidence indicating that the lost colony of Atlantis, featuring an advanced civilization, did exist 12,000 years ago.

The Cult of Venus
Templars and the Ancient Goddess (2017)
https://www.amazon.com/dp/B0767Q4N1S
Set in New England, triggered by the discovery of a medieval journal revealing that the Knights Templar came to America before Columbus because they were secretly worshiping the ancient Goddess.

The Swagger Sword
Templars, Columbus and the Vatican Cover-up (2018)
https://www.amazon.com/gp/product/B07HCRNYVN
Set in Rhode Island and Ireland, inspired by the 1980s Vatican Bank Scandal and featuring a treasure map, carved on a sword, indicating that Christopher Columbus may have aided the Templars in secreting a treasure in America.

Treasure Templari
Templars, Nazis and the Holy Grail (2019)
https://www.amazon.com/gp/product/B07XV9QJNZ
Set in New England, New York and Belgium, triggered by a 15th-century Dutch Masterpiece which Hitler believed was a secret map to the Templar treasure and the Holy Grail.

Watchtower of Turtle Island
Templars and the Antichrist (2020)
https://www.amazon.com/gp/product/B089QWSGM1
Set in New England and Montana, sparked by occultists who believe that a stone tower in Newport, RI—built by the medieval Knights Templar— is a portal through which the Antichrist will appear.

Romerica
Roman Artifacts in America (2020)
https://www.amazon.com/gp/product/B08NZ64T4N
Set in New England and the Ohio River Valley, triggered by Roman-era artifacts—many with Jewish themes—evidencing a secret journey to America by Roman/Jewish survivors of the Bar Kokhba uprising circa 133 AD.

Available at Amazon as Paperbacks and as Kindle eBooks

AUTHOR'S NOTE

Though I am anything but an accomplished cook, I often compare writing a novel to cooking a gourmet meal. An author gathers a collection of tantalizing ingredients, then tries to mix them together in a unique and savory way. In this book, a pair of historical mysteries constitute two of the main ingredients. First, what is the true secret at the center of Freemasonry? Second, where did the Melungeon people of Appalachia originate? Even now, after having conducted hundreds of hours of research, I'm not certain I have 100% answered these questions. But I do believe I have set forth *plausible* possibilities which shed light on these mysteries. I'll let you be the judge as to how far beyond plausible I've moved the ball—or how tasty the meal is.

Of course, a third historical mystery stands tall at the center of the story, as it does in most of the books in this series: What did the medieval Knights Templar discover in Jerusalem in the early 1100s which made them so powerful, and was this discovery the reason the Church turned on the secretive Order almost 200 years later? By focusing on Templar history in Portugal, I believe I've offered plausible insights into this mystery as well.

Finally, a suggestion from researcher and media personality Barbara DeLong gave me another key ingredient to mix into this story: the Hopi

Blue Star prophecy. Though not directly related to the Templars, the prophecy provided an opportunity for Astarte to explore more of her Native American heritage.

As is the case with all the books in this series, if an artifact, site or object of art is pictured, it is real—except as specifically noted otherwise below. And if I claim the item is of a certain age or of a certain provenance or features certain characteristics, that information is correct or believed to be correct. Likewise, the historical and literary references are accurate. How I use these objects and references to weave a story is, of course, where the fiction takes root.

Three significant aspect of this story are fictional. To state the obvious, the assertion that the Tables of Testimony tablet is kept in the Asheville Masonic Temple is not (as far as I know) true. Likewise, I know of no actual painting depicting the likeness of Nancy Hanks Lincoln as a child (thought the DNA evidence is real—see below). Finally, though the Hopi Blue Star prophecy is true, I am not aware of any recent explosion at the galactic core.

Generally speaking, I relied on the following books when researching the major historical plot points in this story:

Melungeons: The Last Lost Tribe in America (Mercer University Press 2004), by Elizabeth Caldwell Hirschman.

First Templar Nation (Destiny Book 2012), by Freddy Silva (discussing the history of the Templars in Portugal).

Earth Under Fire (Bear and Company 2005), by Paul A. LaViolette (discussing the Blue Star prophecy and the possibility of an explosion at the galactic core).

The Secret Society of Moses (Inner Traditions 2010), by Flavio Barbiero (discussing the priestly families fleeing Jerusalem for Rome with Josephus after King Herod's War).

For inquisitive readers, perhaps curious about some of the specific historical assertions made and evidence presented in this novel, more information is available here (in order of appearance in the story):

*For information on the appearance of Nancy Hanks Lincoln, as well as her portrait, see: https://lincolncollection.tumblr.com/post/166252377409/lincolns-angel-mother-nancy-hanks-lincoln

*For information on the Tennessee Supreme Court case discussing the origin of the Melungeons, see: https://www.telegram.com/article/20120525/NEWS/120529602

*For similarities between Melungeon and Jewish religious rituals, see *Melungeons*, at p. 121-122 and p. 129. See also: https://dnaconsultants.com/signs-of-crypto-jewish-heritage/

*For the specific text of the Blue Star prophecy, and information regarding Sagittarius and Scorpio pointing at the galactic core, see video: https://www.youtube.com/watch?v=h_LAFTs53OI

*For the assertion that underground living areas exist in the Hopi cliff dwellings, see: https://www.encyclopedia.com/history/united-states-and-canada/north-american-indigenous-peoples/anasazi

*For the assertion that being a Mason disqualifies members from receiving Communion, see: https://en.wikipedia.org/wiki/Freemasonry#Christianity_and_Freemasonry

*For the Thomas Paine quote that Freemasonry is derived from the Druids, see: https://allthingsliberty.com/2016/11/thomas-paine-deism-masonic-fraternity/

*For a discussion of various world cultures possessing a "fire and flood" legend, see *Earth Under Fire*, at p. 186-87.

*For the quote asserting that Masonic rituals tell the story of Biblical history from the point of view of the priestly families, see *The Secret Society of Moses*, at p. 141.

*For the assertion that Josephus negotiated the freedom of 240 prisoners of the Jewish priestly class, see *The Secret Society of Moses*, at p. 116.

*For similarities between Mithraic ritual and Freemasonry, see *The Secret Society of Moses*, at p. 169.

*For a discussion of the richest people of all time, see: https://www.lovemoney.com/gallerylist/51988/the-20-richest-people-of-all-time#:~:text=King%20Solomon%20of%20Israel%20%E2%80%93%20peak,%242%20trillion%20(%C2%A31.42trn)&text=According%20to%20the%20Bible%2C%20King,billions%20of%20dollars%20in%202016

*For the pillar theme in Tarot practice and Cabalism, see: https://thepointofasharpinstrument.wordpress.com/2016/12/09/the-emerald-tablet-what-is-it/

*For the importance of the priest, Zabud, in Masonic ritual, see: https://crypticmasons.org/9-news/343-who-was-zabud

*For the assertion that a cosmic explosion would cause a gravity wave which would result in tidal waves, tsunamis and enhanced volcanic activity, see *Earth Under Fire*, at p. 72.

*For the quote asserting that the Melungeon people lost their heritage, culture and religion in an effort to assimilate, see: https://www.beautifulislam.net/history/melungeons

*The source of the story told to children, comparing Melungeons to ogres, can be found here: https://www.google.com/books/edition/Comics_and_the_U_S_South/IuTiI-zzjkkC?hl=en&gbpv=1&dq=%22I+

first+heard+at+my+father%27s+knee+as+a+child+in+the+mountains+
of+Eastern+Tennessee%22&pg=PA215&printsec=frontcover

*For the assertion that in Europe the term 'Portuguese' became synony-
mous with 'Jew,' see *Melungeons*, at p. 32.

*For the assertion that the king of Portugal allowed the outlawed
Templars to reconstitute themselves as the Knights of Christ, see *First
Templar Nation*, at p. 337-39.

*For the assertion that the Hopi are the oldest of all Native American
tribes, see: https://www.thevintagenews.com/2019/01/11/hopi/

*For the assertion that the DNA of the oldest member of the Blackfoot
tribe   originated   in   Arizona,   see: https://www.bionews.
org.uk/page_142820

*For the history and details of the construction of the Tomar complex,
including the Charola, see *First Templar Nation*, at p. 241.

*For background information on the Church of Santa Maria de Olival,
"the mother of all Templar churches," see *First Templar Nation*, at
p. 205.

*For the assertion that the medieval Church decreed that all depictions of
the Virgin Mary must be in white and blue, with her hair covered, see
The Woman with the Alabaster Jar (Bear & Company, 1993), by
Margaret Starbird, at p. 123.

*For the assertion that the place name 'Tomar' derives from the name of
the daughter of Jesus and Mary Magdalene, 'Sarah Tamar,' see *First
Templar Nation*, at p. 242-43.

*For information about the two initiation wells at Quinta da Regaleira,
see *First Templar Nation*, at p. 324.

*For the argument that the Tables of Testimony are separate and distinct from the Ten Commandment tablets, see *Bloodline of the Holy Grail* (Barnes and Noble, 2003) by Laurence Gardner, at p. 213.

*For information on the 2020 attack at a church in Axum, Ethiopia, during which militiamen attempted to take the Ark of the Covenant while priests and local villagers defended the church, see: https://nypost.com/ 2021/02/20/at-least-800-ethiopians-killed-after-defending-ark-of-the-covenant/

*For the assertion that the Templars, in the 1180s, built underground churches and chapels connected by tunnels in northern Ethiopia, see: https://thetemplarknight.com/2012/07/09/templars-ark-covenant-ethiopia/

*For the assertion that an Ethiopian king in 1306 sent a delegation to the Pope, beseeching him to leave the Ark in Ethiopia, see *The Sign and the Seal* (Touchstone 1992), by Graham Hancock, at page 160-65.

*For the quote from a professor from the University of London asserting that Prince Henry the Navigator was obsessed with making direct contact with Ethiopia, see *The Sign and the Seal,* at page 169.

*For the assertion that the Portuguese troops sent to defend Ethiopia from a Muslim invasion in the 1500s were led by a member of the Knights of Christ, see *The Sign and the Seal,* at page 173.

*For the quote describing the Lalibela churches, see *The Sign and the Seal,* at page 115.

*For the Dr. Donald Yates quote asserting that Cherokee/Jewish inter-marriage predates Columbus, see: https://www.thejc.com/news/world/ big-chief-rabbi-why-cherokees-could-be-jewish-1.53565

*For the assertion that matrilineal kin of Nancy Hanks Lincoln belonged to rare haplogroup X1c, see: https://geneticlincoln.com/

*For the assertion that the Cherokee name for God is 'Yi-ho-wa,' a name which no common person was allowed to speak, see *Ancient American Magazine*, Issue 86, at p. 43.

*For the assertion that Elvis Presley was of Jewish and Cherokee descent, see: https://ancientamerica.com/anomalous-dna-in-the-cherokee/

*For the Cherokee legend that the tribe possessed and guarded the Ark of the Covenant, see: https://www.bofm.blog/cherokee-ark-of-the-covenant/ (quote paraphrased)

*For the assertion that in the 1930s the Cherokee tribe moved the Ark of the Covenant out of Tennessee, see: https://old.world-mysteries.com/ PhilipGardiner/arkofc_fj.htm

*For the assertion that virtually every town where the Melungeons settled also simultaneously established a Freemasonic lodge, see *Melungeons*, at p. 103.

*For the quote about the Jews of Newport, RI practicing Freemasonry in 1658, see: https://freemasonry.bcy.ca/ history/history_of_rhode_island.html

*For information on, and translation of, the *Ha-Magid* Hebrew newspaper article discussing Abraham Lincoln asserting his Jewish heritage, see: https://jewishreviewofbooks.com/articles/5068/was-lincoln-jewish/

*For information about Abraham Lincoln's family's Jewish heritage—that the name Abraham is Jewish; that his great-grandfather, cousin and uncle were named Mordecai; that he was the only president not to belong to a church; that the town in England where his family came from had a large Jewish population; and that his ancestors were metallurgists—see

Melungeons, at p. 89-93. See also: https://www.shapell.org/events/
lincoln-and-the-jews-a-history-book-release/?gclid=Cj0KEQjw-
qbLBRD79JWsjuXI784BEiQAftBCIzV7ZBpet7md85X84P6Pb1ScNV1
0SW6IxNhgOzCArqAaAq1l8P8HAQ

*For the assertion that Bernard de Clairvoux defined God as "length,
width, height and depth," see: https://www.google.com/books/edition/
Knights_Templar_Encyclopedia/095EDwAAQBAJ?hl=en&gbpv=1&
dq=freemasonry+%22number,+measure+and+weight%22&pg=PT59&
printsec=frontcover

*For the assertion that the Masons credit Josephus with teaching them
about the Pillars of Enoch, see: http://pubs.royle.com/article/The+
Secrets+Of+Enoch+In+The+Masonic+Tradition/1450144/
166570/article.html

*For the assertion that the stained glass in medieval cathedrals glows at
twilight, and that the formula for making this glass has been lost, see
Bloodline of the Holy Grail, at p. 218.

*For the assertion that people of Jewish heritage win a vastly dispropor-
tionate number of Nobel Prizes, see: https://www.cjnews.com/living-
jewish/nobel-prize-and-the-jews

*For the quote asserting that the Cosmic Equations explain numerous
phenomena in nature, see: https://www.4truthseekers.org/articles/
the_importance_of_ley_lines_and_vortices.php (quote paraphrased)

*For the assertion that ancient Pillars of Enoch legends all assert that
people would perish by flood and fire, see: http://pubs.royle.com/article/
The+Secrets+Of+Enoch+In+The+Masonic+Tradition/1450144/
166570/article.html

As you can see from the numerous sources cited above, there is substan-
tial evidence supporting the assertions in this novel. Have I proven my

case? That is for you to decide. But I do feel confident that, even if I got some of the details wrong, there is a fascinating story—involving the Templars, the Freemasons, the Melungeons, the Cherokee, and the Jewish priestly families—to be told here. As I often say, trying to decipher these ancient mysteries is the stuff that keeps me up at night.

Thanks for reading and coming on this journey with me.

David S. Brody, May, 2021
Newburyport, Massachusetts

ACKNOWLEDGMENTS

I am grateful to my dedicated team of Beat Readers. Some are newbies, many are repeat volunteers. But all provide an invaluable service, helping me polish and improve the story before releasing it publicly. I offer my heartfelt thanks—for their astute insights, observations and comments—to the following individuals (in alphabetical order):

Jonathan Blasczak
Ben Brody
Roberto Calo
Ed Correa
Randy Dickey
Kevin Dorsey
Michele Doucette
Jessica Glover
Magda Grover
Michael Hauptly-Pierce
Mark Hickox
Albert Holstius
James Ingalls
Christopher Jordan

Penny Lacroix
Deb Louison Lavoy
Jeremy & Heather Ledoux
Carol MacLeod
Matt McMahon
Paul McNamee
Ron Reed
Brent Reynolds
Brent Robison
Scott Selig
Parker Smith
Carlos Varin
Ted Vaught
Jane Werthmann
John Whitmore
Terry Anne Wildman
Sheila Williams
Mary Yannetti

Any mistakes in the story are mine, not theirs. And the fact that they may have assisted me does not mean they endorse or support any of the things written.

My research is always greatly aided by the extensive files and archives maintained by the New England Antiquities Research Association (NEARA). I strongly encourage anyone who has an interest in ancient sites and artifacts in and around New England to join NEARA (visit www.NEARA.org).

Finally, my wife Kim deserves both thanks and credit. I dragged her down to Asheville, North Carolina at the end of a cold New England winter, only to find that it was twenty degrees colder there than in Massachusetts. Because of the pandemic, we ate outside, bundled against the cold. All so I could research the local sites and history. Not to mention all the help she gave—as always—during the story development and writing stage of this project. Truly, this series of books would not exist were it not for Kim's invaluable assistance, insights and patient support.

PHOTO CREDITS

Coronation of Mary, Quinta da Regaleira, credit Allie Brody

*Church of Saint George, Lalibela (2 images), credit Bernard Gagnon, Wikipedia

*Cherokee Tribal Patch, credit *Ancient American Magazine*, Issue 86, at p. 4

*Vatican Golden Ratio Staircase, credit User:Colin / Wikimedia Commons / CC BY-SA 3.0

*Notre Dame Cathedral and Golden Ratio, credit: https://bleckarchitects.com/math-in-architecture/

Made in the USA
Coppell, TX
06 June 2021